CW01020600

Secrets of the
Toffee Factory Girls

By Glenda Young

Saga Novels
Belle of the Back Streets
The Tuppenny Child
Pearl of Pit Lane
The Girl with the Scarlet Ribbon
The Paper Mill Girl
The Miner's Lass
A Mother's Christmas Wish
The Sixpenny Orphan

The Toffee Factory Girls
Secrets of the Toffee Factory Girls

Helen Dexter Cosy Crime Mysteries
Murder at the Seaview Hotel
Curtain Call at the Seaview Hotel
Foul Play at the Seaview Hotel

GLENDA YOUNG

Secrets of the
Toffee Factory Girls

HEADLINE

First published in 2025
by HEADLINE PUBLISHING GROUP LIMITED

1

Cataloguing in Publication Data is available from the British Library

ISBN 978 1 0354 0255 7

Typeset in in 12.75/16pt Stempel Garamond LT Std by Jouve (UK), Milton Keynes

Printed and bound in Great Britain by Clays Ltd, Elcograf S.p.A.

MIX
Paper | Supporting
responsible forestry
FSC® C104740

Headline's policy is to use papers that are natural, renewable and
recyclable products and made from wood grown in well-managed
forests and other controlled sources. The logging and manufacturing
processes are expected to conform to the environmental
regulations of the country of origin.

HEADLINE PUBLISHING GROUP LIMITED
An Hachette UK Company
Carmelite House
50 Victoria Embankment
London EC4Y 0DZ

The authorized representative in the EEA is Hachette Ireland, 8 Castlecourt
Centre, Dublin 15, D15 XTP3, Ireland (email: info@hbgi.ie)

www.headline.co.uk
www.hachette.co.uk

Author's Note

Please note, in this work of fiction I have used poetic licence to best fit dates to the narrative. If you'd like to discover the real history of Elisabethville, fictionalised in this novel, I highly recommend the books *Who Were the Birtley Belgians?* by Birtley Heritage Group, published by Summerhill Books, and *Of Arms and the Heroes: The Story of the Birtley Belgians* by John G. Bygate, published by History of Education Project.

Acknowledgements

My grateful thanks go to the many local historians who provided their time, advice and help while I was researching the history of toffee factories in the north-east. Thank you to Gavin Purdon, local historian at Chester-le-Street and author of the book about Horner's toffee factory, *It Was Grand Toffee*. Thank you to Dorothy Hall and everyone at Chester-le-Street Heritage Group. Thank you to Val Greaves, Jean Atkinson and Barry Ross, and everyone at Birtley Heritage Group. Thank you also to Sunderland historian Sharon Vincent for her invaluable knowledge of women's social history. And huge thanks to the very friendly, helpful staff at the University of York Borthwick Archives, where I researched toffee factories during the First World War.

Thank you to my agent, Caroline Sheldon, for everything, and to the team at Headline who look after me so well. Finally, thank you to my husband, Barry, for fuelling me with tea, coffee and cheese scones when I lock myself away to write.

The Story So Far

The Toffee Factory Girls:
Book 1 in the Trilogy

Hetty, Elsie and Anne start work at Jack's toffee factory in the Durham market town of Chester-le-Street when war breaks out and men leave to serve in the forces.

Hetty Lawson is the breadwinner at home, working to pay debts her father left when he died. She wins a competition at the toffee factory to become the face of the new brand of toffee, which is named Lady Tina. Hetty lives with her overbearing mother, Hilda, and younger brother, Dan, who is her mother's favourite child. When Hetty's boyfriend, Bob, goes off to war, she falls for a Belgian man, Dirk, who lives in the nearby village of Elisabeth-ville. Hetty writes to Bob to call off their relationship, but unbeknown to her, her letter is lost before it leaves the country.

Elsie Cooper has had a rough upbringing. She meets Frankie, a minor criminal, and ends up agreeing to take the blame for a crime he commits. Frankie's hold over Elsie results in heartbreaking consequences. Meanwhile, Elsie's factory colleague, Stan, will do anything for her, but she sees him only as a friend, blind to the fact that he's the right man for her.

Anne Wright starts work in Mr Jack's office as a typist. She is efficient and organised and whips the office – and Mr Jack himself – into shape. However, behind her businesslike facade, she hides a heartbreaking secret. She had a baby out of wedlock, had no choice but to sell him and now struggles to live with her decision. She channels her sorrow and energy into her work and impresses Mr Jack with her energy and enthusiasm for the toffee factory. She also develops feelings for him, and he feels the same for her. However, he is already promised to a society lady, and if he doesn't marry her, her father won't invest in the factory to secure its future.

Chapter One

January 1916

Anne Wright rented a cramped room on the top floor of a terraced house on Victor Street. Her landlady, Mrs Fortune, had an annoying habit of entering her room without warning. However, this time when she tried to open the door, she was thwarted. Anne allowed herself a smile as she glanced at the bolt. There was a knock, loud and insistent.

'Miss Wright!' Mrs Fortune yelled from the landing. 'Is there something wrong with your door? It won't open.'

There was more rattling of the handle before Anne slid open the lock. Mrs Fortune, red in the face with frustration, almost fell into Anne's arms when the door finally opened.

Anne, standing tall and straight, smiled serenely. 'Mrs Fortune, how nice to see you this Saturday morning. Was there something you wanted?' She knew she'd have to play it carefully with her landlady, for she didn't want to risk being thrown out. Her little room wasn't plush, but it was the only home she had. However, she was fed up to the back teeth of her landlady barging in. Finally she'd taken steps to ensure it didn't happen again.

Mrs Fortune breathed deeply, nostrils flaring, and narrowed her eyes. 'What happened to your door? Why was it stuck?' she demanded. She looked around the room. 'I hope you're not hiding something in here.'

Anne's shoulders dropped. She'd been living with Mrs Fortune for over a year and was disappointed that her landlady still didn't trust her.

'Mrs Fortune, I am not hiding anything, or anyone. I know you well enough by now to know you're intimating, yet again, that I have sneaked a gentleman in here. I have told you many times that I'm not that kind of girl. You know I'd never break any of your house rules,' she said firmly.

Mrs Fortune's beady eyes landed on Anne's pristine eiderdown. Anne could have sworn at that moment that the landlady looked disappointed not to have found evidence of wrongdoing.

Mrs Fortune was a peculiar woman, she thought. She was short, with grey hair tucked under a small black hat that she wore from first thing each morning to last thing at night. Anne had never seen her without it. 'Mrs Fortune, do you remember our conversations . . .' she began, then paused, thinking of how best to explain why she had installed the lock on her door without permission. 'Our many conversations about you, as my landlady, respecting my privacy as your lodger?'

Mrs Fortune put her hands on her stout hips and looked from Anne to the door, where the shiny new bolt finally caught her eye.

'What on earth is that?' she yelled.

'I think you know what it is, Mrs Fortune.'

'You've damaged the door,' Mrs Fortune said, running her fingers across the bolt.

Anne crossed her arms. 'I've done no such thing. As you can see. I've installed a lock, carefully and neatly.'

Mrs Fortune stepped forward and looked into Anne's clear, bright eyes. Anne stood her ground and pressed her sensible flat shoes against the bare floor to steady herself. She knew she should have asked permission, but had she done so, she feared Mrs Fortune would have said no.

'If I'd asked you about installing a lock, you would have refused me,' she began, pre-empting complaints.

Mrs Fortune shook her head. 'You don't need a lock on your door. You don't require privacy in my home . . . unless you've got something to hide,' she said darkly.

Anne dismissed her comment with a wave of her hand. 'I do need privacy, Mrs Fortune. Everyone is entitled to it. I don't barge into your rooms downstairs, do I? And although I've asked you many times not to enter my room without permission, you've repeatedly ignored my requests. I'm a grown woman, not a child. While I've lived under your roof I've been a model tenant. I always pay my rent on time, I keep my room clean, and I never . . .' she tilted her chin, 'I never bring back gentleman callers. And don't I give you free toffee each week from my work at Jack's factory too?'

Mrs Fortune's right eye twitched. Anne had expected more resistance from the feisty woman. She'd even put money aside from her wages in case the landlady demanded compensation. However, she was both surprised and relieved when Mrs Fortune dropped her gaze. For the first time since she'd moved into Victor Street, Anne felt she'd won a small victory.

Mrs Fortune turned away and carefully inspected the lock. 'You installed this yourself?' she asked more gently now, sounding impressed.

'Yes, I bought it from the Co-op in town, along with a screwdriver and all the fixings,' Anne replied.

Mrs Fortune spun around and her eyebrows shot up into the rim of her black hat. 'You know how to operate a screwdriver?' she said, astonished.

Anne nodded. 'Yes, of course. I'm a woman of many talents, Mrs Fortune. There's a lot you don't know about me.'

Mrs Fortune gave a wry smile. 'There are many things we don't know about each other,' she replied.

Anne immediately wished she could take back her words. Because if Mrs Fortune found out everything about her, she knew she'd be thrown out onto the street. She'd shared her deepest secret with only Hetty and Elsie, her close friends at the toffee factory. They knew about the baby son she'd parted with to be raised by Mr and Mrs Matthews, a well-to-do couple in Durham. That was where she was planning to head this morning. All she wanted to do was take a peek at her boy, just a glimpse over the fence. Some days the heartache of giving up her child wouldn't leave her and compelled her to seek him out, hoping for a glimpse of him through a window of the couple's large, impressive home.

Anne kept other secrets too, things she hadn't even shared with Hetty and Elsie. Things she couldn't share with anyone. The truth was that she'd fallen for the factory owner, Mr Jack, who she worked closely with. However, he was promised to a society lady by the name of Lucinda Dalton and they were to be wed. To complicate matters further, Mr Jack had recently told Anne he loved her, not Lucinda. He'd even presented her with a Christmas gift, a silver brooch with precious stones in the exact shade of blue to match the toffee factory logo.

So far, she hadn't dared allow herself to be swept up in the romance of Mr Jack's heartfelt words. If she did, his marriage to Lucinda might not go ahead, and Mr Dalton's promised investment in the factory wouldn't happen, meaning there was every chance the factory would have to close, particularly if the rumours of sugar rationing were true. All the sugar boilers, chocolate enrobers, wrappers and packers, delivery men and stable men would then be out of work. Anne would lose her much-loved role as secretary to Mr Jack, and every toffee factory girl, including her friends Elsie and Hetty, would lose their jobs too. No, there was no need for Mrs Fortune to know everything.

Anne bit her tongue as Mrs Fortune looked her all the way up from her sensible shoes and her black linen skirt to her cream blouse with its patterned-lace collar and her brown hair elegantly styled in a bun. Aware she was being scrutinised, she felt herself blush and she pushed her small wire-rimmed glasses up the bridge of her nose. Mrs Fortune crossed her arms.

'I won't have you damaging any more of my doors, Miss Wright,' she said. 'Or floors, or windows, or any part of my home. Do you hear me?'

'Loud and clear, Mrs Fortune,' Anne replied. 'Now, was there a reason for your visit this morning? I was about to go out.'

Mrs Fortune nodded quickly, then closed the door.

She indicated the bed. 'You may wish to sit down, Miss Wright.'

Anne shook her head. 'Whatever it is, Mrs Fortune, I'm sure I can remain standing.'

The landlady began pacing. The room was so small that it only took her three steps to reach the window and three steps to return. Anne wondered what was on her mind. She glanced at her wristwatch. The bus to Durham was due soon and she didn't want to miss it. She hoped her landlady would be quick. However, the clouded look on the woman's face suggested otherwise.

'Times are hard, Miss Wright,' Mrs Fortune began, still pacing. 'This dreadful war shows no end and food prices have shot through the roof.'

Anne braced herself. Because of her privileged position at the toffee factory, she knew exactly how much of an increase there'd been in food prices nationwide.

'I understand, Mrs Fortune,' she said.

Mrs Fortune stopped pacing. She looked at Anne. 'Of course you do, you're an intelligent girl. You wouldn't have been taken on at Jack's factory in such a senior role if you weren't.'

'How much more rent do you want?' Anne offered.

A smile came to Mrs Fortune's lips, then she delved into the front pocket of the apron that covered her skirt and blouse. She pulled out a small envelope and handed it to Anne.

'The new terms are in my letter. Please read this and sign it to say you agree, then leave it with me on your way out.'

Anne took the envelope and placed it carefully on the mantelpiece. 'I'll read it when I return, Mrs Fortune. I really should go. I don't want to be late.'

She picked up her handbag and gathered her coat, hat and scarf. It was blustery outside with a strong January wind and she needed to wrap up warmly.

'There's something else I need to tell you,' Mrs Fortune added.

Anne didn't stop in her preparations to leave, hoping the landlady would pick up on the hint. 'Oh?' she said, thrusting her arms into her winter coat.

'I'm taking in another lodger,' Mrs Fortune announced.

This made Anne stop in her tracks. She blinked hard. 'But where will they . . .?' There were no more rooms in Mrs Fortune's house, so where would another lodger live?

'Pearl will live downstairs in my front parlour,' Mrs Fortune said.

Anne was stunned. Not only was Mrs Fortune giving up one of her private rooms, but she'd called the new lodger by her first name. All the time Anne had lived here, she'd been addressed as Miss Wright.

'Pearl?' she said, hoping Mrs Fortune would share some more details about the new girl. However, the land-lady merely pursed her lips and headed to the door. She paused there, holding the handle. Anne followed, know-ing that she'd have to run to Front Street if she was to catch the Durham bus.

'One more thing, Miss Wright.'

'What is it now?' Anne asked impatiently.

'There's a gentleman to see you. I haven't invited him in, as the neighbours will gossip and I won't have that. He's waiting outside on the street.'

Anne's heart skipped a beat. 'A gentleman? Who is it?' she asked.

'I didn't ask his name as I have no time for such callers.

You know my house rules,' Mrs Fortune said sternly. Then she walked from the room and away down the stairs.

Anne was confused. She wasn't expecting anyone. The only men she knew in Chester-le-Street were those she worked with at the factory. Why on earth would one of them come to her home? She racked her brains. Only one person knew where she lived, and that was Mr Jack himself, but surely it wouldn't be him? He wouldn't be so indiscreet as to visit her lodgings. In any case, Mrs Fortune would have recognised him. As the owner of the toffee factory, which employed many in the small market town of Chester-le-Street, he was a familiar face to everyone.

She listened to Mrs Fortune's footsteps disappear downstairs, then heard the door to the parlour open. 'Pearl, my dear!' she heard the landlady exclaim before the door closed.

Her head spun. She couldn't think straight. Another lodger in the small house, especially one so well known to Mrs Fortune, was one thing. And now a gentleman coming to call, well, that was another matter entirely. She took a moment to gather herself and calm her racing heart. She glanced at her watch again, realising she was too late to catch the bus and there wasn't another due for an hour. There was only one thing for it. She headed downstairs to discover who was waiting outside.

Chapter Two

In a terraced house on Elm Street, Hetty Lawson was arguing with her mum, Hilda, again. Their relationship had never been easy, with Hilda favouring Hetty's brother, Dan, who was away fighting in the war. In Hilda's eyes Dan could never do wrong, whereas Hetty, it seemed, could never do anything right. Their already difficult relationship had recently worsened after Hetty had brought her boyfriend, Dirk, home for the first time a few weeks earlier, on Christmas Eve. Christmas was now a fading memory as the harsh, icy winds of the new year blew in, but Hetty and Hilda's argument showed no sign of blowing out.

The women were huddled in front of the coal fire in their kitchen. Lazing by the fire was Hetty's small black dog, which Dirk had given to her; it was how they'd first met. He had found the animal on the street one day, assumed it was Hetty's and handed it to her before walking off. Hetty's heart had melted at the sight of the little stray and she'd brought it home. It was only meant to be a temporary stay, until its owner claimed it. Now, months later, the dog was still living with her, although she hadn't given it a name yet. Well, she'd never thought she'd be keeping it. Now it had settled in as part of the family. To distract herself from her argument with Hilda, she mulled over names in her mind. Tiny? Shorty? Neither of those seemed right, although they did accurately describe the dog. His coat was jet black, the colour of midnight. She wondered how he would respond to a short name like Jet; it seemed a fitting choice.

As the animal snoozed, Hetty and Hilda were busy with their hands. Hetty was darning a tear in her favourite blue skirt while Hilda held a pencil and notepad, writing a letter to Dan.

'You're selfish, Hetty,' she huffed, without looking up.

Hetty laid down her sewing and looked at her mum's lined face. Hilda had aged quickly since Dan had signed up. Hetty glanced at his most recent letter, which lay on the table, and her stomach twisted. It had been a gruelling read, with none of Dan's usual cheery tone. In its place were words that had torn at her heart. It had begun simply: *Dear Mother and Hetty, I do not much care for the trenches*. And in that opening line, Hetty understood how much Dan was suffering.

His letters so far had never contained any complaint, not wanting Hilda to know how desperate his new life was. The one that had arrived today was the first hint that war wasn't the adventure he'd been promised. He'd been signed up by an overeager recruiting sergeant, who'd turned a blind eye to the fact that Dan was only fifteen years old. Just a boy. He was one of the thousands of young men known as 'teenage Tommies' who'd been recruited in the mad dash to enlist as many troops as possible to fight overseas.

Hetty softened a little as she took in her mum's

downturned mouth and sad expression. Hilda was a small woman, thin, all skin and bones. Her sunken cheeks made her look worn and ill. Despite the fact that she was only middle-aged, her shoulder-length hair had already turned grey. Her body was stooped, her shoulders round as she sat forward in her chair, her pencil poised. Hetty knew her mum missed Dan with all her heart. He was all she ever talked about, and she wrote to him each day.

'Selfish, that's what you are,' Hilda went on. 'You've already got a fella, what do you want another one for? You'll get yourself a reputation like your friend Elsie Cooper. Oh, you should hear the gossip from the market about her and her aunt Jean.'

Any compassion that Hetty had begun to feel dissolved at the mention of Elsie's name. Her best friend had been through a dreadful time at the hands of her abusive husband, Frankie. He'd beaten her so hard on their wedding night that their baby had died inside her. It had been a harrowing time, from which Elsie was still not recovered.

'Leave Elsie out of this, Mum. What she does is none of your business.'

Hilda tutted and carried on scribbling on her notepaper.

'I don't want two fellas. I've got Dirk and we're happy,' Hetty said, keeping as calm as she could. She'd been over this many times with her mum, who seemed not to want to hear the truth. 'You know I've written to Bob to break things off with him.'

Hilda tutted out loud. 'And yet he still writes to you.'

'He sends me cards that the army give him,' Hetty said sternly. 'All he does is cross out those parts that aren't relevant. He doesn't write anything else. There's never been any romance in anything he sends me.'

11

She sighed. There had never been any romance in Bob, never mind his cards, although she was surprised he kept sending them after she'd written to end their relationship.

'Dirk is the only man in my life,' she continued. 'I wish you'd accept it. Why can't you support me? Why must you make things so hard? Life's difficult enough with the war. Plus there are rumours going around that the toffee factory might be on its last legs once sugar rationing hits. There's even talk about it closing down until the war's over. I've got a lot on my mind, Mum, and the last thing I need is for you to ban Dirk from our house.'

'It's *my* house,' Hilda said firmly, keeping her gaze on her letter to Dan. 'And while you're under my roof, you'll live by my rules. One of those rules is that I won't let you bring anyone here that I don't approve of.'

Hetty crossed her arms. 'You mean because Dirk's Belgian.'

'He's different, Hetty,' Hilda said.

'He's a man, isn't he? What's so different about that? He's got two arms, two legs, and all the right equipment in all the right places.'

Hilda's face turned to thunder. 'There's no need to be crude,' she hissed.

But Hetty's dander was up and she wouldn't be stopped.

'He's a human being. He's a wonderful person. He's kind and sweet and he makes me laugh. He treats me well, takes me to the cinema, to dances, and he's never forced himself on me, not like some men try to do.'

She reached a hand out to gently touch her mum's arm.

'I love him, Mum, can't you see?' she implored, but Hilda sharply pulled her arm back and Hetty's hand fell. She knew her mum wouldn't be moved.

'He's one of the Belgians, Hetty. Now, I gave him a chance when he came here for tea. That's as much as I promised I'd do.'

'But what did he do that was wrong? Why have you taken against him? He was perfectly polite. He even brought you an iced bun from the baker on Front Street. And yet you treated him like he was dirt. You couldn't even be nice to him for my sake, could you? You didn't even try. Why not let him come again, Mum? You'll soon see how lovely he is.'

'He spoke funny,' Hilda muttered.

'Of course he did, he's foreign, he's got an accent,' Hetty cried, exasperated. 'But he speaks perfectly good English. He's got an important job, he's a teacher. Why won't you let him visit again?'

Hilda jabbed her pencil in Hetty's direction. 'I should stop you from seeing him altogether. If your father was still alive, he'd have words to say about it. He wouldn't have accepted a foreigner in this house.'

At the mention of her late father, tears pricked Hetty's eyes. She missed him every day.

'Dad was kind and considerate, he would have accepted Dirk, but you're narrow-minded. You can't see past the end of your nose when it comes to him. I know the real reason you don't want him back. It's because of the neighbours, isn't it? You're frightened of what they'll say, what they'll think about your daughter courting a fella who's not a local lad. You'd deny me happiness and love because you're afraid of being gossiped about.'

Hilda reached under her chair and pulled out a rolled-up copy of the local newspaper. She held it up in front of Hetty's face and brandished it like a weapon.

'Do you know what they're saying in here about the Belgians?'

Hetty knew only too well about the angry, bitter letters printed in the local paper about the Belgian community who lived in the nearby village of Elisabethville. Thousands of Belgians had been brought to England by the British government after the war began, to work in the munitions factories. They'd built their own village and named it after the Belgian queen. Elisabethville was run under Belgian law, as a military base. It had its own school, hospital and church. It had a dance hall and community centre, blocks of accommodation for the single men, where Dirk lived, and rows of wooden huts for families. These huts were the real reason that the letters to the newspaper were full of anger and spite, because locals were jealous. Not only did the wooden huts have electricity inside – no oil lamps for them – but they also had running water with the luxury of an indoor bathroom. These were things that none of the older houses in the town had. The petty jealousies had made some locals, including Hilda, suspicious and hostile over anything related to the new community. There were even rumours that real bacon was offered for sale in their village shop. This further stoked tensions among some Chester-le-Street residents.

'You're desperate to believe anything other people say that backs up your horrible mistaken ideas!' Hetty yelled.

Hilda gasped at Hetty's outburst, then turned her head away. Hetty knew she'd hit on the truth. How she hated arguing with her mum, though. She was frightened she might say too much, something that might force Hilda to throw her out. It wouldn't be the first time her mum

14

had threatened such a thing. There was only one thing for it: she had to calm down, before she said something she'd regret. Her mum was aching over Dan fighting in the war and Hetty knew how much she worried, how little she slept for fear of something happening to him. She had no wish to make things worse.

She picked up her darning and attacked the skirt with the needle, making uneven stitches. There was silence between the women, the only sounds in the room the crackling of the fire and the ticking of the clock. Finally Hetty could take it no more. She threw down her sewing and leapt to her feet.

'I'm going out!' she said, glancing nervously at the window, where tree branches bent in a gusty wind.

Hilda looked up, alarmed. 'Going out in this weather? Don't be daft, lass.'

'I'll get wrapped up,' Hetty said, as she walked from the kitchen into the hall. The dog stood and followed her, looking at her with pleading eyes. She softened and bent down to him.

'Do you want to come outside too?' she said. His tail wagged furiously. 'All right then. But you're going to have to get used to your new name. I'm going to call you Jet.'

He cocked his head to one side.

'Jet!' Hetty said, louder.

This time the dog responded to her voice and sat obediently as she tied a string leash around his neck. She rewarded him with a stroke and decided to keep on rewarding him each time he responded to his new name. She took down her dad's coat from the peg behind the door, breathing in the smell of it, always hoping for a reminder of him. But she was always disappointed; it just smelled of damp. She wrapped a knitted scarf around her neck and pulled on an old woollen hat.

'I'll be back soon,' she called before she stormed from the house with the dog, letting the front door slam; she was in no mood to close it quietly.

She headed along Elm Street, intending to walk to the river to help clear her mind. When she reached the Co-op on Front Street, she stopped and waited for a cart to go by. And that was when she saw her friend Anne, walking arm-in-arm with a man she immediately recognised from the toffee factory. Hetty did a double-take; she couldn't believe her eyes. The two of them looked cosy, chatting amiably as they walked, heads close together. She was confused. Well, Anne was a dark horse, she thought. She hadn't once mentioned she was stepping out with some-one, especially not *him*. Mind you, she didn't think he would have been her type at all. He was rough around the edges while Anne was elegant and poised. Hetty would even have called her posh. So what on earth was she doing with him?

Chapter Three

That night, Elsie Cooper puckered her lips in front of a small square mirror and began painting them scarlet. She was so engrossed in creating a perfect bow that she didn't notice her aunt Jean watching.

'Who are you getting all dolled up for?' Jean asked.

Elsie immediately picked up on her suspicious tone. Determined not to let it get to her, she smacked her lips together. She popped the lipstick in her bag, then turned to face her aunt. Jean wore a white dressing gown that trailed to the floor and floated behind when she walked, like a long wedding veil. The gown was a gift from a tall, muscular man called Alfie. He was one of Jean's regular visitors, the only one of her men she allowed to stay overnight, therefore Elsie knew he was special to her aunt. Jean's long brown hair was tied up in a bun and her face was scrubbed clean. But within hours, Elsie knew, her whole appearance would change when she'd head out to walk the streets to lure a man to pay for her company. Then her face would be painted, her clothes showy and brash and her heels as high as she could bear.

'I'm not getting dolled up for anyone, I'm just going out,' Elsie replied breezily.

Jean walked towards her and sank into a chair. She looked into Elsie's dark eyes. 'I hope you're not going out to meet who I think you are,' she warned.

Elsie tried to stand, but she was stopped by Jean's firm hand.

'Tell me you're not going to see Frankie.'

She shrugged her aunt's hand away, stood and walked across the room.

'Elsie! Love!' Jean cried.

Elsie spun around and glared at her aunt. 'Since when have you been interested in who I go out with or what I do? Ever since you took me in when Mum and Dad died, you've treated me like a burden to shoulder. You've ignored me and blanked me. You used to lock me in my room when you brought fellas to the flat. Now that I'm older and know what you do for a living, I have to leave when you bring business back here. I spend so much time walking up and down Front Street to keep out of your way while you entertain men in your room that people are starting to wonder if I'm looking for fellas on the street too.'

Jean stood and walked towards her. 'Haven't I provided for you, always?' she said gently.

Elsie hung her head and felt a twinge of guilt. Jean was right. She'd taken Elsie in when her parents had died and had given her, without complaint, shelter, food and a bed.

'Haven't I fed you and kept you warm? I've done my best, Elsie. Oh, I mightn't have cared for you, loved you in the way other women love their own children. I know I haven't given you as much affection as you wanted.'

'Or needed,' Elsie said quietly.

Jean acknowledged the comment with a nod of her head. 'I'm not the maternal type and never have been. You know that. Why now, all of a sudden, are you throwing this back in my face? You've lived here rent-free all your life. Since you started work at the toffee factory and began earning your own wages, I've never once taken money off you. I've never asked you for a penny, and let me remind you that you've never offered. You're free to come and go here and do as you wish.'

'Only when you're not working,' Elsie said.

Jean took a breath and carried on. 'And now you're wanting things from me that I can't give. I can't give you love and affection, Elsie. It's not how I am. You know me too well for that.'

She reached for Elsie's arm and gently placed her hand there. This time Elsie didn't pull away.

'You know what I am. The only affection I give is in exchange for cold, hard cash. I've never made any secret of what I do for a living. It's either that or starve. My job at the market selling linens and cloths doesn't bring in enough to put coal on the fire. Men pay me for sex, it's as easy as that, uncomplicated, no strings, no emotional ties. No tears. No heartache. Mind you, Alfie's not so bad. He doesn't sponge off me or raise his fists—'

Jean stopped dead as Elsie began to sob. Elsie felt herself being drawn into her aunt's warm embrace. She could smell her familiar lily-of-the-valley perfume, another gift from Alfie.

After a while, she pulled away and dabbed her eyes with her tissue. 'My face must look a mess,' she said, walking to the mirror.

Jean followed, stood behind her and laid her hands on her shoulders. Both women were reflected in the small square of glass.

'You never look anything but beautiful,' Jean said to Elsie's reflection. 'Now please, be honest. Is it Frankie you're going to see?'

Elsie stiffened and didn't reply.

'Turn around and look at me, Elsie.'

Slowly Elsie turned. At first she dropped her gaze, but Jean gently tilted her chin with her finger until she had no choice but to look into her eyes.

'I'll ask you again, Elsie. Are you going to meet Frankie?'

Elsie squeezed her eyes shut. She nodded. When she opened them again, a tear made its way down her cheek. Jean brushed it away with her fingertip.

'If I ask you not to go, would you change your mind?'

Silence.

'All right, you've given me your answer. You're a grown woman, Elsie Cooper, a married woman, too. I can't stop you from doing what you want, even if I don't agree with it or understand.'

'I have to see him,' Elsie said, but her words came out in a whisper.

'No you don't,' Jean said firmly. 'Frankie Ireland is a monster.'

'Aunt Jean, he's my husband!' Elsie cried, stepping away.

'A husband who beat you so badly you lost your child.'

Elsie's hands flew protectively to her stomach, but Jean wasn't finished.

'A husband who touched up your best friend on your wedding day.'

She put her hands over her ears. 'Stop it!' she yelled.

'A husband who stole from the factory and tried to pin the blame on you. A husband who's involved in all kinds of petty crime. A husband who got Hetty's little brother into trouble with the police. Do you want me to go on? Because I could, you know. There's more I could tell you about your beloved husband!'

Jean's face was flushed red; tendrils of hair escaped around her face. She laid a hand on her heart as she ran out of steam.

'Well, I've said my piece. If you're determined to see Frankie, so be it. But don't come crying to me when he raises his hand again, and he will, just mark my words.'

'He won't! He's promised me that he's changed!' Elsie cried.

Jean dismissed the comment with a wave of her hand. 'Pah. That's what they all say. Why do you think I stay single and live on my own? Fellas? They're not worth that.' She clicked her finger and thumb.

Elsie picked up her coat and bag and ran to the door, but Jean reached it first and blocked her way.

'Please, Elsie, don't go back to him, not after what he did. Have some self-respect,' she pleaded.

Elsie thrust her arms into her coat and wrapped her scarf around her neck. 'He begged me to meet him,' she said, her words this time a whisper.

Jean stood to one side, away from the door. She pulled her dressing gown protectively around her. 'Then you're a fool, Elsie Cooper,' she said.

'I'm Mrs Elsie Ireland now!' Elsie yelled.

She stormed past her aunt, pulled the door open and stepped onto the cold landing. An icy wind blew in from a broken window as she hurried down the stairs and onto the street.

On Monday morning, Elsie arrived at the toffee factory for the start of her working week. She joined a throng of women milling through the tall, wide iron gates, swaddled against the weather in thick layers of woollens, coats, hats and scarves. Under their coats and jumpers the women wore their khaki and red overalls with the Jack's logo in blue.

As they pushed through the gates into the cobbled yard, they headed in different directions. Some were bound for the toffee stores, others the enrobing, packing or delivery rooms. Elsie began marching to the wrapping room, where her job was to wrap thousands of toffees, every single one by hand. It was a dull job made bearable by working alongside her best friend, Hetty. Suddenly she felt herself being jostled. At first she was surprised, but then she beamed widely when she saw Hetty on one side and Anne on the other.

'Morning, girls,' she said.

'How was your weekend?' Hetty asked.

Elsie shrugged, unwilling to give anything away. She knew she couldn't tell Hetty she'd seen Frankie, because her friend would say words as harsh as those she'd received from Jean.

'Quiet,' she replied.

'Go anywhere nice? See anyone?' Hetty asked.

Elsie shook her head and quickly changed the subject. 'Did you go dancing with Dirk at Elisabethville on Saturday night?'

Hetty rolled her eyes. 'No, because Mum kicked up a

fuss about me seeing him, again. She's terrified about what the neighbours will say and doesn't give two hoots about my happiness.'

Elsie laid her hand on Hetty's arm.

'Anne and I care about you; we girls should look after each other.'

Hetty patted Elsie's hand.

'Thank you.'

Elsie turned to Anne. 'What about you, Anne? Did you have a nice weekend?'

Anne didn't answer. Instead she pointed to the reception building in the courtyard. 'I must dash. Mr Jack's called an important meeting this morning and I need to prepare.'

'Is it about the future of the factory? It is true we might close?' Elsie asked.

Anne leaned forward and whispered, 'You mustn't tell anyone, right? But you might as well know, because you'll find out this morning anyway. Mr Jack's going to make an important announcement that will affect the future of the factory – and all of our lives.'

Chapter Four

Hetty linked arms with Elsie as they walked into the wrapping room.

'What do you think Mr Jack will say?' she whispered. 'I've heard that sugar rations are going to hit. If the factory closes, what'll we do?'

The girls stopped at the coat racks, removed their coats, hats and scarves and hung them on pegs. Hetty shivered and rubbed her arms.

'It's freezing in here.'

Elsie wandered to the table, where a mountain of smooth caramels lay in wait to be wrapped. Hetty followed her friend.

'You're quiet this morning, Elsie. Everything all right at home with your aunt?'

'Jean's fine,' Elsie replied dully.

Hetty pulled an armful of soft toffees towards her, then a cardboard box of waxed wrappers. Mechanically, automatically, she and Elsie began to work. They didn't need to think as they twisted the ends of each wrapper to enclose the delicious creamy toffee inside.

'Guess who I saw Anne walking with on Saturday,' Hetty whispered.

She knew Elsie normally lapped up gossip, so was surprised when she kept focused on her task.

'Go on, guess!' she said.

When Elsie still didn't reply, Hetty gave in. She leaned close to her friend.

'I saw her with Stan Chapman, the gardener.'

At this, Elsie turned, eyes wide. 'Stan? Are you sure it was him?'

'I see I've caught your attention finally. One mention of Stan Chapman and you're all ears.' Hetty noticed Elsie blush. 'I'm positive it was him. I didn't see them kissing or anything, but they looked deep in conversation, as if they were sharing a secret.'

Elsie frowned. 'Stan . . . and Anne?' she said sulkily.

'Are you OK?' Hetty asked, glancing sideways at her friend.

'I saw Frankie at the weekend,' Elsie said quickly.

In shock, Hetty dropped the toffee she was wrapping. She felt sick at the sound of Frankie's name.

'Did you speak to him?'

'Shush! We'll get told off by Mrs Perkins if she hears us talking,' Elsie hissed.

Hetty glanced across the room at their supervisor. Then she snapped out of her shock and picked up the toffee again.

'Well? Did you speak to him?' she whispered.

'I might have, what's it to you?' Elsie hissed.

'I'm your best friend, Elsie, and I care for you deeply. I don't want you to get hurt. You know what he did last time. Who's to say he won't do it again, or worse? Does your aunt know that you saw him?'

'Leave me alone,' Elsie whispered. 'I shouldn't have told you.'

Across the table from Hetty and Elsie, some of the other girls looked up. One of them put her finger to her lips and nodded to where Mrs Perkins was sitting at her desk in the corner of the room. The last thing Hetty wanted was to get a telling-off. Her eyes pricked with tears at the thought of her friend demeaning herself to see Frankie, after the pain and misery he'd caused. He'd beaten Elsie black and blue, and she was so poorly she'd had to take a week off work to recover.

'Yes, Aunt Jean knows, since you ask.'

Their whispered conversation was brought to an abrupt halt when a large, swarthy man entered the room wheeling boxes of unwrapped toffees. He stopped at the head of the table where Hetty and Elsie worked and hoisted up a box, then emptied the brown sweets into a small mountain in front of them, ready to be wrapped.

'Come on, girls, hurry up. We're making them faster than you can wrap them today,' he teased.

Hetty noticed him take a good look at Elsie. Her olive skin, dark eyes and shapely figure always received attention from men.

'My word, so you're the beauty in the wrapping room that all the sugar boilers are talking about,' he leered. He sidled up to her. 'Why don't you come out with me this weekend? I'll show you a good time.'

Elsie stepped away. 'In case you haven't heard, I'm a married woman,' she said firmly, but the man didn't back off.

Hetty watched in case Elsie needed her to intervene. She'd always known her friend could handle unwanted attention from the factory men, but there was something cowed about her since she'd married Frankie. She seemed less sure of herself.

An evil grin spread across the man's face. 'Married? That'll not stop *you*. You're nothing but a common tart, lass. We all know what your aunt Jean does at night.'

'Leave her alone,' Hetty yelled,

He turned to look at her and gave an evil laugh. 'Oh, just look who it is! Miss High and Mighty, the girl with her face painted on our tins of toffee. Lady Tina herself. Think you're a cut above, do you?' he taunted. Hetty was aware that the girls around the table had slowed in their work to listen to the exchange. 'I wonder if Mr Jack knows his Lady Tina is stepping out with a Belgian man. Those Belgians are out to take our girls, everyone knows that. Can't trust any of them.'

Hetty's face grew hot with anger. First the man came in here calling Elsie a tart, and now he was dismissing the Belgians who were working hard at the munitions factory, making arms for British soldiers at war.

'How dare you!' she yelled, then clamped her mouth shut. She was aware of the swish of blue cloth at her side. It was Mrs Perkins, in her blue skirt and blouse, positioning herself between Hetty and Elsie.

'What's going on here?' demanded the supervisor.

'I'm done here,' the delivery man said, eyeing Elsie's cleavage. 'But if you change your mind, lass, you know where I am.'

'Get out and leave my girls alone,' Mrs Perkins ordered.

The man walked away, but Hetty noticed him turn

to look at Elsie with a smirk. She felt Elsie's hand on her arm.

'Are you all right?' her friend said.

Hetty nodded. 'You?' she asked.

'I'm fine,' Elsie replied.

Mrs Perkins clapped her hands. 'Girls, back to work!' she called.

Each girl took a pile of toffees and a box of wrappers, concentrating hard on their work, but Hetty knew that what had just happened would be the talk of the canteen at lunchtime. Elsie's aunt Jean would be the topic on everyone's lips, and they would all know about her Belgian boyfriend too. Oh, it wasn't that she wanted to keep Dirk a secret, far from it. If she could, she would climb up the factory chimney and yell from the top about how happy he made her feel. It was just that some of the local people – her own mother included – were narrow-minded and suspicious when it came to the Belgians.

She noticed that Mrs Perkins didn't walk back to her desk, but instead lingered at the table, inspecting the wrapped toffees. The supervisor was middle-aged, much older than the girls who worked in the wrapping room. She wore her long brown hair plaited down her back and her face was always set in a stern expression. When Hetty had first started work, she'd heard whispers from the other girls that it wasn't a good idea to get on the wrong side of her. If Mrs Perkins thought any of her girls were slacking, she'd go straight to the top, to Mr Jack himself, to complain. However, Hetty had found her to be firm but fair.

The supervisor had proved herself supportive and

protective of the wrapping room girls, more so since the death of one girl, Anabel, whom she had sent to work in the cutting room one day. Unbeknown to Mrs Perkins, Anabel had been exhausted that day, half-starved from not having enough to eat at home. She had fallen, hit her head and never regained consciousness. Ever since, rules at the factory had changed, ensuring that no one went hungry or thirsty at work. Free milk was offered in the canteen each lunchtime, and for the first time in the history of Jack's factory, toffees were given away. These were the ones that would have been rejected for being the wrong colour or size. There used to be strict rules concerning rejected toffees: they could only be eaten at work, and under no circumstances were they allowed to leave the factory. This was to protect the quality of the brand, of which Mr Jack was extremely proud. But now workers were allowed to take home toffees for their families.

After Anabel's death, a rose bush had been planted in her memory in the factory gardens, which were tended lovingly by Stan Chapman and his team.

Hetty shifted away from Mrs Perkins when she picked up a handful of toffees to inspect.

'Good work, girls,' the supervisor said approvingly.

Hetty's heart lifted at the compliment. It was good to feel as if the day was returning to normal after the ugly scene with the delivery man. However, Mrs Perkins then gently tapped Hetty and Elsie on their forearms.

'I want a word with you two about what's just happened and what I overheard. Follow me to my office.' She glowered at the other girls. 'What are you all gawping at? Get back to work.'

Hetty glanced at Elsie, who looked nervous. She reached for her friend's hand as they followed Mrs Perkins to the sturdy wooden desk covered in neat piles of papers and dockets. The supervisor sat down, leaving Hetty and Elsie standing in front of her with their backs to the room. Hetty knew the other girls were too far away to be able to hear what was said.

Mrs Perkins turned her stern face to Hetty, then Elsie. She laid her hands on the desk and straightened her back. Hetty gulped.

'Girls, you know I run the wrapping room under strict conditions, don't you?'

'Yes, Mrs Perkins,' Hetty and Elsie chorused.

'Then you'll know I don't like chatter and gossip, won't you?'

'Yes, Mrs Perkins.'

'Would you care to explain to me what was going on just now with the delivery man?'

Hetty looked down at her boots.

'Hetty Lawson,' Mrs Perkins snapped. 'You won't find the answer on the floor. It was your shouting that alerted me. Was the man abusive in his language to you?'

Without waiting for Hetty's response, she turned to Elsie.

'Was he inappropriate with you?'

Hetty opened her mouth to reply, but Mrs Perkins was looking beyond her. She turned her head to see what had caught the supervisor's attention and was surprised to see Anne standing in the doorway. Mrs Perkins stood, walked to her and shook her hand. As Mr Jack's personal secretary, Anne was afforded a great deal of respect in the factory.

She was direct with what she had to say. 'Mrs Perkins, gather your girls and bring everyone to the canteen for an all-staff meeting. Mr Jack has an important announcement.'

Chapter Five

Anne was impressed by the efficient way Mrs Perkins walked to each table and instructed the girls to file out to the canteen. They moved silently, heads down, wondering what was going on.

'Will we lose our jobs?' they asked Anne as they filed from the room. However, Anne was under strict instruction from Mr Jack not to breathe a word. She knew exactly what he was going to say, as she'd help him draft his speech.

'We'll find out soon enough,' she replied, then turned to Hetty and Elsie. 'Let's go,' she said.

The three girls walked from the wrapping room with Anne taking the lead. Within minutes they had reached the canteen, which was a buzz of muted, nervous chatter. Men from the sugar-boiling room stood along one wall with their arms crossed, wearing troubled expressions on their faces. Women from the chocolate-enrobing room and the slab room, where freshly made toffee was cut into bite-sized pieces, were huddled together. Without a word, Anne peeled away from Hetty and Elsie. She headed to the front, where a makeshift stage had been erected for

Mr Jack to address his workforce. On her way, she passed head gardener Stan Chapman. He stepped forward as if to say something, but Anne held up her hand and discreetly shook her head.

'I can't talk now, Stan. Meet me after work, we'll chat then.'

Stan backed away. Anne reached the raised platform where Mr Jack was standing, his normally cheerful expression replaced by a look of concern. His pristine blue bow tie was askew, caused by him nervously pulling at his collar that morning. At the opposite side of the stage, the factory's creative designer, elderly Mr Gerard, with his white hair and bushy eyebrows, was standing next to business manager Mr Burl, one of the most handsome men in the factory but also, Anne knew, a brute who treated his staff badly. His secretary, a mature, handsome woman called Meg, had recently expressed her displeasure to Anne about working for him. She'd complained about his intolerance to junior staff, especially the women in the typing pool, and his bullying manner. He swore at the women too, and upset them to the point where they were often in tears.

'It's water off a duck's back to me,' she'd told Anne. 'Mr Burl can't upset me and he knows it. I've worked here longer than him. I've seen the likes of him come and go. But the younger women don't know how to handle his insults, and frankly, there's no reason why they should. He shouldn't be allowed to get away with such dreadful behaviour.'

Anne and Mr Burl had never got along in all the time she'd worked at the factory. Without meaning to, she'd managed to rub him up the wrong way right from the start. Unbeknownst to her, Mr Burl had planned to install his fiancée in the role as Mr Jack's secretary. Indeed, he'd even promised her the job would be hers. Anne had heard on the factory grapevine that his fiancée had threatened to call off their engagement because he hadn't secured her the job. Mr Burl had treated Anne badly since and had spoken out against her, even in front of Mr Jack. He had gone out of his way to make her life a misery, but Anne had done her best to rise above his petty behaviour.

Anne saw Mr Jack raise his hand, and suddenly a hush descended. She looked at the faces of the work-force, men and women, boys and girls, then closed her eyes and breathed deeply as a lump came to her throat. She knew what was coming and it wasn't good news. When she opened her eyes, she saw Mr Jack glance at her. She nodded briefly in support, and he took a deep breath.

'First of all, can everyone hear me? Those of you stand-ing at the back, can you hear?' he said.

'Aye!' came the reply, all the way from the back, from the women who served in the canteen.

Mr Jack held a sheet of paper in his hands; it was the speech that he and Anne had prepared. Anne saw him glance at it, then he folded it and placed it inside his jacket. Instead of reading from the script, he was going to speak from his heart. Anne's own heart filled with respect and admiration. She pushed back her shoulders and watched.

'Ladies and gentlemen, our country is at war, of that I don't need to remind you. And yet I must state that it is the war that has caused us to gather today, as I need to give you news about the future of the factory.'

'Are we closing?' a man yelled from the side of the room.

'Can't we manufacture munitions instead of sweets?' another called.

Mr Jack held up his hand and silence reigned.

'This is difficult for us all, but please let me speak. The board of directors has been doing its best to steer the factory through troubled times. The war has taken many of our men to fight overseas. We've managed so far to replace them with local women, who are doing sterling work.'

'Hear, hear!' a woman yelled from the centre of the room.

'I'd like to invite Mr Burl to say a few words at this point.'

Mr Burl stepped onto the stage to stand beside Mr Jack. He cleared his throat, pulled a folded sheet of paper from his jacket pocket and began to read.

'I would like to talk about the female workers at the factory, those taken on to replace the men sent to war. At first we were not inclined to take the idea seriously of women coming to work here.'

Anne remembered what Meg had told her about Mr Burl's treatment of the women in the typing pool. She felt sick to her stomach that he was giving praise to the factory's women when he treated the ones he worked with so badly.

'Hypocrite,' she muttered under her breath.

'But we were proved wrong,' Mr Burl continued. 'Because not only do the women do their work well, they also do it with a smile.'

Anne gritted her teeth.

'They do it with a spring in their step, with good heart and good cheer. We applaud each and every one of you for stepping into the roles left by our brave men who are fighting at the front. And we trust it won't be long before those men return safe and sound to their families and loved ones. And when they return, we will thank the women workers, who will, I am sure, be relieved and happy to go back to looking after their families at home.'

'Not on your nelly, mate! Have you seen my old man?' one of the canteen women yelled.

Mr Burl didn't crack a smile though many in the canteen broke into laughter. He stepped away from the stage and Mr Jack waited for the laughter to subside.

'Thank you, Mr Burl, for your contribution to this difficult statement we must make today. Now, we all know that the war has begun to cause problems with sugar rationing and our output is expected to reduce . . .' Mr Jack paused before delivering the next word, 'substantially.'

There was a collective gasp in the room.

'However difficult it will be, and I make no bones about how hard things will become, we intend to keep the wheels turning. We will hold Jack's toffee factory together until this wretched war is over. I promise each one of you that it will not defeat us. The country will always need toffees and sweets, now more than ever. The pleasure of confectionery can help the nation through difficult, dark days ahead. But we must be realistic. With rationing and reduced output, we cannot continue to operate as normal.'

Here Mr Jack paused and glanced again at Anne. She nodded, encouraging him to carry on, knowing how difficult the next part of his speech was. Knowing how much it would affect, even destroy, the livelihoods of the people standing in front of her. She couldn't bear to look, and she dropped her gaze for a moment, trying to gather herself and force herself not to cry. When she looked up again, she saw the expectant faces of the workforce waiting to hear what Mr Jack would say.

'Closing the factory is not an option,' Mr Jack asserted loudly.

Chatter rippled through the canteen before quickly dying away.

'Turning it over to making munitions is not viable either,' he added. 'The sugar we use here has a deadly side that prevents such a change. The merest hint of sugar coming into contact with the acid used to make bombs would blow this factory sky-high. Just a few days ago, Mr Burl read of a munitions worker in Liverpool who was fined a week's wages after being found with a barley sugar in his pocket. One single barley sugar! Such a foolish action could have killed himself, his colleagues and friends. We have too much sugar in the factory, in the fabric of the building, in every single room, to consider making munitions. It is too dangerous by far.'

He paused, and there was dead silence. When he began speaking again, Anne could tell he was struggling with what he had to impart. The quaver in his voice gave him away, and he kept touching his blue bow tie, which he always did when anxious. She'd seen him do this many times in board meetings when he had to negotiate difficult conversations, especially over factory finances. He'd done it a lot more recently since rumours of sugar rationing became a startling reality.

'Before I continue, let me repeat what I have just said. I want you to remember this always. Jack's toffee factory will *not* be defeated by war. We will *not* close down. And we will *not* be turning our machinery over to make munitions. We will continue to produce toffee as best as we can using what is available. The good news, my friends, is that great quantities of toffee have been ordered by our government to send to troops in all parts of the world. Our brave boys and men, all the Tommies in the trenches, will receive parcels of Lady Tina toffee, sent in our trademark tins. We all know that toffees last longer than chocolates, and our boys fighting overseas will receive their share. We aim to fulfil as many government orders as we can while our rations last. But there is bad news too, alas. Because ports are blocked and sugar is unable to arrive as it once did, so too our output will decrease and there will be hardship ahead for us all.'

Anne bit the inside of her cheek to stop herself from crying.

'To steer us through this uncertain time, to keep the factory open and our machines turning, sacrifices need to be made. It breaks my heart to give you this news, but I must. Unlike the toffees we make, I cannot coat my words in chocolate. I will not give you a sugared version of the truth.' Mr Jack's hand flew to his bow tie. 'Until further notice, we will be manufacturing on a much-reduced scale. It is the first time in the history of the factory, a factory that my father proudly built many decades ago, that we have taken such drastic measures. Therefore . . .'

Anne heard the crack in his voice.

'Therefore from next Monday we will operate for only three days each week.'

That was when the canteen erupted into noise, and tears made their way down Anne's face. When she looked at Mr Jack, she saw that he was crying too.

Chapter Six

As Anne left the canteen, Stan walked towards her.

'We need to talk,' he whispered.

She shook her head. 'I can't speak now. Meet me by the gate after work.'

Hetty watched as Anne left the canteen with Stan Chapman. They looked to be whispering to each other, heads close together. It was exactly as she had seen them on Saturday morning in town, arm in arm. Was something going on between them? Well, it wasn't her business if there was, she knew that. But still, she was surprised. She hadn't thought Anne would lower herself to court a gardener, someone who worked with his hands in the soil. She'd pegged her as more gracious, even courting one of the smartly dressed gentlemen who worked behind the counter at the Co-op.

Anne strode ahead, leaving Stan behind. She had more important things on her mind. She walked into reception to find Jacob at his desk. He was a skinny man with black hair, thin lips and narrow eyes. His countenance was always grim and he rarely smiled, despite Anne's frequent attempts to lighten his mood. His job was to meet and greet factory visitors and record their details and appointments in the company ledger. He took great pride in his work, but he wasn't the friendliest person and Anne felt him ill-suited to his role. It was something she had often spoken to him about, chastising him for not being more welcoming. However, Jacob wasn't for changing his ways and remained as surly as ever. Anne noticed he was working on the appointments diary. He looked up when he saw her.

'What will you do when the factory closes for two days each week?' she asked him, concerned. 'How will you cope?' She knew it was a question that would be repeated all across the factory. Workers would be anxious about earning less money. Men would have time on their hands that they wouldn't know what to do with. Women would be forced back to the drudgery of housework instead of being productive, meeting friends and earning their own money for the first time in their lives.

'I'll survive, Anne. Don't worry about me. I have my mother to care for, she'll be glad of the company. What about yourself?'

Anne's shoulders dropped, because she had no idea. Even though she'd known Mr Jack's announcement was coming and had been aware of the plans for the three-day week since the last board meeting, her head spun when she thought of her future. All she had was her small room at Mrs Fortune's. She had no skills except organising, typing and administration.

'I don't know,' she replied sadly.

As she turned away to head to her office, Jacob called out to her.

'Anne, a visitor arrived just before you returned. She's here to see Mr Jack and demanded to wait in his office.'

'But we're not expecting anyone, are we?' she said, confused.

He glanced at the diary and shook his head. 'This particular visitor doesn't make appointments in advance,' he said.

Anne noticed a wry smile make its way to his lips. A look passed between them, and in that moment she knew it must be Mr Jack's fiancée, Lucinda Dalton. She was the only person who ever turned up unannounced, apart from Mr Jack's father. After a terrible start to the day with the announcement, handling Lucinda Dalton was the last thing Anne wanted. Her stomach fluttered with nerves. How could she face the woman knowing where Mr Jack's true feelings lay?

'Thank you, Jacob,' she said politely, then made her way out of reception, walking along the hallway panelled with caramel-coloured wood, the plush carpets a deep shade of toffee brown.

When she reached Mr Jack's office, the door was closed. Her own office was in an anteroom with an adjoining door, so she had no choice but to enter and greet Lucinda. Her stomach turned with anxiety as she pushed open the door, but she held her head high,.

Lucinda was a striking woman, and the sight of her sitting in Mr Jack's chair made Anne stop in her tracks. Her shoulder-length blonde hair was curled, her dark eyes exaggerated by pencil and shadow and her lips painted blood red. Anne could smell an overwhelming lemon perfume that left a bitter tang in the air. Lucinda was tall and willowy, and even behind the desk she gave off a sense of her stature and long, slender limbs. She wore a severe black jacket, and a pair of black gloves and a small cloche hat lay on the table.

Anne forced a smile, feeling treacherous to this woman who had no clue about her fiancé's true feelings. She walked to Mr Jack's desk and held out her hand. 'Miss Dalton, how lovely to see you.' She cursed herself for lying, but what else could she do?

Lucinda extended her own hand with its long, bony fingers and shook Anne's lightly. It felt to Anne as if she was being dismissed instead of greeted.

'Where is he?' Lucinda demanded.

'Mr Jack? Why, he's just delivered bad news to the workforce in the canteen. He could be there a while answering questions. I'm sure everyone's head is spinning.'

Lucinda sank back into the chair and regarded Anne coolly. 'Then bring me a cup of coffee while I wait. One of the good china cups, not those mugs you bought that William is so fond of. I often wonder, dear Anne, if you know him better than I. Oh, and don't bring me any damn toffees, they're no good for my figure. If I keep on eating them, I won't fit into my wedding gown.'

'Of course, I'll do it straight away, Miss Dalton,' Anne replied.

She left the office and headed to the small kitchen. When she reached it, she closed the door to shut herself away. Her head spun and she took a breath to steady herself. She had struggled to keep a lid on her feelings for Mr Jack since their heartfelt conversation, but seeing Lucinda in the flesh again, whilst knowing what she knew about

Mr Jack's true feelings, having to be polite and smile and pretend all was well . . . She wasn't sure how she'd cope when she returned to the office.

When she did return, she was heartened to see Mr Jack there. His presence acted as a welcome buffer between her and Lucinda. He was greeting his fiancée with a chaste kiss on her heavily powdered cheek. Anne laid the tray down on the desk.

'Darling, sit here in your chair,' Lucinda said. She stood to allow Mr Jack to take his seat. Anne watched with interest. It was as if she was granting him permission to take up his rightful position. He sat and rubbed his temples. Anne was aware of the strain that the meeting in the canteen had caused. However, Lucinda seemed in no way concerned. Instead, she wittered on about how her father's Rolls-Royce would need to be thoroughly polished before her wedding day. Anne noticed she never once called it *their* wedding, just hers. She wondered if the woman cared about what Mr Jack had been through that morning.

'Sir, would you like coffee too?' she asked.

'No coffee for me, Anne,' Mr Jack replied, looking at her.

Anne returned to her own office and closed the connecting door. However, she could still hear Lucinda through the wood-panelled wall. She sat down at her desk and opened a folder of papers, ready to type a report. But before her fingers hit the typewriter keys, she heard her name mentioned. She paused to listen further.

'You seem happier since Anne began working for you,' Lucinda was saying.

Anne was intrigued. She guessed that Lucinda had no

idea how much sound travelled between the offices, although she was aware Mr Jack would know. She waited for him to ask his fiancée to keep her voice down, but no such request was forthcoming. Lucinda continued.

'You're more calm, productive, more yourself somehow. You're more like the old William I knew.'

'The old William? We've only been together a few months, Lucinda,' Mr Jack replied curtly.

'Of course, when we marry, you'll have to get rid of her,' Lucinda continued. 'Life will be different then. You won't need to work here at this dreadful noisy factory. Father plans to sell it off after the war ends. Until then, he's talking about digging up the garden. He wants all the flowers ripped out.'

Mr Jack's voice was cold. 'Well, one thing's for sure, Anabel's rose bush is going nowhere.'

'Who on earth is Anabel?' Lucinda sounded puzzled.

'You know very well that Anabel is the young girl who died in the wrapping room last year. We planted a rose bush in her memory.'

'Well, Daddy will decide, of course. He's also talking about building a new machine shed for making munitions, a safe place not contaminated with sugar.'

'He hasn't mentioned any of this to me,' Mr Jack growled. 'How long have you known he wants to sell the factory? When did he tell you?'

Anne had never heard him sound so angry.

'Oh, calm down, dear,' Lucinda said, irritated.

'Calm down?' Mr Jack exploded. 'Your father said he wanted to invest in the factory, not sell us to the highest bidder.'

'Sit down, William,' Lucinda said sternly.

Anne listened in shock as their argument unravelled. She could picture Mr Jack pacing the floor, agitated and upset by the news.

'Stop fiddling with your bow tie!' Lucinda snapped.

'Your father hasn't been honest with me, Lucinda.'

'Don't be so naïve, darling. Daddy's a businessman. Most of them are liars,' Lucinda replied. 'Look, why don't you stop marching up and down. Watching you is making me dizzy. I want to talk about my wedding. Once Daddy sells the factory, you'll no longer need to work. We can travel, William, and see the world.'

'We can't travel while there's a damn war on, woman,' Mr Jack said, his voice rising again.

'Well, how else will I take you away from this dreadful place?' Lucinda said. 'It's all you think about, all you talk about. Your mind is always here, stuck in toffee.'

Anne felt guilty about continuing to listen to such an intimate conversation, but she had no choice as their voices carried through the thin wall.

'And yet . . .' Lucinda paused. Anne leaned forward, ear cocked. 'And yet you seem happier here in the factory than you ever do with me. You're at home here. You've got Anne tending to your needs, bringing you coffee in a mug instead of the china cups I prefer, for instance. You allow her to attend the management board meetings, where she's privy to all kinds of things about the factory that I'm not aware of. And you sing her praises often. Have you noticed that she blushes when you walk into the room? If I didn't know better, I'd say she was sweet on you. Oh, dear William, just look at your face. It's as if you're blushing too.'

Anne flinched as Lucinda carried on, her voice shrill and harsh.

'I sometimes wonder why you don't take up with her instead. But then why would you stoop to a girl who works as your secretary when you could have me? I've got a glittering circle of friends and my family is wealthy. In fact, I was wondering what I should give you as a wedding gift, my dear man. How about a new pen? No?' She laughed, but the sound was false. 'Then I could offer you my family estate in Scotland. And where will we go on honeymoon? I was thinking of—'

'Stop, Lucinda,' Mr Jack urged. 'This can't go on any longer . . . *We* can't go on. There is something I need you to know.'

Hetty found herself wondering again about Anne and Stan Chapman. Well, now that men were going to war, there were slim pickings left in Chester-le-Street as far as fellas were concerned. Was that why Anne had cosied up with the gardener? She was glad that she had met a good fella in Dirk, even if his work teaching boys at the school in Elisabethville kept him busy. She hadn't seen him since Christmas. She worried it was because Hilda had ignored him when he'd visited and he didn't want to return.

She walked out of the canteen with Elsie at her side. 'What'll we do for money when we earn only three days' pay?' she asked.

Elsie shrugged. 'Aunt Jean will make sure I don't go without.' She slid her arm through Hetty's and snuggled close to her side as they walked back to the wrapping room. 'Listen, Hetty. You asked me what happened when I met Frankie at the weekend. I owe you an apology for snapping at you. I also owe you an explanation. See, he swore to me that he'd changed and begged me to see him. He was desperate, crying, on his knees when he asked. That's why I had to hear what he said.'

Hetty gently stroked Elsie's hand. 'Elsie, love, after what he did to you, aren't you scared he might do it again? You can't tell me you love someone so brutal and vicious.'

Elsie pulled away and looked into Hetty's eyes. 'You're right. I'm terrified of him. Scared that he'll hit me again. Scared that his temper will spiral out of control and he'll beat me until he can't stop. That's why, after I talked to him at the weekend, I made an important decision.' She stuck her chest out. 'I'm never going to see him again.'

Hetty felt relief flood through her.

'Aunt Jean and I had a long talk about it after I returned home from meeting him on Saturday night. She said she'd keep me safe if he turns up at the flat.'

'I'm pleased to hear it, love. But if you ever need me, for anything, I'm here for you always.'

Elsie gave her a wide smile.

As soon as the girls walked into the wrapping room, Mrs Perkins swept across the room in a swish of blue skirt and demanded they follow her to her desk. 'Girls, we need to talk. Our conversation was interrupted earlier.'

'Oh crumbs, we're for it now,' Elsie muttered.

Mrs Perkins sat at her desk, with Hetty and Elsie standing shoulder to shoulder facing her. 'I heard some of what was said by the delivery man this morning,' she began. 'Your business is your own, of course, but I don't want gossip spreading around the factory that my girls are . . .' she looked from Elsie to Hetty and paused briefly before continuing, 'common tarts, or that they're sneaking into Elisabethville to meet a boyfriend when they should be there on factory business delivering tins of toffee.'

'I didn't! I'd never do that!' Hetty cried.

'Go back to work, this instant.'

'Yes, Mrs Perkins,' they chorused.

Before they could leave, however, a girl marched up to the desk to hand the supervisor a delivery docket. 'Mrs Perkins, your signature's needed,' she said.

Mrs Perkins didn't read the docket, having seen hundreds of them before, and quickly signed her name on the sheet in a swirl of black ink. *Mrs Pearl Perkins*, Hetty read. In all the time she'd worked at the factory, she had never known the woman's first name. Pearl. It made her seem almost human.

Chapter Seven

The factory was abuzz all day with talk of the new arrangements for the three-day week. Anxiety led to a dull acceptance that this was the only way things could be. All agreed it was better than the factory closing down. And so, at the end of the day, it was a quiet, resigned work-force that left through the gates. Usually men and boys would run out to head home for tea; women would join hands or link arms and rush to the tea rooms and cafés with friends. Today, however, the atmosphere was subdued.

Hetty and Elsie walked out together in silence. Then suddenly Hetty's blood ran cold. Waiting at the factory gates was a tall man with receding black hair and dark eyes. A man who had once worked as a sugar boiler at the factory but was sacked when he was caught stealing. Frankie Ireland. She had no idea what he did now to earn a living, or where he lived. She'd heard rumours that he hadn't signed up to join the army like most of the other men in town, because he claimed he had a weak chest. She wondered if that was really true, or just another of the lies he told. All she knew was that his brother, Jim, had thrown him out of his room at the Lambton Arms, the pub Jim ran with his wife, Cathy, after he discovered what Frankie had done to Elsie.

Hetty glanced over her shoulder. That was when she noticed Stan Chapman lingering outside reception. She saw Anne step out and glance nervously around, then she and Stan walked off together.

'I'm sorry to bother you, Anne,' Stan began. He had to hurry to keep up with her. 'But you know how worried I am about Elsie. I don't know who else to talk to about her.'

Elsie Cooper was the last thing on Anne's mind after the announcement of the three-day week and Lucinda's visit. However, she too was worried about the girl. When Stan had come to see her at Mrs Fortune's house on Saturday, he'd intimated that Elsie was in danger. Anne needed to know what was going on.

'We can't talk here,' she said. 'There are too many colleagues around.' She pointed ahead to the Lambton Café on the corner of Front Street and High Chare. 'Let's go for a pot of tea; we'll have privacy in the café. I doubt it'll be busy with factory girls after Mr Jack's announcement. They'll all have gone straight home to give the bad news to their families.'

'It was a shock, all right,' Stan said. 'How will any of us manage on three days' pay?'

Anne looked at him as they crossed the road. He was a thickset man with hands like shovels, a broad chest and strong arms. His face was open and honest, weather-beaten and ruddy from years spent working outdoors. His brown hair was cut short and his eyes were hazel.

As they entered the café, Stan removed his flat cap.

They were shown to a table in the window by a young, miserable-looking waitress in a green apron. However, Anne knew that if they sat there, it would put them in full view of the factory workers as they waited for buses on Front Street or walked past on their way home. She pointed to another table, tucked away at the back.

'Could we sit there instead, please?' she asked.

The waitress looked affronted. 'What's the matter with this one?' she demanded. 'Not good enough for you?'

'We'd like that one,' Anne said calmly.

'Please yourself,' the waitress huffed.

Anne and Stan settled themselves at the table and Anne lifted the menu. 'What will you have, Stan?'

'Just tea for me, thanks.'

Anne perused the menu, knowing it would be much easier to eat dinner in the café than cook in Mrs Fortune's kitchen at home. Thinking of Mrs Fortune's house made her wonder when she would meet the new lodger.

'I think I'll have a leek pudding. Sure you won't join me?'

Stan shook his head. 'I'll be quick in what I've got to say. We didn't have much time to talk on Saturday. I can't apologise enough about coming to your lodgings, but I didn't know what else to do. I tried to see you at work, but Jacob wouldn't let me in without an appointment. Elsie's in danger. I feel it in here and I want to do all I can to help.' He held his hands to his heart and looked imploringly at Anne.

'You really care for her, don't you?' she said.

Stan sat up straight in his seat. 'I'm a concerned friend, that's all,' he said abruptly, then his face softened. 'But I know something about her, Anne, something that no one else does. It's something she didn't want anyone to know after what Frankie did. She begged me to keep it to myself and I have done so far.' He sighed heavily. 'I'm wrestling with my conscience. Because if I tell you what I know, I'll have to break Elsie's confidence.'

Anne patted his hand. 'Whatever you tell me remains a secret,' she assured him.

Stan took heart and carried on. 'Thank you, Anne. You see, I've heard from the lads in the sugar boiling room that Frankie's out to win Elsie back. He swears he's changed and won't raise a hand to her again. From what I know about Elsie, she wants to be loved so much that she might just believe him. But if anything happens to that girl, I'll burn for ever inside.'

'Tea? Coffee? We've got no sugar,' the waitress barked. She had appeared without warning, and Anne hoped she hadn't overheard Stan's words.

Anne ordered tea for two and a leek pudding. She waited for the waitress to disappear, then leaned forward to Stan. 'I appreciate you coming to me. I want to help Elsie too. I had no idea what Frankie was up to. Please tell me what you know.'

Elsie steeled herself when she spotted Frankie at the factory gates. She hadn't expected to see him again after Saturday night. When they'd met then, Frankie had pleaded with her to take him back. He'd promised he'd changed; he'd even cried, again, and said how sorry he was for what he'd done on their wedding day. Elsie had listened to his impassioned pleas and declarations of love, and with every word, the crack in her heart began to feel as if it might mend . . . and that was what had scared her the most. She had no one else in her life who cared about her the way Frankie said he did. He was the only person who told her the things she longed to hear. However, while his lips had promised one thing, his brutal actions had said another. If only she had someone to talk to, to confide in, someone who would wrap their arms around her, hold her and tell her everything would be all right.

She knew that if she succumbed to Frankie's words, she would end up suffering the temper and brutality that she now knew was part of him. Her emotional scars were too raw to accept him back into her life. This was the man who'd kicked her and punched her. The man who'd beat her so badly she'd lost their baby. The man his own brother and sister-in-law had shunned from their family. Her aunt had warned her not to take him back and Hetty had said the same. Elsie had told him on Saturday night that she was staying put with Aunt Jean, whether they were married or not. But now he was waiting at the factory gates, unexpected and unwanted.

'Are you all right?' Hetty asked her, nodding at Frankie.

'I'm a big girl, I can take care of myself,' Elsie replied with more confidence than she felt. 'Go home, Hetty. I'll deal with Frankie.'

Reluctantly Hetty turned away, but when Elsie glanced over her shoulder to see if she had gone, she was grateful and relieved that her friend was still there, watching vigilantly.

When Elsie reached the gates, Frankie stepped forward, throwing his arm around her shoulders. She tried to shrug him off, but he held tight.

'What are you doing here?' she asked him. 'I told you, we're over! I never want to see you again!'

He ignored her. 'Where do you want to go? You name

it, I'll take you,' he said. 'I've found a room in a house on Pine Street. I thought we'd go there so I can show you where I'm living. Once you see it, you'll love it, Elsie, and then you can move in.'

She felt his grip on her shoulder tighten, then he leaned in to her, breathing in her face, and she could smell the stench of beer.

'I'll do anything for my wife. Want to come to see my new home?' He sneered. 'Or do you have somewhere else you need to be?'

Elsie's heart plummeted, for that was the crux of it. She had nowhere else. If she went home to the flat, Aunt Jean would either be locked in her room with a man she'd met on the street, or at work on the market. Elsie would be left to her own devices, reading in her room, cooking her own dinner, suffering another lonely night curled up on her bed with only a novel for company.

Frankie dropped his arm from her shoulders, then stopped dead on the pavement. He stood in front of her, preventing her from walking on. 'Cheer up, love,' he said. Then he grabbed her hand and broke into a run. Elsie had to sprint to keep up.

'Stop, Frankie! You're hurting me,' she said, trying to pull away, but he wouldn't let go. She called out, hoping one of the women leaving work might hear her and help, but no one wanted to get involved. She shouted for Hetty, but her cries were carried away on the wind as Frankie dragged her along.

Panting and out of breath, they arrived outside a house at the end of Pine Street. The front door was splintered at the bottom, as if someone had kicked it. The windows were grimy, with no curtains or nets, and roof slates were missing. Frankie let go of Elsie's hand and pushed open the battered door.

'Get inside, lass,' he ordered.

Elsie didn't move. She glanced at the doorstep. It was covered in muck, as if someone had scraped mud off their shoes. She knew what stepping over the threshold would mean, what Frankie was hoping for. If she entered the house, there would be no turning back. She didn't need to think twice; she wasn't prepared to take another step.

'No.'

Frankie's face dropped. 'No?' he said, incredulous. 'Are you defying your husband?'

'I've already told you I don't want to be with you,' Elsie began, but Frankie moved quickly and wrapped his arms around her.

'Please, Elsie,' he begged. 'Give it a try. Come in and see for yourself what we could do with this place. It's just one room, but between us we could turn it into our home.'

She felt herself softening and hated herself for it, but he was saying words she longed to hear. A home of her own and someone to care for her was all she had ever wanted.

'Believe me, Elsie. Trust me,' he cooed. 'I'm a changed man, I swear. Haven't I told you this already? I'll never raise my hand again. I love you, Mrs Ireland. Isn't that what you want? What you've always wanted? Someone to love you? You've never had your own family, just your aunt Jean. Well, we're family now, you and me. We could even try for another baby. What happened last time was wrong, I know that. I wasn't in my right mind. I was troubled and lost. I'd been drinking too much. Believe me, Elsie, please.'

At this, tears rolled down her face. The thought of

trying again for a baby was too much to bear, and her heart broke all over again. She wanted to walk away, leave the dirty house on Pine Street and leave Frankie too. But her legs wouldn't move. She felt dizzy, light-headed, and began to shake. She was scared that she might fall to the ground. In her confusion, Frankie pulled her to him, embracing her, caressing her as her tears fell. She looked into his face and saw he was crying too.

'Come on, Elsie, please, just take a look at the room. If you don't like it, you don't have to return,' he begged.

Elsie felt as if she was watching herself standing on the pavement, as if it wasn't really her. She steadied herself, determined to walk away and get as far as she could from Frankie and the awful house. But he grabbed her by the shoulders, pushing her across the threshold, and she stumbled inside.

Chapter Eight

Anne left Stan at the café and walked home with a heavy heart. He'd told her everything, and now she knew the awful truth. He had explained that after Frankie had beaten Elsie on their wedding day, she had gone to the river, desperate and alone. Stan had been walking his dog, Patch, there, as he did most nights, and found Elsie wandering in the cold night air. She'd seemed eerily calm, he'd told Anne, but when he'd called out her name, surprised to see her, she hadn't responded. Alarmed, he'd followed her and was horrified to see her heading into the treacherous river, as if she was sleepwalking. She seemed not to notice the icy water hit her skin or care that her feet stumbled over rocks and stones. Without a thought for his own safety, Stan had run into the freezing-cold river, caught Elsie up in his arms and carried her sobbing to safety. After she'd calmed down, he had walked her back to the Lambton Arms, where she'd been living with Jim and Cathy.

As he'd revealed the distressing events, Anne could tell by his tone and the way he kept pausing, as if unsure how much he should say, that he cared for Elsie deeply.

Now she struggled with the weight of information he had given her, trying to work out how best to offer Elsie support. Had she been about to take her own life? It was too dreadful to consider. She needed to speak to her, but what if Elsie told her that what went on between her and Frankie was none of her business? He was still her husband. She might fall out with Anne and Stan and tell them to leave her alone.

Thoughts whirled in Anne's head as she processed the news. Her confused feelings about Elsie collided with how she'd felt earlier that day seeing Lucinda and overhearing her words. Elsie, Lucinda, Mr Jack and Stan spun around in her mind, and she could feel a headache pulsing. How she wished she had someone to talk to who might help her understand her emotions, especially regarding Mr Jack. It was too confusing, and pointless, to admit how she felt about him. What good would it do either of them? A shiver went down her back when she recalled Lucinda's words about her father's plans to close the factory. That had been a huge shock for Anne and, from the reaction she'd overheard, for Mr Jack too. Everything seemed difficult, a weight on her shoulders that she couldn't unload. All she wanted was to return to her room at Mrs Fortune's house, collapse into her bed warmed by her hot-water bottle and try to make sense of the thoughts that were causing her so much distress.

She turned the corner of Victor Street, heading home. An oil lamp glowed in the window of Mrs Fortune's downstairs parlour, giving a welcoming light. She wondered if the new lodger was home. It would be good to meet her finally, as their paths hadn't crossed yet. As she walked along the dimly lit street, she saw a figure outside

Mrs Fortune's house. It was a man. She slowed her pace, trying to work out who it was. At first she worried it was Stan, waiting to give her more news about Elsie, but as she drew near, she could tell it wasn't him. He was shorter, less stocky than Stan. He wore a hat and a long dark coat. Anne eyed him carefully with every step that took her closer. Then he turned and she stopped dead, for she recognised him immediately. At first she thought it was a trick of the light that was making her see someone who shouldn't be there, but when he spotted her, he raised his hat. Now that Anne was close, she saw he wore a worried expression. Concerned that Mrs Fortune might see him, she pulled him gently away from the house.

'Mr Jack, what are you doing here?' she gasped.

She glanced at the window, and her heart fell as she saw a curtain twitch. The light from the oil lamp brightened then faded as the curtain fell.

'We've been seen,' she whispered. 'Please, come away from here. My landlady doesn't allow gentleman callers. If she recognises you, she'll have a field day spreading gossip that the toffee factory owner was here.'

'We can tell her I'm here on factory business,' Mr Jack replied softly as Anne led him away. 'And it's true, in a way.'

Anne's head spun. 'Couldn't it wait until tomorrow?' she asked.

'Anne, my dear. I can't contain my feelings any longer. I have spent a miserable afternoon with Lucinda.'

She looked into his eyes. What was he saying?

'I had no choice but to break off our engagement.'

Anne was shocked. Of course, she'd heard some of his conversation with Lucinda through the adjoining wall of their offices, but she'd never dreamed it would lead to him breaking off his engagement. All she knew was that the two of them had left the factory together after he'd told her he had something important to say.

'But what about your wedding? It's all arranged,' she managed to say.

'There will be no wedding,' Mr Jack said firmly. 'I was being dishonest to Lucinda, and to myself. I was also being utterly unfair to you. I will do the decent thing and accept the blame for calling it off. I will write letters of apology and make visits to those invited to explain that the fault is all mine. I will send flowers to Lucinda's mother and take the worst from her father that I know will be coming my way. But my word, I will give him hell too. He misled me about his plans for the factory. The management board, of course, will demand an explanation as to why Dalton won't be investing, and I will tell them the truth. Once they hear about his scheme to sell the place as soon as the war ends, they will understand.

'As for Lucinda, she has agreed to let me go without a fuss. She knows gossip will be rife within her circle, but she's made of stern stuff. In fact, she's already talked about visiting her aunt in Inverness until the worst blows over, and she admitted some relief at not having to go through with the charade. She was never invested emotionally in me. It was all her father's idea. I'd always had my suspicions that the man was up to something, and now I know the awful truth. He never wanted the factory, or a son-in-law, just the land the factory sits on. But the main reason I've called the wedding off is that I can't marry Lucinda when I have strong feelings for someone else.'

Anne gulped. 'Someone else?' she breathed. Her heart skipped a beat.

Mr Jack leaned forward and planted the softest kiss on her cheek. Anne was stunned at his public display of affection, but felt secretly happy too.

'Someone beautiful and clever,' he said, stepping away a respectable distance. 'You know it's you I want. From the first moment I laid my eyes on you when you came for your interview, I knew you had something about you. I felt it in here.' His hands flew to his heart. 'And I've felt it ever since, every day. When we work together at the factory, your enthusiasm and insight spur me on to be my best. We work well as a team, but just think what we could do as a partnership, as a couple. You and I could take on the world, Anne, the whole world.'

He stepped back and tilted his chin. In the dim light, Anne saw his eyes sparkle.

'The next few months will be tricky; I won't lie to you. Lucinda's father will give me hell for breaking off the engagement. My own father will have strong words too. My poor mother will be inconsolable; she's already bought a new hat.'

Here he paused a moment with a slight smile on his face.

'But seriously, Anne, the immediate future will be hard. With your help, I will have to navigate the factory through difficult times. There will be greater changes, more restrictions until the war is over.'

'Mr Jack, I don't know what to say,' Anne said, then stepped away as a passer-by walked along the other side of the street. 'We shouldn't be seen talking like this,' she went on. 'It will do your reputation no good if someone spies the toffee factory owner chatting to a girl on a dark street corner. Why, you'll be the gossip of Chester-le-Street for months.'

He smiled. 'I don't care who sees me with you.'

Anne gasped. 'Mr Jack . . . please . . . You've had a difficult conversation with your fiancée today; don't rush into anything, please. Don't say things you might regret.'

'My dear Anne, know that I am yours, if you will have me.'

Anne was dumbstruck. She couldn't make sense of what was happening, right here on the street where her lodging house was. It all seemed unreal.

'Mr Jack, I . . .' she began.

He shook his head. 'Please, don't say a word. Make the right decision with your heart and your mind. I'll leave you now and head home to the Deanery. Call on me any time if you would like to talk. We will not be alone there, as my housekeeper will be on hand and I trust her implicitly. Everything will be proper and above board, as it was on the day you came to tea before Christmas. However, I think it best not to talk of this at work. We must remain dispassionate at the factory, as if nothing has changed.'

He raised Anne's left hand to his lips and gently kissed her fingers as he gazed into her eyes.

'I'm yours, Anne. All you have to do is say the word.'

With that, he tipped his hat and walked away into the night. Anne was left speechless and stunned . . . and very happy too.

Chapter Nine

Meanwhile, across town, Hetty was banging on a door on Front Street. Behind the door was a steep staircase that led to the flat where Jean and Elsie lived above a dressmaker's shop.

'Jean! Get down here!' she yelled. She glanced up at the window, but there was no movement, so she looked around for a stone and picked it up. Her aim was perfect, and within seconds Jean's head popped out of the window. Her hair was unpinned and she held what looked like a bedsheet against her bare skin.

'Who the devil's throwing stones at my window?'

Hetty waved both hands. 'Jean! Elsie's in danger. You've got to come, now! She's with Frankie. He turned up at the factory and dragged her away.'

The window slammed shut, and a few moments later the door in front of Hetty opened and a smartly dressed man walked out, buttoning an expensive-looking coat. Behind him walked Jean, fully dressed now, stuffing her hair under a hat.

'Bye, love, see you next week, same time,' she said,

kissing the man on the cheek, then she threaded her arm through Hetty's.

While Hetty knew what Jean did for a living, she was surprised to hear her use such a term of endearment. 'You called that man *love*. Do you really love him?' she asked.

Jean looked at her askance. 'I love them all, Hetty, for as long as it takes them to pay me. Apart from a fella called Alfie, who I'm growing quite fond of. Anyway, enough of talking about men. Take me to Elsie. We've got to get her away from that monster.'

Hetty felt conspicuous as she walked down Front Street with Jean. She felt men's eyes bore into her and noticed looks of disapproval from women who passed her by. She felt as if everyone knew who Jean was, what she did, and were judging her too as she walked with her. But she was too worried about Elsie to care.

'Where's Frankie taken her?' Jean asked.

'I don't know. I followed them as far as Front Street, but I lost them when I bumped into Mum. She was taking Jet for a walk, but her chest isn't good and she was struggling to breathe. I took her home and had to stay with her until she felt all right, then I came straight here. I'm worried sick about Elsie.'

'We'll ask Jim; he might know where Frankie is.'

Jean manoeuvred Hetty across the road to the Lambton Arms and knocked loudly. Jim's wife, Cathy, opened the door. A short, stocky woman with dark hair swept back from her face, she was wearing a brown apron over a blue dress and had a tea towel slung across her shoulder. She narrowed her eyes at Jean.

'We don't want your kind of business in here, Jean, I've told you before,' she said firmly.

Jean shook her head. 'I'm not here to cause bother. I'm here to ask if you know where we'll find Frankie. He's got Elsie.'

Hetty stepped forward. 'He turned up at work tonight and grabbed her. I followed them for a while but couldn't see where they went,' she explained.

Cathy's mouth opened in shock. 'The poor girl, after what he did to her,' she muttered. She turned her head and shouted behind her. 'Jim! Get yourself here!'

Jim Ireland was as short and wide as his wife, with a pot belly from too much beer. When he walked, he rocked side to side. He was completely bald and his round face was pink. He wore a pair of black trousers and a white shirt with the sleeves rolled up to the elbows. He nodded towards Jean.

'What's she doing here? I thought we'd barred her after she used our pub for picking up men.'

'Leave it, Jim,' Cathy warned. 'They're looking for Elsie. Frankie's got her.'

'Do you know where we'll find him?' Hetty begged.

Jim thought for a moment. 'The last I heard he'd moved to live in a room at the far end of Pine Street.'

'Thanks, Jim, we'll look for her there.'

As Hetty and Jean turned to walk away, Cathy called out, 'Lasses, wait!' She peeled her apron over her head, flung the tea towel at her husband, then stuffed her arms into a long black coat. 'I'm coming with you, for support.'

Jim laid his hand on her arm. 'Be careful, lass, you know what my brother's like.'

Cathy gritted her teeth. 'Only too well. But he won't stand a chance against three of us. If you had anything about you, Jim Ireland, you'd come and help.'

'I'm not going up against my brother.'

'Coward,' she hissed.

'He's more scared of you than he'll ever be of me,' Jim said. 'Besides, one of us has to stay here to deal with the drayman. If there's no one here to let him in, we'll have no beer to sell tonight.'

Cathy tutted, then she, Hetty and Jean set off at speed for Pine Street.

When they reached the house at the end, Hetty raised her fist to thump on the door, but Jean pulled her back.

'No, let's not cause a scene. If Frankie hears banging, he'll know it means trouble and he might not open up. If he sees you or me, he'll know immediately we're here to get Elsie.'

She gently pushed Cathy forward.

'Cathy, you're family. Knock and call for him. Tell him there's a problem, tell him Jim needs him. It's the only way he'll come to the door. Then when he opens it, we rush at him and force him to the floor. Pin his arms behind his back, sit on his legs. Do whatever it takes to stop him from lashing out and hitting us. Me and Cathy will sort him out. Hetty, you race inside and find Elsie, then we'll all run like hell.'

Hetty looked at her, astonished. 'You make it sound easy.'

'In my line of work I'm used to handling fellas when they get out of line.'

'Can we really do it?' she asked.

'We've got no choice. Elsie's in there, in danger,' Jean replied sternly.

Cathy looked from Hetty to Jean, then knocked politely at the door and called for Frankie, telling him she'd been sent on urgent business from Jim. It took a while, but finally the door opened and Frankie stood there glassy-eyed and swaying. Hetty knew straight away he was drunk. He glared at each woman in turn, leered at Jean, then tried to slam the door in her face. But Jean was one step ahead; she'd stuck her boot in the door to stop it from closing. She pushed Frankie's chest, shoving him forcefully against the wall. The beer had upset his balance, and he stumbled and fell.

'Hetty, find Elsie!' Jean ordered. 'Cathy, help me keep him down.'

As Jean and Cathy struggled with Frankie in the hallway, Hetty ran into the house. The walls were damp and unpainted, the floorboards bare. There was a stained and dirty mattress on the floor of a foul-smelling room. Elsie was curled up on it, asleep. Five empty beer bottles lay on the floor. Hetty flew to her friend.

'Elsie, wake up. We're taking you home. Elsie, love, please wake up.'

Elsie's eyelids fluttered and Hetty helped her to stand. She slung Elsie's arm around her shoulders and put her own arm around Elsie's waist, supporting her friend, who was groggy and stank of beer. When she reached the hall, what she saw made her gasp. Frankie lay prone on the floor with Cathy sitting on his legs. She'd even pulled off his shoes and socks in case he kicked out or tried to run off. Jean had his arms pinned behind his back. He couldn't move an inch, but that didn't stop him from swearing revenge.

'I'll get you back for this,' he yelled at Jean.

Jean stood, then delivered a swift kick to Frankie's ribs. He doubled up in pain.

'Run, girls!' she commanded.

On Victor Street, Anne slid her key into the lock, then pushed the door open and stepped into the hall with its scent of lemon wax polish. As she began to climb to her room, she heard the clink of glasses. She paused on the staircase, listening.

'Cheers, my dear Pearl,' Mrs Fortune said. 'I hope you'll be happy living here.'

'I'm sure I will, Avril. This is fine sherry, by the way,' a second woman replied.

Anne's eyebrows shot up. Avril? She'd never heard her landlady's first name before. She'd never been asked to address her as anything other than Mrs Fortune. She was curious as to why the new girl was allowed to be so familiar. And as for having sherry, well, that was something Anne had never been treated to, except on Christmas Day. How very odd it was.

She turned back towards the door, daring herself to knock in the hope she could introduce herself to Pearl. But then she stopped. If either Mrs Fortune or Pearl had seen her talking to Mr Jack, she'd have some explaining to do.

She was halfway up the stairs when she heard the new lodger speak again.

'A fine sherry indeed, with complex flavours,' Pearl said.

Anne gripped the handrail. There was something about the woman's voice that sounded familiar. She was certain she'd heard it before. She shook her head. She was tired. It had been a dreadful day. Her mind was busy with the announcement at the factory, Stan's disturbing news about Elsie, Lucinda Dalton's visit, and now Mr Jack turning up at her lodging house to reveal that he'd broken off his engagement. Her stomach turned with anxiety. All she wanted to do was go to bed and think, to process what had happened, especially the bombshell of Mr Jack's declaration.

Mulling over his invitation to visit his home at the Deanery, she was surprised and pleased. She never imagined she'd return after taking tea there several weeks ago. It had been a chaste event then, with Edith Brown, his housekeeper, in attendance, pottering around the room, lifting cups, placing slices of cake. There had been little conversation between her and Mr Jack. Now things had changed, and she decided that returning to talk to him was an excellent idea.

She crawled into bed, exhausted, and watched the flickering light from the oil lamp at her bedside illuminate her small room. The enormity of Mr Jack's words flattered her in every way, yet troubled her at the same time. He'd proved his love for her without her asking. He'd called off his wedding for her. She already admired and respected him, and, she admitted, the stirrings of love were there too. They had been for longer than she cared to admit, though she'd had to suppress them and push them deep inside her heart because of Lucinda Dalton. But now there were no obstacles in her way.

She closed her eyes, knowing that her future, should she choose it, could be different . . . better. However, when her son had been born and the baby's father had disappeared, she'd sworn to herself she'd never become involved with another man. She'd been too badly hurt. Her gut twisted painfully. Her son was a secret of which Mr Jack was unaware, and oh, how guilty she felt at not being able to tell him. However, she'd made a promise to Mr and Mrs Matthews that she'd never reveal their connection.

Chapter Ten

After Hetty, Jean and Cathy had rescued Elsie from Frankie's evil grip, they returned to Jean and Elsie's flat on Front Street. There they sobered Elsie with coffee and made sure she was unhurt. Once Elsie reassured them that she was fine, and swore she'd never see Frankie again, Hetty and Cathy left and headed home. As she walked, Hetty crossed her fingers and secretly prayed that Elsie had meant what she'd said. She knew how vulnerable her friend could be, and she was worried for her.

Hetty had still not seen or heard from Dirk. His absence hurt deeply, for she'd thought there was something special about him, and that they'd forged a bond. Apart from Bob, Dirk was the only man she'd kissed, the only man she'd felt anything for. Surely he wasn't going to end things without an explanation. Had she said something that had upset him? Had he been stringing her along all this time? Was she nothing more to him than a girl he'd had fun with? With all her heart she hoped not. While Dirk was free to visit her at any time at home, or turn up at the factory gates, she couldn't go to Elisabethville to see him. Although she had a pass from the factory that allowed her into the village on business, she hadn't been asked to deliver toffee there for weeks. She'd tried to distract herself from thoughts of him, though it proved hard, for he was constantly on her mind.

As the harsh winter began to loosen its grip, war continued to rage. Jack's toffee factory settled uneasily into its new work pattern. It wasn't a simple transition, with many issues to be resolved around staffing and shifts. However, Mr Jack ensured that robust structures were put in place. It was an unprecedented time in the history of the factory, and he was determined to keep it open any way he could. 'I'll show Dalton! How dare he even think about closing this place down after he said he was going to invest!' he complained bitterly and often to Anne. Now that the investment from Lucinda's father was no longer an option, Mr Jack began work on developing more modest financial procedures.

During this time of great change, Anne gave much thought to Mr Jack's declaration of love. Each night, when she returned alone to her small room at Mrs Fortune's, it felt as if she'd left part of herself at the factory. Soon, all she wanted was to be with the man she now realised she loved, carrying out the job she adored.

She had still not met Pearl, and this unsettled her too. It felt as if there was a stranger living in the house. Their paths hadn't even crossed in the kitchen or in the hall outside the bathroom the women shared.

One Saturday morning, Mrs Fortune knocked on Anne's bedroom door. Anne slid the bolt and opened it.

'Morning, Mrs Fortune. How are you?'

'I'm very well, Miss Wright,' the landlady replied,

peering into the room. Anne stood her ground with her hand on the door, not allowing her to enter. 'I wondered if you might have some time today to help me fix a shelf on the wall in Pearl's room?'

'Me?' Anne said, surprised.

Mrs Fortune peered around the door at the lock Anne had fixed. 'Well, you did say you knew how to use a screwdriver,' she said. 'Perhaps you have other skills that might assist me.'

'I'd be happy to help,' Anne said.

And so later that morning, she and Mrs Fortune entered Pearl's room, downstairs at the front. Anne was hoping to meet the mystery woman for the first time, but was disappointed.

'Isn't Pearl here today?' she asked as she looked around.

'She's visiting family,' Mrs Fortune replied, giving nothing away.

Installing the shelf was an easy task for Anne with a hammer and nails. As she worked, she tried to get a sense of the woman. The room was tidy. Books lay in a box on the floor, to be placed on the new shelf once it was up. Clothes were neatly folded and a heavy coat was slung over the wardrobe door. There was something about the coat that looked familiar to Anne, but she felt it rude to stare.

Once the shelf was in place, Mrs Fortune expressed her gratitude and ushered her from the room. Anne wondered where Pearl worked, for she must have a job if she could afford to rent a room. She asked Mrs Fortune, but the landlady shrugged off her question.

'I'm sure she'd tell you if she wanted you to know.'

'But I never see her,' Anne pointed out. 'She must leave

the house before me each morning. When I return home from work at night, I hear your voices coming from the front parlour. Perhaps . . .' She paused. 'Perhaps I could join you both one night for dinner? I'd like to meet Pearl, very much.'

Mrs Fortune straightened her small black hat and Anne noticed her face cloud over. 'Perhaps,' she said cagily.

It felt to Anne as if Mrs Fortune and Pearl were hiding something from her. Then she dismissed the foolish notion. War was making everyone paranoid, even her.

During this difficult time at the factory, Anne threw herself into her work supporting Mr Jack and the board of directors. Along with everyone else at the factory, her hours and pay had been cut to three days. However, this didn't stop her from working five days a week as before, even though she was being paid less. Well, she had nothing else to do and willingly, happily dedicated all her time and energy to Mr Jack. They worked more than ever as a team, both of them turning up early each morning and staying late at night. They became closer, bonded by the struggle the factory faced and determined to work as hard as they could. On the days when they were the only two there, they pored over finance figures, schedules and plans and the government orders that were keeping the factory afloat.

One day, unable to stay quiet any longer, she tackled Mr Jack on the subject of Lucinda's father and the lack of investment. Setting two cups of coffee on his desk, she sat opposite, then lifted her cup and gently blew the surface to cool it.

'Do you ever regret turning down Mr Dalton's offer of

investment to keep the factory open until the end of the war?' she asked.

Mr Jack's face blanched and he looked straight at her. 'Never,' he said firmly, holding her gaze. 'Now I know the truth from Lucinda's mouth. His investment was offered to the board under false pretences. He never had a desire to be involved in the confectionery business. He wanted to close down the factory, sell the land, dig up the gardens I created and destroy the rose bush planted in Anabel's memory. Dear Anne, you know I could never have taken his money, especially when I didn't love his daughter.'

He stood and walked around the desk, gently placing his hand on her shoulder.

'There's only one woman I love. With you by my side, we'll get through this damn war.'

Anne felt reassured beyond measure. She patted his hand, then looked into his eyes. 'In that case, let's get back to work.'

Mr Jack returned to his seat, all business now. 'Could you bring me the advertising folder, please? I need to peruse it before the board meeting next week.' He sighed heavily. 'The damn board meeting. They'll give me a rough ride for turning down the investment from Lucinda's father. They'll want an explanation and also expect my business plan for steering us through the next months. Think you can help me compose a persuasive report?'

'I'm sure I can,' Anne said confidently. 'And once the announcement is made to the board that you and Lucinda are no longer to be married, perhaps I could take up your invitation to join you at home for dinner.'

Mr Jack's face softened. 'I'd like that very much. And

you must call me William at home. However, for the time being, let's keep things formal and professional at work.'

Anne smiled widely and gave a mock salute. 'Yes, sir,' she said. Then she glanced at the clock on the wall. 'Now then, I must go, as I have a memo to deal with.'

Mr Jack raised his eyebrows. 'Oh?'

'It's a formal request from Mr Burl's secretary, Meg. She's asked to speak to me again in confidence about him. From what she's intimated so far about their working relationship, I fear it won't be good news.'

Hetty was at home, scanning the positions vacant column in the newspaper. Hilda was sitting at the kitchen table writing to Dan. Jet lay under the table.

'Mum, there's a job here looking after a small boy for a couple in Durham city. Apply to Mr and Mrs Matthews,' Hetty said, running her finger across the ad. But then her heart sank. 'Aw, no. It says girls who apply must be experienced in looking after children, and I'm not. They also want someone to live with them, and oh, crikey, they're moving to Scotland and will expect the girl to accompany them. I don't much fancy Scotland. That's no good for me. Plus I only need a job for two days each week while I'm not at the toffee factory. I've got to earn money to feed us both and buy coal. Now, what else is on offer?'

She ran a finger down the column. 'Mum!' she cried excitedly. Hilda looked up, annoyed.

'What is it? Can't you see I'm busy?'

'There's a job here I think I can do.'

Hilda laid down her pencil and glared at her. 'Oh Hetty! You've made me lose concentration,' she complained. 'What is it that's got you so giddy?'

Glenda Young

Hetty read from the newspaper. 'Girl wanted for domestic work at Lumley Castle, two days per week. Apply in person to Mrs Doughty, housekeeper. Reference required. Must be clean, tidy and hard-working.' She put the newspaper down. 'This is perfect.'

Hilda shot her a look of disdain. 'Hard-working? You? I wouldn't call wrapping toffees hard work. And when you're not at work, you're gadding about with your Belgian fella or sulking here at home. Mind you, you haven't seen Dirk in ages. Has he gone off you? I told you not to mess with those Belgian men.'

Hetty knew how hard she worked at the toffee factory, how tired she was at night after standing all day at the wrapping table. After she finished at the factory, she worked at home too, with Hilda's bad chest preventing her from carrying out the simplest of chores, which all fell squarely on Hetty's shoulders. But while she shrugged off Hilda's comments about work, being used to her constant criticism, the comments about Dirk stung. She missed him a lot and wasn't sure when, or if, she would see him again.

'I'm going to apply for this job,' she said. 'If the two days a week are the same two days I'm not at work at the factory, why, it'd be perfect.'

She stood and began to pace, thinking through all she needed to do. She hoped it would keep her mind busy and stop her from dwelling on Dirk.

'I need to speak to Anne at work to ask if she'll write my character reference. And I need to clean my shoes and wash my hair before I meet the housekeeper.' Her eyes shone as she picked up the newspaper again. 'Wow! A castle. This isn't any old job. The Earl of Scarbrough and his family live at the castle. I wonder what he's like?'

78

Hilda shifted in her seat and picked up her pencil, returning her attention to writing to her beloved son.

'You'll never get to find out. You'll be cleaning his privy, not serving his meals. Don't get above yourself.'

A rattle at the door stopped their conversation. Hetty left the kitchen and walked into the hallway to see who was there. Her heart fell when she saw that a small square card had been pushed through the letter box.

'Is that the post, Hetty? Is there a letter from Dan?' Hilda called.

Hetty picked up the card. 'Nothing from Dan,' she replied.

She slipped the card into her pocket and climbed the stairs. When she reached her bedroom, she closed the door and sank onto her bed. Pulling the card out, she scanned it in confusion. It was another card from Bob. She couldn't understand it. She'd written to him months ago, a long letter in which she'd agonised over each word as she ended their relationship. She'd wished him well and sent her love, hope and prayers that he'd keep safe in the trenches. And yet he still kept sending the cards. One arrived each month, as regular as clockwork. There was nothing written on them; that wasn't Bob's style. The cards were army-issue, designed for the soldiers to strike through words that didn't apply to them, letting the reader know they were safe or in the hospital or moving to a new address. However, what Hetty couldn't understand was why he was so intent on staying in touch.

Chapter Eleven

The next morning when Hetty set off for work, Jet followed her from the house. She tried shooing him away, but he wouldn't leave her side. She resigned herself to having him walking with her, knowing he was capable of finding his own way home once he'd accompanied her to the factory. She lifted her chin and continued slowly along Elm Street, thinking of Bob and his cards that kept arriving. She was so lost in her thoughts that she didn't notice a man calling her name.

'Hetty!'

Jet barked to get her attention.

'Hetty, wait, please!' the man shouted, and this time Hetty turned. She heard the accent in his voice and knew immediately it was Dirk.

Her heart beat wildly at the sight of him, and she paused, ready to run to him, then stopped herself. She had too much pride to throw herself at him when he hadn't bothered to see her in weeks. However, Jet ran rings around his legs, barking with glee. Hetty pushed on, determined. If Dirk wanted to speak to her, he'd have to do so on her terms.

Soon he was at her side and he fell into step. She was aware of him striding alongside her, conscious of the height of him, his long legs and sturdy boots. Over the last few weeks, her mind had spun with questions about why he was avoiding her. She'd felt angry and upset that he hadn't been in touch. But now she was determined not to give away her feelings. He tried to take her hand, but she pulled it away and pushed it into the pocket of her dad's coat, then marched on, waiting for him to speak. When he kept quiet, she risked a glance at him, and her anger began to give way to something else, something softer, as she took in the blue of his eyes and his gentle, open face. It was like falling in love all over again. She suddenly felt vulnerable and raw and knew she had to be careful.

'Don't you have somewhere to be?' she said, trying to keep her voice neutral.

Dirk's face creased with confusion. 'Hetty, what's wrong? I want to explain why I haven't had time to visit.'

Hetty picked up her pace again. 'I can't talk now; I'll be late for work. You've picked the wrong time to chat,' she said.

'Hetty, please, I need to speak to you.'

She glared at him. 'You've had weeks to speak to me, but you've chosen not to,' she said, her anger building again. 'I thought we had something special, but you've ignored me since Christmas. You haven't called at my house or waited for me at the factory gates. And you know I can't come to see you at Elisabethville. Was it my mum?'

'What?' Dirk said, confused.

'My mum. When you came to my house at Christmas. I know she wasn't nice to you. I warned you about her.

She's prickly, always has been.' Her boots slapped the ground as she hurried on, Jet running at her side.

'Hetty, slow down,' Dirk said, and he gently reached for her arm.

She stopped and looked into his blue eyes.

'I'm sorry I haven't been to see you,' he began. 'Work is so busy. The war affects us all. The boys I teach have lost fathers and brothers. They need my care right now.'

Hetty's glance fell. She understood and suddenly felt guilty. Dirk leaned forward and kissed her on her cheek.

'I want to spend time with you, Hetty Lawson,' he said. 'I want to see you soon. Please know that I think of you always and I will do everything I can for us to be together again. But now I must return to work. My boys are waiting in the school and I need to prepare lessons.'

'When will I see you?' she asked.

'Soon, I promise,' he replied.

He gently tilted her chin to raise her lips to his for a lingering kiss. Then he turned on his heel and disappeared, leaving Hetty alone. She heard Jet whining as he walked away.

Elsie was at a loose end. Unlike Hetty, who had to find a second job to top up her factory wages, she was in a more comfortable financial position. With the money that Jean earned on the market and from her work at night, they had enough to manage day to day. Elsie had always trusted Jean to deal with their finances, and never once questioned their arrangement.

She was curled up on the sofa after snoozing for an hour. She'd fallen asleep reading a novel that she'd bought from the market. It was a story of a woman being saved from danger by a strong, handsome man. Now she stretched her shapely legs along the sofa and let out a long, low sigh. She caught sight of the book's cover with its romantic title in bold print. It was as if the words were taunting her. Why couldn't real life be as romantic as that, she wondered. She'd love a tall, dark hero to look after her.

She glanced at the clock. It was time for Jean to return from the market. Elsie stood, yawning, pushed her novel to one side then tended the coal fire. She filled the kettle with water and arranged mugs on a tray. When the kettle boiled, she filled the teapot, then placed a knitted red and white striped cosy on top. Jean was normally as regular as clockwork, but today she was late and Elsie wondered what had held her up. She returned to reading her novel, but as the clock above the mantelpiece ticked the minutes away, she began to grow concerned. Looking out of the window, she searched for her aunt along Front Street, but there was no sign of her. She decided to walk to the market to find her.

She placed the fireguard against the fire, put her coat and shoes on and headed out onto the landing. As she made her way down the stairs, she heard a noise at the front door. Her heart lifted, relieved at the sound of Jean coming home at last. She waited for her aunt to walk in as she did every day. But the door didn't open. There was another noise, scratching, then a hoarse cry.

'Elsie!'

Elsie quickly ran down the stairs holding tight to the handrail, and flung the door open. To her horror, Jean stumbled forward, then collapsed into her arms. Her face was bloodied and her clothes were torn. Her hair had been pulled from its neat bun and was straggling down her back. Elsie drew her indoors and shut the door.

'Lock it,' Jean urged. 'He's out there!'

'Who?' Elsie said. 'Which one of your men did this to you?'

Jean shook her head. 'It was Frankie,' she said. 'Help me get upstairs, please.'

Elsie was horrified. She locked the door, then put her arms around Jean and slowly they climbed the stairs. She helped her aunt to the sofa, then poured boiled water into a bowl, took cotton from a drawer and began to clean the blood from her face.

'What happened?' she asked as she carefully tended her.

'He caught me when I left the market,' Jean said, wincing. 'Ouch. Careful, Elsie, it hurts. He pulled me behind the Lambton Arms and gave me a good hiding.'

'Oh Jean, no!' Elsie cried.

'He said it was revenge for what we did to him when he took you to Pine Street.'

Tears pricked Elsie's eyes. Guilt and shame flooded through her. 'This is all my fault. You kept warning me about him. Why didn't I listen?'

Jean tried to sit up, but let out a cry and put her hand on her side. 'It's *not* your fault, Elsie. Now, I'm going to lie still for a while, until the pain goes.'

'Should I call Dr Gilson?' Elsie asked, her stomach twisting with anxiety.

Jean grabbed her hand with such force that it took her by surprise. 'No one needs to know about this,' she said sternly. 'It's our secret. It's just a few scratches. I'll mend.'

Elsie brought a mug of tea for Jean, who drank it carefully, grimacing each time she took a sip. She noticed that her aunt's stockings were ripped and her skirt twisted.

'He didn't . . .?' she began, afraid to voice the question that was forming. She was relieved when Jean shook her head.

'No, lass. He didn't hurt me that way. He gave me a kicking. I tried fighting back, but I was no match. I yelled for Jim and Cathy, hoping they could hear me, but no one came. I curled up in a ball and put my hands over my head until he'd finished and stormed off. It took me all my strength to stand up and stagger home.'

'I wish I'd never met Frankie Ireland,' Elsie spat.

'There's nothing we can do about that,' Jean said. 'We can't change the past.'

'Can't I divorce him?' Elsie asked.

Jean attempted a smile and her hand flew to her face. 'Oh, that hurts,' she said, then she turned her red and swollen eyes to Elsie. 'Listen to me. Lasses like you can't get divorced, it's far too expensive. I know plenty of women whose fellas beat them up, but they all keep quiet about it. Who's going to help them?'

'What about the police? We have to do something!' Elsie cried.

But Jean shook her head. When she began to speak again, her voice was hoarse and her words came out slowly. The effects of Frankie's beating were obvious. Elsie had suffered once at Frankie's hands and knew exactly how much pain her aunt was in.

'If you think the police will do anything, you're wrong,' Jean said. 'Oh, I know a couple of coppers in Chester-le-Street. I daresay if I offer them a favour, one of them might have a word with Frankie. If we were rich, it'd be different. Money's power. If a lass from a good family gets beaten up, the fella might be locked up for assault.'

Elsie felt wrung out. She looked at her aunt, who was battered and bruised, shaking with pain and shock.

'Let me put you to bed, Jean,' she said.

When Jean not only agreed, but allowed Elsie to help her from the sofa, Elsie knew her aunt needed more help.

'Please let me call the doctor,' she insisted, but Jean shook her head.

'No, Elsie. I'll be right as rain tomorrow,' she said as she limped across the living room to her bedroom. Elsie held tight to her, supporting her every step of the way. She helped her out of her bloodied clothes and slid a cool silk nightgown over her head. Then she pulled back the eiderdown and sheets, closed the curtains and made sure Jean was comfortable.

'I'll bring you something to eat,' she said. She kissed her aunt on her swollen cheek.

'I'll be fine, you'll see. It'll take more than Frankie Ireland to knock the stuffing out of me. Now go, leave me be, let me sleep.'

Elsie left the room feeling anxious and scared. She sank onto the sofa and sipped her tea. Jean had always been robust and energetic, her protector and provider. Now she was beaten and broken, lying in bed unable to move, and Elsie didn't know what to do.

That night, Elsie looked in regularly on her aunt and each time found her sleeping. Jean hadn't touched the food she had brought her, so Elsie took the tray away. Later, when she went to bed, she couldn't sleep. Her thoughts about Frankie tormented her, about how evil he was and how stupid she'd been not to listen to Jean and Hetty's warnings. She'd thought she'd known better, but how wrong she had been. Her breath caught in her chest. She'd been pathetic to marry him. And now she was stuck with him for life.

When she checked on her aunt first thing the next morning, she was relieved to find her awake. However, when she walked to her bedside, she gasped in horror. Jean's eyes were blackened and one was so swollen that Elsie wasn't sure if she could even see. Her lips and cheek were swollen too and there was fresh blood on the pillow. Elsie sank to her knees and held her aunt's hand.

'Please, I beg you, let me call Dr Gilson,' she pleaded.

This time Jean didn't resist. Elsie flew to the doctor's house, urging him to come as soon as he could, then ran back to the flat. She lifted a cup of water to Jean's lips and Jean attempted to sip but it proved too hard. Elsie put the cup on the nightstand.

'I need you to do something for me, love,' Jean said. Her voice was a whisper; she barely had the strength to talk.

'Anything, just name it,' Elsie said.

'Go to the market and tell Florrie Smith I won't be at work for a day or two.'

Elsie knew that with the extent of her injuries, Jean wouldn't be going anywhere for a lot longer than that.

Later that day, Dr Gilson arrived and carefully examined Jean. Elsie stood by her bedside and watched.

'I'll prescribe painkillers,' he said. 'Your body needs to mend, and that means complete bed rest for a couple of weeks.'

'But Doctor, I need to work,' Jean protested.

Dr Gilson stood and packed his stethoscope into his bag. 'You're not to leave this flat, you hear me?'

He turned to Elsie.

'Make sure she stays in bed. When the swelling goes down and she's able to eat properly, only then can she think about work.'

He left Elsie his bill and she showed him out. When she returned to Jean's bedside, her aunt took her hand.

'There's something you should know,' she said.

Elsie gently stroked her aunt's hand as she began to speak.

'Until I get back to work, we're reliant on your wage from the toffee factory.'

Elsie's heart dropped. She'd had no idea things were so tight.

'But I thought we were all right for money,' she said, confused.

Jean shook her head. 'No, lass. I always said we had enough to get by on as long as I worked day and night. If I can't get out to do either of those jobs, money will be scarce. Look, love, I didn't want to worry you. You've enough on your plate with the insecurity at the factory. The truth is that the landlord's already threatened to throw us out. Plus we need to pay for food, coal for the fire and now the doctor's bill.'

Elsie dropped her head and stared at the worn carpet. She was shocked. Her blood ran cold. Aunt Jean had always taken charge of their finances, paid the bills and dealt with the landlord. She was horrified to hear that they had debts, and worse, that they'd spiralled out of control. She gripped the doctor's bill in her hand.

'This is why you didn't want me to fetch Dr Gilson, isn't it?' she said softly. 'You knew we couldn't pay him. But I *had* to call him after the state you woke up in. I can't bear to see you suffer. Oh Jean, I'm so sorry. If it wasn't for me, none of this would have happened. Frankie wouldn't have touched you. It's all my stupid fault.'

'Elsie, how many times do I need to tell you? You must never blame yourself.'

Elsie forced herself to look at Jean's battered face. Her right eye had almost disappeared behind folds of swollen skin. An idea began to form in Elsie's mind, but the thought of it made her feel sick. However, there was no choice.

'I know one way I could earn enough money to pay Dr Gilson's bill and the landlord,' Elsie said. She paused, trying to gather the courage to say the next words. 'I could walk the back lane at night.'

The two women looked at each other, letting the enormity of her words sink in. Jean's mouth hung open in shock.

'No, love . . . I can't let you. I won't. Can't you get a job in one of the munitions factories instead? Don't they need girls to work there? There must be something else you can do. I'd never ask you to walk the streets.'

'You're not asking. I've offered,' Elsie said, more confidently than she felt. 'And what else can I do? It's not as if I could slip into your job at the market, is it? Florrie Smith won't allow it. We know she's a mean old bird. Besides, it'd only be for a few days, until you're back at work.'

'No!' Jean cried.

'Please let me,' Elsie begged. 'It's our only chance. Either I work on the streets or we starve and become homeless. I can't put it plainer than that.'

Jean didn't reply or protest; she simply turned her head

away. Elsie left her bedside and walked to the living room, reeling from the enormity of her decision. Her eye was caught by the front cover of her novel with its hero and heroine falling in love.

'Love and romance, what a joke,' she muttered. Then she picked up the book and flung it into the fire.

Chapter Twelve

In the coming days, spring was ushered in on a stiff breeze and weak sunshine. At Mrs Fortune's house, Anne had still seen nothing of Pearl. This puzzled her a great deal, and one day she decided to do something about it. She knocked on Pearl's door, ready to introduce herself. She even carried a box of Lady Tina toffee as a welcome gift. But she was disappointed when there was no reply. The days went by and she was aware of the times Pearl was in the house as she could hear conversation between her and Mrs Fortune drifting up the stairs. She didn't feel it was her place to interfere in the women's friendship, but surely Pearl knew she lived upstairs, so why was she keeping her distance?

One morning, when Anne arrived at work, she saw the first daffodil shoots pushing through the soil in the factory garden. It warmed her heart to know that some things carried on as normal, oblivious to the ravages of destruction and war.

'Morning, Anne,' a friendly voice called as she gazed at the garden. She spun around to see Stan. He raised his cap to her as he walked past on his way to the gardening sheds.

'Morning, Stan. I'm just musing on the cycle of life,' she said.

He paused and turned back to her. 'Heard anything from Elsie recently?' he asked.

Anne shook her head. 'I feel dreadful as I haven't seen her in ages. I've been too busy helping Mr Jack.'

'I'll keep you updated if I hear anything,' Stan said.

Anne headed to reception, where Jacob was working on his ledger.

'Morning, Jacob, how are you?' she said as cheerily as she could, but he didn't look up or reply. Anne paid him no mind, for she knew he was unlikely to respond when he was in a surly mood. As she headed to the door that led to the corridor, he finally spoke.

'Mr Burl's secretary is waiting in your office.'

Anne thanked him and noticed that Jacob was blushing. 'Are you feeling all right?' she asked.

'Perfectly fine,' he replied, but Anne noticed his voice quiver. He gave a small cough as if to pull himself together. 'As I said, er . . . Meg . . .' he pulled nervously at his shirt collar as he said her name, 'is waiting for you.'

Anne looked at him for a long time, wondering what had ruffled him so much. Then she brushed it from her mind and set off along the carpeted corridor. Mr Jack's office was empty, as he was away at Bournville attending a high-level meeting with chocolatiers to discuss distribution problems caused by the war. Her own office door was ajar, and she saw Meg waiting patiently.

'Morning, Meg, thank you for coming to see me,' she said, businesslike. 'I'm sorry I can't offer you a cup of coffee. I've only just got in and—'

Meg held up her hand. 'It's all right, I'm fine,' she said.

Anne hung up her coat and hat, then sat down at her desk. Meg was older than her, a handsome, slim, mature lady with shoulder-length curled dark hair.

'You asked to see me . . . about Mr Burl,' Anne began. She glanced at the closed door. 'Whatever you tell me in here is confidential. I understand how difficult he can be.'

'He's a brute, Miss Wright,' Meg declared.

Her forthright response took Anne by surprise. 'The war affects us all in different ways,' she said, trying to be diplomatic, but Meg crossed her arms defensively.

'Burl shouts at his staff, did you know that? The typists in the sales team came to see me again for advice, as I'm the eldest woman and the longest-serving. They've asked me to speak up on their behalf. It's time someone took a stand against him. He's a bully who's had his own way too long. Even the men in the team can't abide him, you know. He's quite cruel to some of them. Oh, you should hear what he says if they don't jump at his command.'

Anne listened intently as Meg continued, wondering how best to help. One option would be to speak to Mr Jack when he returned from Bournville the following day, but if she went to him with this, when he had much else on his mind, he might not thank her for it. She decided she would tackle Mr Burl herself. She just had to find the right time.

The following week, Anne was preparing for the board meeting. She set the table with glasses, jugs of water, pencils and notepads. The boardroom was panelled with caramel-coloured wood and it always felt cosy and warm. However, there was nothing cosy about the meeting ahead. It would be one of the most difficult in the toffee factory's history. Mr Jack would need to explain to his peers and shareholders why he wasn't taking the investment offered by Lucinda Dalton's father. For the first time in his tenure as the factory owner, he would have to admit to the board that he'd suffered a personal crisis: that his wedding had been called off and there would be no investment as planned. He'd discussed this in advance with Anne, and she supported his decision to tell them that it had been Dalton's plan all along to close the factory after the war.

She went through to his office and he looked up. 'Ready to go into the meeting?'

She nodded, then handed him a file of papers. 'One moment,' she said. She straightened his blue bow tie and he thanked her with a smile.

Anne steeled herself for what lay ahead. She had butterflies in her stomach. Mr Jack held the office door open and together they headed to meet the board of directors. Inside the boardroom, Mr Jack banged his gavel on the table and called the meeting to order.

'Gentlemen, you will notice that Miss Dalton is not present today,' he began. 'She will not be returning to our board meetings and our engagement has been called off.'

A gasp went around the room. Anne stared hard at her notepad, making unnecessary notes, anything to keep her gaze from the men around the table. She felt her face burn, certain that they could all tell, that they all knew about her and Mr Jack. Mr Jack's father, Albert, was seated directly opposite and she felt his eyes on her. He was the only one at the table who knew that Mr Jack had feelings for her.

The factory's legal director spoke next. 'Let the minutes

of this meeting show that Miss Dalton was never an official member of the board of directors. A vote was never taken for her to be accepted onto the board.'

Mr Jack tapped his gavel on the table again. 'Gentlemen, I have another announcement to make. It has recently come to my notice that Bertram Dalton's offer of investment in our factory was nothing but a bare-faced lie.'

There was another gasp. Mr Gerard leaned forward as Mr Jack continued with the shock news. Anne sat nervously at his side, keeping her gaze focused on her notepad. Mr Jack outlined his own modest financial projection should the war be over in six months, and another plan if it lasted longer than a year. Mr Gerard and Albert supported these proposals and they were passed, but Mr Burl grew red in the face with rage.

'We've lost a major opportunity not having Dalton's investment!' he cried.

Mr Jack handed out sheets outlining his financial projection to all at the table, then a full and frank discussion was held.

'Will the factory have a future without Dalton's investment?' the legal director asked.

Mr Jack's face was stern, but he nodded. 'I give you my word that I will do everything in my power to keep it open,' he said.

It was the creative director, Mr Gerard, who spoke next, changing the subject and the mood in the room.

'We need to advertise more,' he said.

Anne was relieved at the change of focus. All eyes turned to Mr Gerard. But then Mr Burl banged his fist on the table and everyone turned to stare at him instead.

'More advertising while the war rages? Are you

95

completely mad? The government's talking about cutting off sugar supplies to confectioners. I suggest we turn over the sugar boiling rooms to manufacture soup instead of toffee until the war is done!'

Albert shook his head dismissively. 'My dear man, everyone knows the government is likely to change its mind about cutting off sugar supplies. There's already been an outcry from the public. Plus, the orders we're receiving to supply toffees to our servicemen will keep the confectionery trade, including this factory, limping along until war is over.'

Mr Gerard pulled a folded newspaper from under his file of papers. He slowly stood, using the table for support. His shaking hands unfolded the paper then held it high for everyone to see the front page.

'This is the country's most influential national newspaper,' he said. 'It contains a full-page advertisement placed by our competitor, the self-styled king of toffee in Yorkshire. In it, he offers his brand of sweets at good prices to cheer up the nation while we're at war.'

'What's that got to do with us?' Mr Burl snapped.

Mr Gerard curled the newspaper into a roll and held it like a weapon, brandishing it in Burl's direction.

'We need to take lessons from this. If any toffee company is to be on the front page of the newspapers, it should be us. We've let this toffee king reign for too long. Now it's our turn to wear the toffee tiara and confectionery crown. We need to produce adverts to make every sweet-buyer in this country recognise Jack's toffee and position Lady Tina as the only brand to choose.'

Mr Jack leaned forward, his eyes sparkling with excitement. 'Mr Gerard, tell us more.'

Chapter Thirteen

Later that week, Anne called into the wrapping room and asked Mrs Perkins if she could speak to Elsie in private. The supervisor gave her permission, and Elsie followed Anne to her office.

'Is anything wrong, Anne?' she asked nervously. 'I'm not in trouble, am I?'

'No trouble at all. I just want a word.'

Anne showed Elsie into the office and indicated to her to sit. She herself sat the other side of the desk, but with the typewriter between them, it didn't feel right, so she scooted her chair round to the side of the desk so that their knees were almost touching.

'Elsie, I wanted to ask if everything is all right with you.'

'With me?' Elsie said, sitting straight in her seat. 'Of course. Why wouldn't it be?'

Anne noticed her defensive tone, so she tried again. All the while, Stan's words about Elsie walking into the river were uppermost in her mind. But she couldn't – wouldn't – break Stan's confidence and let on to Elsie that he had told her.

'The welfare of the women at the factory is one of my

priorities,' she began. 'But the welfare of my friends means much more. Oh Elsie, I've been so busy with Mr Jack that I haven't had time to speak to you about this until now. I just wanted to make sure that you were feeling all right after what happened with Frankie. I know you were off work for a week.'

Elsie crossed her arms under her bosom. 'I'm all mended now,' she said. 'There's no need to worry. Now, is that all you wanted to say, or was there anything else?'

Anne shook her head. Her words hadn't come out with as much tact as she'd hoped, judging from Elsie's body language. She really needed to work on that if she was to be of help not just to Elsie, but to the other factory girls. She thought of Anabel, who'd died in that terrible accident in the slab room, and Beattie, who'd been attacked in the back lane. She was determined to learn, to help the girls as much as she could.

'I think that's all, Elsie,' she said.

Elsie got up to leave, but Anne stopped her by gently placing her hand on her arm. 'I'm always here if you need someone to speak to.'

Elsie nodded and walked from the room.

Later that day, Anne returned to the wrapping room and marched straight to the corner where Mrs Perkins sat behind her desk.

'Good morning, Mrs Perkins, I've been sent by Mr Jack.'

She handed over a brown folder. As Mrs Perkins took it, she smiled at Anne, which caught her off guard.

'Good morning, my dear, how are you?' the supervisor said.

Anne rocked back on her heels. It was unlike Mrs Perkins to be friendly. Also, she looked softer, happier, more welcoming than Anne had ever known. Anne pulled herself back to the task in hand.

'These are the proposed changes to your room while the factory continues on reduced hours. It's been approved by the management board. You're to lose girls from the wrapping room to send to the packing room and it will be your choice which girls are sent. Mr Jack has full confidence that you'll choose the hardest workers, who can lift boxes and tins. It will improve productivity until such time as we're operating as normal again.'

She watched Mrs Perkins slide a sheet of paper from the file and read the instructions.

'Let's hope the war will be over soon,' the supervisor said. 'The changes are noted, Miss Wright. I will implement them immediately.'

'Thank you,' Anne replied, and turned to leave. But something about the way Mrs Perkins had spoken made her stop dead.

'Could you repeat that, please?' she said.

Mrs Perkins looked flustered. 'Why, yes, I simply said I'll implement the changes immediately.'

Anne listened intently. There was a familiarity to Mrs Perkins' voice that she couldn't pin down.

'Thank you,' she said again, and walked out of the room, puzzled. 'I need to get more sleep, I'm starting to hear things that aren't there,' she muttered to herself as she returned to her office.

In the wrapping room, Hetty gently nudged Elsie. 'Look out, Mrs Perkins is coming,' she whispered.

Hetty straightened her shoulders and smiled when the supervisor reached the table. Mrs Perkins clapped her hands, demanding attention. Work came to a standstill, and waxed papers and soft caramels were laid down.

'Girls, there are changes to be made in the wrapping room,' Mrs Perkins declared.

'Are we to be laid off?' someone called.

'No,' Mrs Perkins said firmly. 'But some of you will leave the wrapping room and go to work in packing instead. I've been asked to choose ten girls who are capable of lifting heavy boxes and tins, and who will be precise when packing Lady Tina. As you know, we're now working on orders for the government, and our toffee is being shipped all over the world.'

She glanced at the sheet of paper in her hand. 'The girls I've chosen to work in the packing room are as follows.'

Hetty reached for Elsie's hand. She hoped with all her heart that if her name was called, then Elsie's would be too. She couldn't bear the thought of not working alongside her best friend. However, she needn't have worried, for her name was called first and Elsie's second.

When all ten names had been read out, Mrs Perkins raised her arm and beckoned the girls to her. 'Follow me. I'll take you to the packing room. Your supervisor there will be Mr Hanratty. I will introduce you, and he will then explain the work.'

A ripple of chatter went around the wrapping room between the girls left behind.

'Girls! Back to work!' Mrs Perkins called to quell the noise.

Hetty and Elsie followed the supervisor out of the room.

'What's Mr Hanratty like, do you know?' Hetty asked.

Elsie shrugged. 'No idea.'

Hetty looked askance at her friend. 'That's not like you. You're normally full of gossip about the men at the factory and know where to find all the handsome ones.'

Elsie's face clouded over. 'That was before I found out how evil some men are; before I married Frankie,' she said sadly.

Hetty threaded her arm through her friend's. 'I'm sorry, love. You must think I'm insensitive. My mind's all over the place at the minute.'

'Is it because you're missing Dirk?' Elsie asked.

'Partly,' Hetty admitted. 'It was weird. He turned up and apologised for not coming to see me. He said he'd been busy at work. Then he kissed me on the cheek and disappeared. I've not seen him since.'

'You should go to visit him at Elisabethville,' Elsie suggested.

Hetty shrugged. 'You know I can't turn up there out of the blue. It's a military base with strict rules.' She decided to change the subject. 'Are you managing all right on reduced wages?'

Elsie turned her head away. Hetty was about to ask what was wrong when they reached the door to the packing room.

Mrs Perkins marched ahead with the girls behind her in single file. She stopped at a small cubicle in the corner of the room and knocked on the glass door. An old man with white hair was hunched over a desk. He smiled when he saw her.

'Come in, my dear Pearl,' he greeted her.

'Arthur!' Mrs Perkins replied. 'I've brought ten of my

girls from the wrapping room. They're hard workers and strong.'

Hetty watched the exchange with interest. Mr Hanratty was the first person she'd heard address Mrs Perkins by her first name, and she wondered if they were old friends who'd worked at the factory together for years.

Then Mrs Perkins leaned across the desk and muttered loudly enough for Hetty to hear, 'The girl at the front is Hetty Lawson, the face of Lady Tina. A word of warning. Keep your eye on her friend Elsie, the dark-haired beauty at her side. She's keen on the fellas and is easily distracted. She and Hetty often chat when they should be concentrating on work. My advice would be to keep them together so you can watch them both.'

Hetty looked at Elsie, who was glancing around the wrapping room and didn't seem to notice, or care, that she was being talked about. It wasn't like her to be so distracted, Hetty thought.

Mrs Perkins left the room and the girls waited for Mr Hanratty as he slowly stood from his desk, shuffled to the door and asked them to follow him.

The first thing Hetty noticed about the packing room was the noise. Where the wrapping room had been quiet and calm, with just the gentle swish of waxed paper, the racket in here attacked her from all angles. Women pounded nails into boxes and crates, and shouted to each other as they heaved boxes to horses and carts waiting outside. She had heard that some of the strongest of the factory horses had been shipped overseas with the soldiers to war.

'It's very different to the wrapping room,' she whispered.

'What? I can't hear you!' Elsie replied.

Hetty and Elsie stood together as Mr Hanratty began to separate the girls, sending them to work in different parts of the room. At last he approached the two of them.

'Mrs Perkins tells me you're good friends. I might be old, but that doesn't mean I don't have a heart. If you'd like to stay together . . .'

'Oh, we would, sir, yes,' Elsie said.

'Very good. I want to keep my workers happy. You can both work on the packing line for Lady Tina. Here, let me show you what you need to do.'

Hetty and Elsie followed him to a long table, not too different to the one they'd worked at in the wrapping room, only this one was narrower, and a line of girls stood only on one side of it. However, the most astonishing thing to Hetty was that the table moved. A belt conveyed tins and wrapped toffees slowly down the line. She knew the factory had an electrical power house, but this was the first time she'd been close to an electrified machine. She stepped back, suddenly afraid of the power of the moving table. Then she looked at girls younger than her casually picking toffees, weighing them and packing them. None of them looked scared. She gingerly stepped forward again.

'You each use one of these,' Mr Hanratty explained, handing metal scoops to Hetty and Elsie. 'We pack four-pound tins of Lady Tina here. They're the tins that go overseas to the soldiers. And it must be four pounds exactly, not one toffee over, not one toffee less. You'll soon get the hang of it. Once you've scooped up the toffees and weighed them, then you fill the tin.'

He took a tin from a stack in the middle of the table. Hetty noticed a well-built woman with rolled-up sleeves placing more tins on the belt at the end of the table to replenish those the girls had filled. She caught Hetty looking and smiled.

'Hey, it's the Lady Tina girl!' she called out over the din.

Hetty saw girls at the table turn and stare. Some smiled, others waved, while one or two ignored her. Her face burning with embarrassment, she turned her attention back to Mr Hanratty.

'When you've filled the tin, put the lid on, make sure it's tight, then off it goes to be packed in straw and sent overseas in a crate. You might be slow at first, but you'll soon speed up. Think you can manage it?'

'Yes, sir,' they chorused.

Mr Hanratty left them. Hetty and Elsie looked at one another, then held their scoops aloft.

'Might as well dig in,' Hetty said, and with that they were off, scooping, weighing and filling the colourful, pretty tins of Lady Tina.

Hetty was concentrating so hard on making sure she had exactly four pounds of toffees in her tin that she didn't notice a woman sidle up to her. It was the well-built woman who'd recognised her as Lady Tina.

'My name's Barbara,' she said. 'It's good to have you here. You're something of a celebrity at Jack's toffee factory. Here, you might like this.'

She slipped a small piece of paper into Hetty's hand and another into Elsie's. Hetty looked at the paper, on which had been written: *Whoever finds this slip would they please correspond.*

Barbara leaned close so they could hear her clearly above the hubbub in the room. 'These are the tins we send to the soldiers. You can slip one of these notes in with the toffees if you like. All the girls do it. My sister got a letter from a chap out in France. If you do it, be discreet. It's our little secret, so don't let Hanratty know.'

Chapter Fourteen

Elsie added her name and address, then slid the note into the toffee tin.

'Elsie Cooper, you're terrible!' Hetty chided.

Elsie shrugged. 'So what if I want a fella to write to me? Maybe he'll turn out to be decent.'

'Have you heard from Frankie lately?' Hetty asked.

Elsie swallowed hard. To mention Frankie and the beating he'd given Jean would be to open up a can of worms she didn't want to talk about. She was still feeling raw with guilt and shame, blaming herself for what had happened. The pact she'd made with her aunt to take her place working the streets was sacred, their secret. She couldn't tell Hetty about it for fear she'd be shocked and think badly of both her and Jean. She returned her attention to work, scooping the wrapped toffees with force and clattering them into the tin.

'I don't ever want to see Frankie again and I don't want to talk about him,' she said, closing the subject. But when she looked into her friend's kind face and saw concern in her eyes, she felt bad for being so curt. 'Sorry, Hetty,' she said gently.

The girls continued scooping toffees, weighing and filling the tins.

'Not one toffee over, not one toffee less,' Elsie said, imitating Mr Hanratty, knowing it would make Hetty smile. She glanced at her friend. 'So come on, tell me more about how you intend to see Dirk.'

Hetty kept quiet.

'Well?' Elsie prompted.

'It's never-ending,' Hetty sighed eventually.

'What is? You and Dirk?' Elsie said, puzzled.

Hetty laughed out loud. 'No, silly. I mean the toffees.' As the girls scooped, weighed and packed, the table in front of them was constantly refilled with toffees and tins. 'Me and Dirk . . .' She paused, and Elsie shot her a look of concern. 'He told me he was busy with work, which can't be right, can it? He doesn't work weekends or evenings, so he could see me then if he wanted to.'

'How many times must I say it? You've got to ask him directly. Go to see him at Elisabethville,' Elsie urged.

Hetty shook her head. 'I've already told you I can't. Before the factory went down to working three days a week, Mr Jack used to send me there to deliver Lady Tina. But now we're focusing on sending tins to the forces, and I haven't been asked to take toffee to Elisabethville. Plus, the Saturday-night dances there have stopped, so I can't even meet Dirk at a dance any more. I can't turn up to the village without being sent on business.'

'You've got an official pass, Hetty. It can't be that difficult to get inside,' Elsie said impatiently.

'I'm not doing anything to jeopardise my pass, it's too

important to the factory,' Hetty replied sharply, and Elsie knew she'd gone too far.

She thought for a moment, wondering what she would do if she was in Hetty's shoes. 'Why not slip a note to the sentry at the gate and ask him to give it to Dirk?' she suggested. 'You could even take a tin of Lady Tina with you as a bribe. When the guard sees your face on the tin, he'll be impressed.'

Hetty was silent for a moment, and Elsie watched as she returned to scooping and weighing.

'Well? Are you going to do it?' she pushed.

Hetty sighed, then looked at her. 'Oh, all right. You're never going to shut up about it if I don't, are you?'

'Go straight after work,' Elsie suggested, but Hetty shook her head.

'I can't. I'm going after a job at Lumley Castle and I have to meet the housekeeper. I've already tried once to meet her, but when I turned up she wasn't there and I was asked to come back. Would you like to come with me? They might have a job for you too.'

Elsie could feel Hetty's eyes on her. Just then, Barbara reappeared, reaching across them both to lift filled toffee tins. She placed them on a barrow, which she wheeled to the dispatch dock, to the men waiting with the horses and carts.

'Although you probably don't need another job, do you?' Hetty went on. 'You and your aunt Jean seem to manage all right for money. She's always looked after you.'

Elsie thought about what she'd offered to do to earn money. Jean had tried to talk her out of it, but she was determined to make amends to her aunt for the beating Frankie had given her. She bit her tongue. A part of her wanted to confide in Hetty about what had happened, about how evil Frankie was and how desperate the situation was for them at home. But she had sworn to Jean that she would keep their arrangement a secret. She turned away from her friend, unable to look her in the eye.

When Hetty finished work, she walked from the factory to the riverside. The air felt mild, a definite sign that spring was on its way. From there, she could see the imposing towers of Lumley Castle, and her stomach fluttered with anticipation. She'd been excited about presenting herself to the housekeeper, but now the castle was in front of her, she began to feel daunted. Just as on her first visit, when the housekeeper had been away, she was intimidated by the size of the place and the number of windows in its thick stone walls.

She walked past a grand door under a stone arch. This was the main entrance, and Hetty knew that domestic staff would never be allowed to use it. She continued around the perimeter, marvelling at the lush green lawns that fell away to the river. When she reached the back of the castle, surrounded by trees, the paved pathway petered out and she carried on along a grass verge. On the ground floor she saw two windows thrown open and a door in between. Sitting on the doorstep was a stout woman with a round face. She wore a pristine white apron over a black long-sleeved blouse and a black skirt. Her feet were clad in sensible black shoes and her legs in black stockings. Her grey hair was uncovered, done up in a bun from which strands of hair fell around her chubby face. Hetty guessed she was older than Hilda, but her expression was more pleasant than her mum's ever was.

She smiled as Hetty approached. 'Hello, love,' she greeted her. 'Now, I may be wrong, but I'm guessing you'll have come about the job.'

'Yes, I came a few days ago but you weren't here and I was asked to return. I saw the ad in the paper. I've brought a reference from Jack's toffee factory where I work three days a week.' Hetty held out an envelope containing the character reference that Anne had typed for her. It was signed by Mr Jack.

The woman took the envelope, then shuffled along the doorstep. She patted the empty space by her side.

'Take the weight off, have a seat,' she said.

Hetty was taken aback by such a friendly greeting. She'd expected something more formal from staff working in a castle.

'I've been asked to report to the housekeeper, Mrs Doughty,' she said.

'Then consider yourself reported,' the woman said, holding out her hand. 'I'm Mrs Doughty, but you can call me Sheila.'

'I'm Hetty Lawson,' Hetty said, shaking her hand.

Sheila opened the envelope and scanned the reference, written on Jack's toffee factory paper with its logo in blue.

'A toffee factory lass, eh? I heard you lot were working only three days a week now. Want to work another two days a week here?'

'Yes, that would be—' Hetty began, but Sheila cut her off. She pointed ahead to the trees at the back of the castle.

'See that, Hetty Lawson?'

Hetty wasn't sure what she was supposed to be looking at. 'The trees, you mean?'

'Aye, the trees,' Sheila sighed. 'I never want to catch you canoodling out there with the chef, the gardener or the earl's chauffeur. Got it?'

Hetty was about to reply, to say she wouldn't dream of doing such a thing, and besides, she had her own fella – or at least she thought she had. She ached to know the truth about what Dirk was really up to.

'And keep your eye on the man who looks after the horses,' Sheila continued. 'He drinks and he's got a bad temper. My advice is to stay out of his way. If you get any trouble from him or any of the men, come straight to me and I'll sort them out. Now then . . . have you got nits?'

'No,' Hetty replied, her head reeling.

Sheila squinted at her. 'You look familiar. Have we met?'

'I don't think so.'

But the housekeeper continued to stare at her for a long time. Finally a satisfied smile spread across her face.

'I know who you are. You're that girl, aren't you? You're her on the tins of Lady Tina.'

Hetty felt herself blush. 'Yes, that's me,' she admitted. 'There was a competition at the factory and Mr Jack chose me to be the face of Lady Tina. He had my likeness painted and it's now on all the tins.'

Sheila slapped her thigh and laughed out loud. 'Lady Tina of the Castle,' she said, laughing. 'Oh Miss La-di-da, you'll fit right in here.'

Hetty wasn't sure if the woman was poking fun. She wasn't even sure if she had been offered the job. She didn't like to ask, it didn't feel polite, but she needed to know. If she hadn't got it, she'd have to find something else. She and her mum needed to eat.

'When can you start?' Sheila asked.

Hetty smiled widely; she couldn't help it. 'You really want me to work here?' she said, overjoyed.

'You're the best I've seen so far. Your reference from the toffee factory is first-rate, and you're the only one I've seen without nits. Don't make me regret taking you on.'

Hetty left the castle with a spring in her step and returned home to give the good news to her mum. Hilda, however, received it with little enthusiasm.

'Make sure you don't neglect your chores around the house,' she moaned.

Jet bounded up to Hetty and she stroked him behind his ears.

'Well, at least the dog's pleased to see me,' she muttered.

After tea, she caught the bus to Elisabethville. She'd taken Elsie's advice and written a note to leave with the guard at the gate. It was a short note, asking Dirk to get in touch, and she didn't put a kiss at the end. However, when she alighted from the bus in Birtley for the short walk to the military base, she stopped dead in her tracks. Ahead of her, unmistakable, was Dirk. Her Dirk. He was walking with a girl, slow and casual, his arm draped across her shoulders.

Hetty was horrified. She wanted to call out to him, but she couldn't as her mouth had gone dry. Her stomach turned over and she felt sick. She couldn't move, her legs wouldn't carry her. She watched as Dirk and the girl greeted the guard on the gate, who allowed them to enter without checking the girl's pass. Did this mean she was Belgian and lived there too?

'Dirk!' she managed to call, finally, but he didn't turn around.

Chapter Fifteen

Hetty struggled to make sense of it. Was it really Dirk she'd seen? Or was it just someone who looked like him? If it was him, was there a good reason why he'd been walking with his arm around a girl? As questions rushed through her mind, however, she knew she was trying to deny the awful truth that she'd seen with her own eyes. Suddenly Dirk's absence from her life made sense. He hadn't been busy at all; he'd been courting another girl! He'd lied to her all this time! She felt her face burn with embarrassment.

'Miss, do you have business here?'

A sharp voice at her side brought her to her senses. It was the guard, demanding to know what she was doing there. She gripped the envelope in her hand.

'No, I need to go,' she said, and turned to walk away. She was distraught. She'd thought she and Dirk had an understanding. But as she headed back to the bus stop, her despair and confusion gave way to anger. How dare he do this to her! How dare he cheat on her and treat her so badly! He'd sworn that he loved her; they'd kissed more than once. She wasn't prepared to let him go without giving him a piece of her mind. There was unfinished business between them. She needed to clear the air and hear it from his own lips. Oh, and she was determined to give as good as she got. She'd tear him to pieces for treating her so badly, lying to her and cheating, betraying her trust. She spun around on her heel, marched back to the sentry and thrust the envelope into his hand.

'I need you to give this to Dirk Horta the school teacher.'

Then she stormed back to the bus stop.

Later that week, in her room at Mrs Fortune's, Anne squinted at her reflection in the mirror. She picked up her small, round wire-framed glasses and put them on. Smacking her lips together, she applied lipstick in delicate pink, then brushed her hair, pulled on her coat and picked up her handbag. Before she left the room, she checked her reflection one last time.

'Come on, Anne, you can do this,' she told herself. She was surprised how confident she sounded, for she felt anything but. She had a difficult meeting ahead, but this time it wasn't a board meeting at the factory. This time she was meeting Mr Jack's parents in their own home While she already knew Mr Jack senior from having encountered him at work, she'd never met Mr Jack's mother before and was feeling nervous.

'My mother may be particularly frosty with you after I called off my engagement to Lucinda,' Mr Jack had warned. 'But I want you to meet her. You've become the most important person in my life.'

Anne had felt heartened by his words.

She walked from her room and headed downstairs. When she reached the hallway, she heard a noise from behind the door of Pearl's room. She paused, hoping she would finally meet the new lodger. She was rewarded for her patience as the door opened, but when it did, she was struck by a peculiar sight. At first she thought she was imaging things. She was already feeling nervous over the meeting with Mr Jack's parents and her stomach was in turmoil. Was this vision in front of her simply her mind working overtime? Was her home life clashing with work in the most unusual way? She felt lightheaded as the woman in front of her smiled and held out her hand.

'Good afternoon, Miss Wright, we meet at home at last.'

'Mrs Perkins?' Anne cried.

She was stunned. She held Mrs Perkins' hand as if to steady herself. Her legs began to shake. What on earth was going on? Why was Mrs Perkins living in Mrs Fortune's front room? She gripped her handbag tightly. She was really taken aback.

'I thought you lived . . .' She racked her brains to remember where Mrs Perkins lived. 'Elsewhere,' she said at last.

'My good friend Avril allowed me to rent a room here. My landlord in Birtley increased my rent and I could no longer afford to live there.'

A noise behind Anne made her start. It was Mrs Fortune, shuffling into the hallway. She wore a blue apron over a smart blouse and skirt, with her small black hat clamped to her head.

'Ah, you've met,' she said stiffly. 'Miss Wright, this is

my good friend Mrs Perkins. Mrs Perkins, this is Miss Wright, who works directly for Mr Jack at the toffee factory, though I suspect you already know that.'

'Call me Pearl at home, please, though never at work; only a few of the old-timers at the factory call me by my first name,' Mrs Perkins told Anne with a smile. 'We've all got to have our little secrets.'

'Pearl, of course. Thank you,' Anne said, glancing between the two women. She noticed they were the same height and roughly the same age, which she guessed was somewhere on the far side of fifty.

She tried to make sense of the pair being friends. Questions raced through her mind. How long had they known each other? Had they been friends as girls? Were they both widows? She knew that many women lived together these days; it wasn't uncommon with the huge numbers of men at war. She shook her head. It was none of her business.

'You look very smart, Anne. Are you meeting a friend?' Pearl asked.

Anne noticed a look pass between the women. She remembered the night Mr Jack had come to see her, and the curtain twitching at the window. Had one of them spotted her with the factory boss? Were they alluding to him now? She tilted her chin. Where she was going and who she was seeing was her secret.

'Yes, a friend,' she replied, revealing nothing, then turned to walk along the hallway.

'Will you be home in time to take dinner with Pearl and me?' Mrs Fortune asked.

This was unusual, as the landlady had never invited her to dinner before, but it was a welcome invitation.

Anne decided she'd like the chance to get to know both women better and become friendly with them.

'We've been able to buy a chicken from a farmer I know. I thought I would rustle up a stew. And there'd be apple pie for dessert,' Pearl said kindly.

Anne smiled at both ladies. 'I'm afraid I won't be back in time for dinner, but it does sound wonderful. Perhaps I could join you another time.'

She saw another look pass between the women.

'We'd like that very much, and you must call me Avril from now on, Miss Wright,' Mrs Fortune said.

Anne smiled. 'Only if you call me Anne.'

Avril stuck out her hand and Anne accepted it, shaking it heartily.

'It's a deal, Anne,' said the landlady.

'I must go, otherwise I'll be late,' Anne said, excusing herself as she headed to the door. She heard footsteps behind her and knew both ladies were following her. As she stepped outside, she glanced back to see them standing shoulder to shoulder, waving her off with a smile.

Walking along Victor Street, heading to the factory, she felt confused over what had just happened. Mrs Fortune and Mrs Perkins were now Avril and Pearl, treating her as if she was a friend rather than a lodger or colleague. It felt as if the ground had shifted beneath her feet, but instead of being shaken, she felt very happy indeed.

That evening, Elsie applied a thick layer of make-up. She wanted to hide behind a mask, to play a role rather than being herself. She wasn't nervous about what lay ahead; it was only meeting a fella, something she'd done many times before. However, this time she'd be paid, and would go further than usual for a first date. This time she had to bring a man back to the flat, where he'd take his pleasure and she'd take his cash.

Before she left the flat, she made sure Jean was comfortable, then she stepped onto the street. She knew exactly where to go, as Jean had advised her, and she bore her aunt's warnings about staying safe in mind. She headed to the toffee factory, behind which was a narrow lane that ran along the railway sidings where trains brought goods into the factory and took filled tins away. The railway ran as far as London to the south and Scotland to the north. One of the girls in the wrapping room, Beattie, had been attacked on the dark lane, and after a campaign led by Hetty and implemented by Anne, Mr Jack had had gas lights installed. It helped the girls feel safe when they walked to work on dark mornings or returned home at night. However, there was one part that remained dark despite the lights. It was at the spot where the lane went under a bridge, a spot hidden from view except from the men who knew where to look. And it was here that Elsie waited for her first customer to arrive.

Chapter Sixteen

Anne steeled herself as William's car made its way along a private drive bordered by trees. Inside the car they were seated so close that their shoulders touched. Apart from a couple of stolen kisses at the factory, this was the most intimate they'd ever been. However, Anne was nervous of what lay ahead, especially meeting William's mother. She knew she looked smart and presentable and was confident that William's parents would not find her lacking in that department. She sat up straight, trying to clear her mind for the meeting ahead.

The car slowed to a halt outside a two-storey house surrounded by trees. Anne was immediately struck by the beauty of the house and its setting. It was built of dark brown bricks the colour of toffee, and caramel-coloured bricks surrounded the window panes. The whole effect was of a charming, comfortable home.

'It was built by my father with the money he made when he first started the toffee factory,' William said, as if reading her mind.

Anne peered from the car window, taking it all in. 'It

looks idyllic; I've never seen anything like it. Did you grow up here?'

William nodded and pointed to an upstairs window at the front. 'That was my room, up there. But living here, in the woods, was too quiet for me. That's why I enjoy being in Chester-le-Street, close to the factory. Come on, let's go in and I'll introduce you.'

Anne waited until William opened the passenger door for her. She appreciated the way he held out his hand as she stepped from the car. He was always so attentive, which she enjoyed a great deal. Once out of the car, she pushed her glasses up the bridge of her nose.

'How do I look?'

He gave her an admiring glance all the way up from her smart brown shoes to her matching cream skirt and jacket. Then he slid his arm through hers.

'You look perfect, as always. Now, shall we go in?'

She took a deep breath as they headed to the door, above which was a portico supported by columns. William held the door open and Anne stepped inside. Although the house was large, inside it felt cosy and warm, and this helped put her at ease.

'Ah, you're here at last!' called a voice, and Anne saw Mr Jack senior walking towards them.

She'd met him a few times at the factory when he'd attended board meetings or called in unannounced to see William. He was a short man, just like his son; a few inches shorter than Anne. Although he was elderly, his mind was still sharp and he often had a mischievous glint in his eye. His face was long and narrow and he wore a tidy white moustache and beard.

Anne held out her hand. 'It's good to see you again, Mr Jack,' she said formally.

He took her hand and gently held it with both of his own. 'No need to stand on ceremony, Anne. You must always call me Albert from now on.'

'Thank you . . . Albert,' she said.

'And where is Mother?' William asked.

Anne noticed Albert's cheerful face turn glum.

'She's having trouble processing all of this, son,' he admitted. 'The Dalton family won't speak to her after you called off the engagement. She's taking their rejection badly.'

'Is she up to seeing us . . . to meeting Anne?' William asked.

Albert walked to a closed door in the hallway, indicating that Anne and William should follow. 'Oh, she'll see you all right, I made sure of that, but she might have some strong words to say.'

He leaned close to Anne.

'Take whatever my wife says to you with a pinch of salt. She'll come around in the end.'

William stepped forward and took Anne's arm again. 'She'll have to, for I have no intention of giving Anne up. She's the woman I want to marry.'

Anne's heart skipped a beat. 'Marry?' she said, shocked. They'd never talked of marriage! Her head reeled and she shot a look at William. She was aghast that he should blurt out the word when they hadn't discussed such a thing. But he didn't acknowledge her and she felt fury building up. How dare he take her for granted! 'William!' she hissed in his ear, determined to reprimand him, just as the door opened and she was ushered inside. Her admonishment would have to wait, and she did her best to calm herself down.

When she entered the room, the first thing that hit her was the heat. A coal fire blazed in a wide stone hearth and the room was uncomfortably warm. The second thing she noticed was that Mrs Jack was seated with her back to the room in a high-backed winged chair. Anne took her cue from Albert and William, who walked to the fireplace to face Mrs Jack.

'Mother, I'd like you to meet Anne,' William said. He stood to one side of the chair.

Anne stepped forward and placed herself in front of William's mother, ready to greet her. Clara Jack's face was lined; she was in her late sixties, Anne guessed. Her black hair was styled neatly around her face. Anne could see the look of William in her, especially in her sparkling dark eyes. However, she didn't look up or acknowledge Anne.

'Oh, so *you're* the woman who's disrupted our lives!' she hissed.

Anne was horrified. She quickly glanced at William, hoping for his support, and she wasn't disappointed.

'Mother, that's no way to speak. None of this is Anne's fault,' he said sharply.

'I know this must be difficult for you, Mrs Jack,' Anne began.

'Pfft! You can say that again!' Clara spat, still refusing to make eye contact.

'Mother!' William cried, exasperated.

He indicated for Anne to sit on the sofa that faced his mother's chair. Anne sank down, keeping her knees together, and placed her handbag by her feet. When her hand brushed the carpet, she felt the thick pile of it, and she wondered how much such luxury cost. She allowed herself a quick glance around the room. Albert stood by the fireplace with one arm along the mantel, while William sat at Anne's side. Mrs Jack was swaddled in blankets, and Anne wondered if she was ill. Closer inspection led her to realise it was a soft wraparound cloak the woman wore, its folds of material swallowing her up. Then she saw a walking cane propped by her chair.

Mrs Jack turned, and this time she looked straight at Anne. Anne attempted a smile and sat straight in her seat.

'What family are you from, girl?' Mrs Jack demanded.

'Family?' Anne said, flustered. 'Well, my parents were the Wrights, from Sunderland. They died of Spanish flu.'

Mrs Jack waved her hand dismissively. 'Never heard of them,' she said.

Anne was hurt by her curt tone. 'They were very well respected,' she said, holding her nerve.

'Do you enjoy working as a typist?' Mrs Jack demanded.

Anne couldn't miss the sarcasm in her tone, but she wouldn't allow herself to be talked down to. She was extremely proud of the work she did at the factory and wouldn't let anyone, even the woman in front of her, belittle it.

'Yes, my job involves typing, Mrs Jack. As I'm sure you're aware, there's a lot more to it than that. I worked as a high-level secretary for Mayfair Toffee in Sunderland for over five years, and I'm very proud now to work for your son.'

'She could run my factory single-handed, she's wonderful,' William said proudly.

'The management board think highly of her, as do I,' Albert added.

Mrs Jack narrowed her eyes at her husband. 'Albert, I think one of my migraines is coming. I don't think I'm well enough to join you for dinner after all.'

Albert rolled his eyes and nodded at William and Anne. 'That's enough for today. We'll leave your mother in here and the three of us can talk over dinner.'

Albert held Anne's arm and escorted her from the stuffy room. Closing the door behind them, he took her to one side, allowing William to enter the dining room.

'You'll have to excuse my wife. The situation with the Daltons has affected her badly.'

'Do you think she'll ever accept me?' Anne asked.

Albert gently patted her hand. 'Give her time, my dear. I knew there was something special about you when William hired you. I was impressed with how quickly and efficiently you settled in at the factory. And oh my word! Your idea to hold a competition to find the face of Lady Tina toffee was inspired!'

'Thank you,' Anne said.

He gave a wary look at the door to the room where they'd left his wife sitting by the fire, then lowered his voice.

'I've known for a long time that my son was smitten with you. I was also aware of his doubts over his feelings for Lucinda and his suspicions about her father's true intentions for the factory. I've had time to get used to all this, but for Clara the situation is raw. I never told her about you right at the start, for I wasn't sure if William would still go through with the wedding to Lucinda, for decency's sake if nothing else.'

'And for the investment for the factory,' Anne added.

Albert's face dropped. 'Well, that's now a moot point. The factory will struggle on through this war and then it will be up to William to steer it into calm waters once the war ends. It won't be easy, but something tells me you're up to the job of helping him. I've long admired your tenacity at the factory, Anne, and the way you've whipped my son and his disorganised office into shape.'

'Father, dinner is ready to be served,' William called from the dining room, putting an end to further conversation.

Chapter Seventeen

As the days went by, Elsie and Jean settled into a new routine. On the days when Elsie worked at the toffee factory, she would cook Jean a breakfast of oats on the fire then serve it to her in bed. Jean was getting stronger now and her bruises had started to fade. She could sit up in bed but was still unable to walk downstairs unaided to use the privy in the yard. Elsie tended her aunt as she recovered, as her penance for what Frankie had done. No matter how many times Jean told her it wasn't her fault, Elsie blamed herself. To make amends in the only way she knew how, she now walked the back lane each night while Jean was confined to her bed.

On that first night of working on the lane, before Elsie left the flat she took a swig from a bottle of whisky Jean kept in the pantry. The whisky was kept for Jean's special man, Alfie, but Elsie needed something to take the edge off her nerves. That night she had been scared as she waited under the bridge. Her heart raced each time she heard a noise, and she wondered if she had the nerve to go through with what she'd planned. But she knew she had to do it. She had no choice. When she'd mentioned to

Jean that Hetty had applied to Lumley Castle to work as a skivvy, and admitted she'd thought of doing the same, Jean had laughed out loud. 'You can earn more from one night on the back lane than you can working three days as a skivvy.' That was enough to banish any lingering doubts in Elsie's mind that she was doing the right thing. She and Jean desperately needed the cash.

Eventually she'd heard footsteps, and a man in a dark overcoat and hat came into view.

'Got a light for my cigarette, mister?' she asked, just as Jean had instructed, but he strode past without a word or a second look.

Elsie stepped back and waited until another man walked by. 'Got a light, mister?' she asked again, but the man didn't offer a light. He dropped his gaze to the ground.

'How much do you charge?' he muttered, his voice so strained Elsie could hardly hear.

She repeated what Jean had told her and named her price. 'I need the money first.'

'Got a room?' he asked.

She pointed along the lane. 'Follow me.'

She pocketed his money, then set off briskly with him at her side. They walked in silence. Elsie's heart beat double-time, and in her mind she practised what she'd say should she bump into someone she knew. She'd tell them the fella was a friend who was taking her to the Lambton Café for supper. No one needed to know her secret. However, to her relief the streets were empty and she didn't need to explain to anyone what she was up to, or who the man was. She hadn't even asked his name. Jean said it was best not to.

When they reached the flat, Elsie led the way upstairs

and showed the man into her bedroom. She popped her head around the door of Jean's room and was relieved to see her asleep. Before returning to her own bedroom, where her customer waited, she headed to the pantry. She opened Alfie's whisky bottle and took another long slug to steady her nerves.

Later that week, at the factory, Anne took Mr Jack's coffee to him on a tray. He barely registered she was there; he was busy poring over figures. However, Anne needed to speak to him about what had happened at his parents' house. There hadn't been the opportunity so far as they'd both been so busy, but she needed to get something off her chest, something that had been rankling with her since that night.

'William,' she said softly.

This time he looked up, alarmed. 'Always call me Mr Jack at work, Anne. You know we must keep our relationship a secret.'

Anne sank into the chair on the opposite side of the desk. 'I need to speak to you.'

'Can't it wait?' he said, glancing at the figures again.

She shook her head. 'If I wait any longer, I'll explode.'

Mr Jack pushed the figures away and leaned forward. 'Then tell me what it is.'

Anne steadied herself. 'When we visited your parents . . .' she began.

'I can't apologise enough about the way Mother treated you,' he replied sheepishly.

'It's not that,' Anne said. 'Although I hope to win her around in time.'

'Then what is it?'

129

'It's you, William,' she said, deliberately ignoring his request to address him formally. 'There's something I want to say to you. We're getting along well, yes?'

Mr Jack nodded.

'We admire and respect one another,' she added.

He reached across the desk to take her hand in his. 'I love you, Anne,' he said.

'And I feel the same,' she replied. 'But you're letting your feelings run away with you. When we were at your parents' house, you told your father that I was the girl you wanted to marry. We haven't spoken of marriage, yet you assumed it was what I wanted.'

His face fell. 'Is it not?'

Anne's shoulders dropped. 'Not yet,' she said cautiously. 'You see, I was hurt badly in the past. There was a man who broke my heart. I need you to be patient. Please don't rush into making plans or tell your parents that there's going to be a wedding. I need time to get used to this . . . to you and me. It's happened so fast. We are a good team, William, just as you promised. We're a partnership through and through. But please don't rush me into marriage.'

Mr Jack leaned back and fiddled nervously with his bow tie. 'The last thing I wanted was to upset you,' he said gently. 'Would you come to the Deanery soon, Anne? Come for dinner one night and we'll talk it through. Perhaps you can tell me about this man who broke your heart.'

She shook her head. 'No, William. That man is in the past and that's where he will stay. But I will come for dinner; it's an invitation I gladly accept.'

* * *

Later that day, glad to have cleared the air with Mr Jack, Anne was called into his office to take notes at a meeting. The factory's creative director, Mr Gerard, had expressed a wish to talk about new lines of advertising during the war. Mr Burl, the sales director, was also due at the meeting but hadn't yet arrived.

'Where the heck is he?' Mr Jack said impatiently.

Anne had noticed that ever since the night with his parents, his temper at work had become frayed and his manner short. When she'd expressed her concern, he'd told her he was still upset because of his mother's behaviour.

'I'll find Burl,' she said. She laid her notepad and pencil down and left the room. It was a relief to be away from his side. When he held meetings in his office, she found it increasingly difficult to hide their relationship. There were times when she wanted to lay her hand on his arm to calm him when he worried that the war would cause production to cease and shut down the factory. There were times when she longed to simply hold his hand in public or straighten his bow tie in view of other members of staff, but she had to suppress her emotions and desires. Their relationship, he insisted, had to be kept secret, until the dust settled and the fallout from his broken engagement with Lucinda had blown over. Anne respected his decision. The last thing she wanted was to be seen by factory staff as the harlot who had come between Mr Jack and Miss Dalton.

She hurried to Burl's office and knocked on his door. There was a scuffling noise from within, then he opened the door. She noticed he looked ruffled, as if something had upset him. He was running his hand through his hair.

'Mr Jack is waiting,' Anne said.

Mr Burl straightened his tie. 'Ah yes, of course. Let me, er, pick up the papers I need.'

While they were alone, Anne took the opportunity to speak up. She'd tried many times to arrange a meeting with him to discuss what Meg had told her.

'Mr Burl, you keep ignoring my requests to talk to you,' she said. 'Is there a reason for this?'

'I'm very busy right now,' he said, distracted.

He turned and headed to his desk. As Anne watched him, she spotted a white feather on his blotter. She'd heard of such feathers being handed out by disdainful women trying to shame men into enlisting in the army. As she walked back to Mr Jack's office with Mr Burl behind her, she wondered where the feather had come from. Had it arrived in the post, or had someone at the factory given it to him? As far as she knew, Mr Burl had no reason to be exempt from conscription. She knew that Mr Jack was medically unfit because of a weak chest, and also exempt on the grounds that as the toffee factory owner, he was overseeing production of government orders. Mr Gerard was too old to be in the army, although his sharp mind was invaluable at the factory.

When she reached Mr Jack's office, she paused a moment, allowing Mr Burl to straighten his hair and pull himself together.

'Are you ready?' she asked him.

He nodded in reply. Anne pushed the door open, walked into the office and took her seat next to Mr Jack.

Mr Gerard was in full flow, excitedly outlining his ideas for a change in the way the factory advertised toffee. Mr Burl took his seat opposite Anne. She picked up her pad and pencil and began to take notes as Mr Gerard spoke. However, Mr Burl rudely interrupted him.

'It's madness to think about increasing our advertising, Gerard! Raw materials such as milk are at unprecedentedly high prices. Sugar is not easy to get – at any price. And our men joining the forces make it difficult to keep the factory running even at three days a week. The women coming in need to be trained.' He sighed loudly. 'And that takes time and effort.'

At this, Anne spoke up. 'May I remind you, Mr Burl, that without the women working at the factory, we would have gone out of business months ago.'

He ignored her.

'Miss Wright has a valid point,' Mr Jack said, but Burl carried on regardless.

'I know we've discounted plans to turn the factory over to munitions, but I hear of other factories being used by the government as recruiting stations. I'd like to propose this as an option for us too.'

Mr Jack shook his head. 'No, Burl. Despite the war and the unsettled market, people still want toffee and sweets. Yes, raw materials are hard to obtain, but we must continue to advertise to keep our brand in the public eye. When war is over, we'll be the first brand everyone turns to.'

Mr Gerard nodded. 'That's why we need to advertise more cannily. We must retain our presence in the market. We must remind everyone that Jack's toffee is the best. I'm not talking about spending more money on advertising. I'm talking about spending the current budget more wisely.'

Mr Jack leaned forward. 'Carry on, Gerard. I'm intrigued to hear your plans.'

'We'll need to increase our prices, of course,' Burl stated firmly.

Mr Gerard walked to a side table and spread a roll of paper on top. 'Gentlemen, my team has drafted new advertisements for your approval.'

Anne walked with the men to inspect the work. When she saw the designs that Mr Gerard's team had created, she thought her heart would burst with pride. There were three separate drawings of a soldier, a sailor and an airman, all of them holding aloft a tin of Lady Tina toffee.

'The wording proclaims that our forces deserve the best,' Mr Gerard said proudly. 'And the best is Jack's toffee, of course. The advertisement is aimed at the families of those in the forces. We're linking our brand with patriotism and family love.'

Mr Jack ran his hand across the ads. 'My word, these are inspired, Gerard,' he said approvingly.

Anne stood back and watched Mr Burl as he looked at the pictures of uniformed servicemen.

'I hope they won't stoke the white-feather brigade to more agitation,' he muttered under his breath.

Chapter Eighteen

Later that week, Hetty woke to a sunny spring day. But when she went downstairs to the kitchen, she found her mum still in her nightgown, sitting in silence. The hearth was empty and the coal fire wasn't set. Normally it would be blazing by now, keeping their spirits high, boiling water and cooking food. Jet lay at Hilda's feet.

'What's wrong, Mum?'

Hilda continued staring out the window. Her hands were in her lap and her face was deathly white. And then Hetty saw two letters on the table. They were official army letters, one addressed to *Mrs Hilda Lawson* and the other to *Miss Henrietta Lawson*.

'They've just arrived. I can't bring myself to look at them,' Hilda whispered.

Hetty backed away, afraid of what the letters would contain. She sat opposite her mum at the empty hearth and took Hilda's small, cold hands in her own.

'Would you like me to open them?' she asked. 'There's one for me too.'

Hilda gave a slight nod. 'Open yours first.'

Hetty walked to the table and picked up the envelope.

Her hands began to shake and she felt sick with anxiety. She braced herself for what the letter would say.

'Mine must be about Bob,' she said, forcing herself to acknowledge the dreadful reality of the news she felt sure she held in her hands. She took a knife from the drawer and slit the envelope open, then sat opposite her mum again. She glanced at Hilda's worried face before pulling the thin sheet of paper from the envelope. She scanned it quickly, not daring to breathe, waiting for the words to hit her with a force she wasn't ready for.

'What is it?' Hilda whispered fearfully.

Hetty handed the letter over for her mum to read. 'It says that Bob's missing, presumed dead.'

She felt the room spin and gripped her chair seat with both hands. She wanted, needed to be held, to be told that everything would be all right, that Bob might still be alive. But she knew better than to expect a hug from her mum, who'd never shown her affection. The only person Hilda had ever cared about was Dan. Her hands remained in her lap.

'Presumed dead,' Hetty repeated, trying to make sense of it.

'Will his sister receive this letter too?' Hilda asked.

Hetty thought of Bob's sister, Marie, his only living relative.

'I'm not sure. Before he went away, Bob told me he'd listed me as his next of kin, in case . . . in case anything like this happened. He said he wanted me to be the first to know.'

She began to cry. She'd fallen out of love with Bob months ago, before she'd met Dirk. Now her tears fell for the kind, solid man she'd once known.

'Would you open my letter?' Hilda said, breaking into her sorrow.

Hetty slowly wiped her eyes, then picked up the knife and slit the second envelope.

'Read it to me. Please,' Hilda said in a tiny voice.

Hetty's heart was on the floor as she pulled the sheet of paper from the envelope and read the heavy black type. It was the news they'd dreaded from the moment Dan had joined the army. She looked at her mum's ashen face.

'My boy's gone, hasn't he?' Hilda said.

'Yes, he's gone,' Hetty said with a catch in her throat.

She held the letter out, but Hilda drew her hands back. Hetty laid it on the hearth along with her own about Bob.

The weight in her heart pulled her chest down and her whole body sank. The news about Bob had been shocking and tragic. But the second letter affirming that Dan was dead was unthinkable. Killed in action, it said. Three little words proclaiming the death of her brother, of Hilda's son, just a boy. Hetty reached for her mum's hands, and this time Hilda didn't pull away. Her frail body began to gently rock back and forth as silent tears streamed down her face.

Hetty had no choice but to force herself to work. When she walked along the streets to the toffee factory, she kept her eyes on the ground. She didn't want to look up to see other people happy and smiling. She couldn't bear to witness the world carrying on as normal. She felt numb with the combined grief of her brother's death and the news about Bob. She thought of Dan, always up to no good, laughing, smiling, whistling, walking along with his hands in his pockets. A young life cut short. She shuffled to the factory gates, not looking at who was around her. She didn't even notice Elsie. She was shrouded in her grief.

Arriving for work that morning, Anne was beckoned to one side by Jacob as soon as she walked into reception.

'Anne, could I have a word with you, in confidence? It's a personal matter,' he said.

She was taken aback by his request, because Jacob was a man who kept his personal life private. She knew little about him other than that he lived with his mother and was often surly, closed and officious.

'Yes, of course. Would you like to come into my office?' she asked. Mr Jack wouldn't be arriving at the factory until later that morning, so she had the place to herself.

She led the way and indicated a chair opposite her desk. As Jacob sat down, Anne took off her coat and hat and laid her handbag next to her typewriter. She sat on the edge of the desk and pushed her glasses up the bridge of her nose. She could see that Jacob looked nervous.

'What is it?' she asked.

He swallowed hard, then sat up straight in his seat. His feet, in black shoes shined to perfection, were placed firmly on the floor, and his black suit and white shirt were pristine.

'Do you promise that what I say in here will not leave these four walls?' he said.

'I swear,' Anne replied, intrigued.

'Well, it's . . . er . . . rather delicate,' he began.

'You can trust me,' Anne said.

Jacob nodded. 'Yes, I believe so.'

'So tell me,' Anne said kindly.

'I don't have much experience with ladies, Anne.'

Whatever she had expected him to say, it certainly wasn't this. She watched with interest as he carried on.

'However, I find that I've fallen for someone at the factory and I don't know what to do. She's someone I've admired for a very long time. I'm not sure how to tell her that I like her, you see.'

He stared so intently into Anne's eyes that it made her uncomfortable. The way he was looking at her . . . Why, it couldn't be, could it? Was she the woman he'd fallen for?

'I want to ask her out on a date, but I don't know where to begin,' he said, becoming impassioned. He leapt from his seat and quickly walked towards her. Anne held out her hands to stop him getting close.

'Now then, steady on,' she said firmly.

Jacob stood stock still. 'Pardon?'

Anne smiled kindly. 'Look, Jacob, I'm flattered, of course, but I'm not the right girl for you.'

He slapped his hand against his forehead. 'It's not you, Anne!'

'It's not?' Her face grew hot with embarrassment. 'Jacob, I'm sorry. I thought . . .'

'It's Meg, Mr Burl's secretary,' he explained.

Anne felt a shiver of relief and pulled herself together. 'Oh. Right,' she said, businesslike. 'Meg, of course. She's a hard-working, forthright woman. I admire her. How long have you been friendly with her?'

'For years. I've carried a torch for her since the day she started work at the factory. I haven't had the nerve to admit it to anyone. But it's this damn war, Anne. It makes a fellow want to make the most of the time he's got left. I need to tell Meg the truth about how I feel.'

He retreated to his seat.

'I wish to apologise for the confusion. It is Meg my heart is set on,' he said formally.

'Would you like me to speak to her on your behalf and put in a good word for you?'

Jacob's normally dour expression broke into a smile. 'Oh Anne, would you?'

Anne winked at him. 'Leave it with me. I'll speak to her.'

'You won't tell anyone else, will you?' he begged.

'You can rest assured your secret is safe with me.'

Jacob stood. 'It seems that we both have secrets to keep for each other,' he said, holding Anne's gaze.

'Secrets? What on earth do you mean?'

He took a step closer and whispered in her ear. 'I know there's something going on between you and Mr Jack.'

Chapter Nineteen

Anne felt the blood rush to her cheeks. 'I'm sure I don't know what you mean,' she said, trying not to sound flustered.

'Anne, believe me when I say I am not a person who passes judgement. However, I have noticed certain things pass between you and Mr Jack. I simply wanted to let you know that if I have noticed these kind looks and gentle words since the departure of Miss Dalton from Mr Jack's life, then others might have noticed them too.'

'You're wrong, Jacob,' she said, but her voice betrayed her and she knew it. Oh, how glorious it would be to unburden herself and tell someone the truth. But she couldn't, not yet, as she and Mr Jack had agreed to keep their relationship secret for now. Yet Jacob was right: if he'd noticed the growing fondness between them, then who else at the factory knew? Was she already being gossiped about in the wrapping room, packing room and canteen?'

'As you wish, Anne,' he said, and he turned to leave.

Anne steadied herself against her desk. 'Jacob,' she called.

He paused with his hand on the door. 'Yes?'

'I need you to promise me that you won't say anything about this to anyone.'

'You have my word. But . . .' He hesitated.

'Go on,' Anne said.

'Well, it's none of my business, but as we're now keeping secrets for each other, I'd just like to say something else. You and Mr Jack make a wonderful couple.' And with that, he left.

Anne sank into her seat with her head reeling, but she didn't have time to think more about it, for there was a knock at her door.

'Come in,' she called. She pushed her glasses up the bridge of her nose and tried to compose herself.

Stan Chapman walked into her office, carrying a file of papers in one hand and stubby pencils in the other. Anne snapped into business mode, remembering she had arranged a meeting with him to talk about the factory gardens. Mr Jack had followed another of her suggestions, this time for the gardens to be made more productive until the end of the war.

'Sit down, Stan,' she said, indicating the chair where Jacob had sat moments ago.

She pulled herself together and forced herself to concentrate. But before they got down to business, she looked at Stan's rugged face.

'Any news on Elsie?' she asked.

'Only that she's not back with Frankie, for which we can be grateful. Frankie's moved to live on Pine Street, so the sugar boilers tell me. It's a hovel. I've seen Elsie around the factory and she says hello when we meet, but she keeps herself to herself these days. She doesn't look the same, not as alert, and she isn't as friendly as she was. There's a blankness to her now; her eyes look dead. The sparkle she once had has gone.'

'Lots of things are different because of the war,' Anne said sadly.

'Including the factory garden,' Stan said.

His mention of the garden, the reason for their meeting, pulled Anne from her reverie about Elsie. She felt terribly guilty for not putting more time aside to speak to her friend, but there'd been little time for anything, or anyone, as work for Mr Jack was all-consuming. She forced a smile as Stan handed over a drawing with the proposed layout. Flower beds and rose bushes were to be dug up and vegetables planted instead.

'It's only for the duration of the war,' Anne said firmly.

'As soon as this is over, flowers will bloom again. I'll make sure of it. Until then, the gardens will flourish with potatoes and carrots, beans and peas, cabbages and cauliflowers. It won't be as pretty as the floral displays that Jack's toffee factory is renowned for, but it will help feed the workers. Mr Jack told me that this was your idea, Anne, and I applaud you.'

'What about the rose bush planted in memory of Anabel, the girl who died in the packing room? I need reassurance that that won't be dug up,' she said. She was relieved when Stan gave her his word that Anabel's rose would not be moved.

At lunchtime that day, Anne made her way to the canteen, where a limited menu was on offer. Portions were smaller than ever, and there were no desserts because of sugar rationing. Every ounce of sugar that came into the factory went into making toffee. She took a tray and joined the queue at the counter, where she chose a suet pudding. As she went to find a seat, she noticed Hetty and Elsie sitting at a table in the corner. It was Elsie who saw her first, and Anne was heartened when she raised her hand and beckoned her to join them.

'I haven't seen you both for so long,' she said as she sat down. 'What have you been up to?'

There was silence from both girls, and Anne was confused. This wasn't like Hetty and Elsie. Normally she'd have trouble getting a word in. She studied Elsie's face. Stan was right: she didn't seem to have the energy she once had, the sparkle, he had called it. Her normally pristine khaki and red overall looked grubby, and her hair, usually carefully styled, was loose and lank around her face. While Anne desperately needed to speak to her again to find out how she was coping, she didn't want to do so in front of Hetty, just in case there was anything Elsie didn't want Hetty to know.

'Are you well, Elsie?' she asked, keeping her tone light.

Elsie picked up a mug with both hands. 'Me? Oh, I'm fine. Aren't I always?' she said breezily.

'And your aunt Jean, how is she?'

'She's well,' Elsie replied curtly.

Anne tried again, this time with Hetty.

'How's Dirk, have you seen him recently?'

She saw Hetty's gaze drop. Anne laid her knife and fork down and pushed her tray away.

'What's happened, girls? You're both quiet, this isn't like you.'

'Hetty's brother died,' Elsie said softly.

Anne's heart dropped to the floor. She stood and walked

around the table to sit beside Hetty, wrapping her arms around her friend. Hetty leaned into her and sobbed gently on her shoulder.

'And Bob's missing in action, he might be dead too,' Elsie added.

Anne racked her brains, trying to remember who Bob was and what he'd meant to Hetty. Then it hit her. He was the fella Hetty had been courting before she met her Belgian friend. He'd been a dull stick by all accounts and Hetty never had much to say about him. But clearly his presumed death had hit her hard.

'I'm so sorry,' Anne murmured as she stroked Hetty's hair, trying her best to comfort her. 'I'm here for you, Hetty. Whatever you need, let me know.'

With her free hand, she reached across the table to Elsie. The girls sat in silence for a long time with the weight of the tragedy on their minds.

'Why don't you go home, take the afternoon off?' Anne said after a while. 'I'm sure your mother must need you.'

Hetty gently pulled away from her. She pushed her hair back from her tear-stained face and shook her head.

'Mum's taken to bed. Dan's bed. She won't leave his room and says she can't face the world. He was her pride and joy, her reason for living. His death has broken her. She's refusing to eat, saying she wants to die too. Nothing I say or do makes a difference.' Hetty dreaded going home. 'I'm better off here, at work. It stops me from dwelling too much on what's happened.'

She gripped her hands at her heart.

'It hurts so much. Dan was just a boy, Anne, only fifteen years old. Oh, we used to fight like cat and dog when we were growing up, and he was always Mum's favourite. When he went off to war, he thought it would be an adventure. He thought it'd make him a man, and now he'll never grow up.' She began sobbing again.

'Oh love,' she heard at her side.

She wiped her eyes and saw Elsie's look of concern.

'I'll pull myself together, I'll be fine,' she said.

'You don't look fine,' Anne said. 'Now, are you sure you don't want to go home? I'll square it with Mr Hanratty in the packing room if you don't feel up to staying.'

Hetty shuffled in her seat, then sat up straight. 'I'll cope,' she said, looking around the canteen. 'Half the people in here are suffering. See the woman in the corner? She lost her husband; he was killed in action last week. Most of the inhabitants of Chester-le-Street are carrying grief or worry in their hearts, but all of them keep going. In private they might crumble, but in public they have to be brave. It's the only way to get through. If other people can do it, so can I. But first I need to mourn Dan in my own way.'

'Will he have a funeral?' Elsie asked.

Hetty knew she'd need to think about a fitting send-off for her brother. Hilda wasn't up to arranging anything in the state she was in, and Hetty knew it would fall on her shoulders. Dan's body, the army letter had told her, would be buried with no distinction of class and rank near the battlefield where he had died. There would be an engraved tombstone to preserve his name. *Daniel Lawson, aged 15.*

Chapter Twenty

At the end of the day, when Hetty and Elsie left the packing room. Mr Hanratty called out a cheery 'Good evening', but Hetty didn't hear. She was lost in grief over Dan and concern for her mum. She was grateful for Elsie's arm to hold as she walked into the cobbled yard. Outside, the weather had taken a turn for the worse. Thick, fat raindrops fell from a grey sky and bounced off the cobblestones. Hetty pulled up the collar of her dad's coat, burying her face inside, and stuck her hands into the deep pockets. As a cold wind blew and rain pelted down, she was aware of a man walking beside Elsie and heard a voice she recognised. When she glanced across, she saw Stan Chapman.

'Everything all right, Elsie?' he asked cheerfully as he marched by.

'Everything's just fine, Stan,' Elsie replied, but her tone was dull.

'Cheer up, Hetty love,' he said, casting a glance at her. 'The weather won't stay this bad for long. We're supposed to have sunshine tomorrow.' And with that he marched off.

Elsie looked at Hetty. 'He's not insensitive, he just doesn't know what's happened.'

'I know,' Hetty replied.

The girls forged ahead through the crowd of women pushing through the iron gates. They walked with their heads down against the heavy rain, and all Hetty could see were the paving stones beneath her feet. She kept her gaze low, her tears falling with the rain, and moved forward as if in a dream, letting Elsie pull her this way and that, taking her away from the factory and setting her on the path home.

When they reached Front Street, Elsie pushed her wet hair back from her face, then hugged Hetty.

'Give my love to your mum,' she said.

Hetty let herself be held, and nestled her face on Elsie's shoulder, on her wet coat. Then she peeled away from her friend as Elsie walked off to her flat. She set off down Front Street, intent on heading home, but her legs didn't feel as if they belonged to her. She had to force one foot in front of the other.

'Keep going, you can do it,' she whispered to herself.

As she walked, the rain continued, heavier now. People scurried past, running into shop doorways for shelter. But Hetty didn't feel as if she could run; it was all she could do to stay upright, and stop herself from collapsing under the weight of her despair. She stared ahead, concentrating on getting home, running through in her mind all the things she'd need to do. She'd set the fire to warm the kitchen. She'd boil water for tea and take her mum a cup upstairs in Dan's room. She'd sit a while with her, then cook her something to eat. After she'd eaten and washed the pots, she'd make a list of people to speak to about arranging a formal goodbye for Dan in place of the funeral he'd never have. She had no clue where to start; it was too overwhelming.

She continued staring ahead as her feet hit the pavement. She was vaguely aware of people around her. The bus to Durham sailed by, spraying up a puddle that soaked her legs. And then she saw a man walking quickly towards her. He wore a wide-brimmed hat, which was what caught her eye, for it was unusual in a town where most men wore flat caps.

'Hetty!' he called.

'Dirk?' she replied.

He ran to her and took her in his arms. 'Let me take you home and out of this dreadful weather,' he said. He removed his hat and placed it on her head, then threaded his arm through hers.

Hetty leaned gratefully in to his side. Over the last few weeks there'd been many questions she'd wanted to ask him. But now that he was here, holding her arm, striding alongside her, nothing seemed important any more. Her grief over losing Dan pushed all other thoughts away. She felt numb. She was aware of Dirk's height, and his long legs and sturdy boots. As they continued to walk, she kept glancing at him and her anger began to stir. Battling against the wind and rain as they headed to Elm Street, she gently removed her arm from his.

'Don't you have somewhere else to be . . . someone else to be with?' she asked.

His face creased with confusion. 'Someone else? No.'

He tried to take her hand, but Hetty pulled it away and pushed it into her pocket. They walked in silence until they reached her house. She pushed open the door and stepped inside, shaking the rain from her coat before hanging it on a peg by the door. She took off Dirk's hat and shook the rain from that too. All the while, Dirk stood outside on the pavement, waiting for an invitation to enter. Hetty looked at him, at the state he was in, his overcoat soaked through and his hair plastered to his head. Raindrops hung from his eyebrows and eyelashes.

'You're determined, I'll give you that. You'd better come in.'

The minute he stepped into the house, Jet bounded along the hallway. Ignoring Hetty completely, he ran straight to Dirk, who fussed over him and stroked him.

'Go through to the kitchen,' Hetty said. 'I need to go upstairs to check on Mum, then I'll make tea. You and I need to talk.'

Dirk gave her a quizzical look. Hetty walked upstairs to Dan's room and found her mum fast asleep in the bed. She quietly closed the door and crept downstairs. Dirk was sitting in Hilda's chair at the hearth with Jet curled on his lap.

'Have you given him a name yet?' he asked, indicating the dog.

'He's called Jet,' Hetty replied dully.

'Jet. It suits him,' Dirk agreed. He began talking to the dog, using its new name.

Hetty started to set the fire. She began rolling and knotting sheets of newspaper, then laid wooden sticks on top. Outside, the wind howled and rain lashed at the windows. As she worked, not once did she look at Dirk, but kept her gaze ahead. A part of her was afraid that if she looked at him fully, she would end up falling for him again. She couldn't allow herself that, not after she'd seen him with another girl. She placed the sticks on the fire, then emptied coal from the bucket on top. She couldn't keep quiet any longer.

'What do you want, Dirk?' she asked.

'Want?' he said, confused. 'Why, I want to see you, Hetty.'

'You must have received my note, then. The one I left with the guard at Elisabethville.'

He delved into his trouser pocket and pulled out the envelope that Hetty had left with the guard.

'Yes, and I am sorry it has taken me this long to visit you. But if you don't mind me saying so, you don't seem happy to see me.'

Jet jumped from his lap and walked away to sit under the table. Hetty lit the fire, setting the newspaper knots alight. As the flames took hold and the room began to warm, she sat opposite Dirk. Looking hard at him, she came out with the words that had been burning inside her.

'I saw you with another girl,' she said. She lifted her eyes and held his gaze as she spoke. 'I came to Elisabeth-ville one night after work. I hadn't seen you for so long. I'd intended to leave my note with the guard and walk away, that's all I was going to do. But then I saw you . . . with her. You had your arm around her. When you both walked into the village, I called out your name but you didn't turn around.'

Dirk shook his head. 'What girl?'

Hetty leaned back in her chair and eyed him cautiously. 'Is this a game to you? Because it's not funny to me. I loved you, Dirk,' she said. Then she gasped and put a hand over her mouth. Her emotions over Dan's death were raw, close to the surface, affecting everything she did and said. She stood.

'I think you should leave. I should never have invited you in. I won't see you again, not after you've cheated on me. I thought you respected me. I thought you liked being with me.'

But Dirk didn't move. 'I don't know what girl it could be,' he said, sounding desperate. He laid both his hands on his heart. 'I swear to you that I have no feelings for anyone but you.'

Then he clamped his hand to his forehead.

'Gerta!' he cried.

'What?'

He reached for Hetty's hands, but she pulled them away.

'Please, Hetty, let me explain. It's not what you think. You saw me with Gerta, she's my best friend's wife. He . . .' He paused. 'Please, Hetty.'

Hetty sank back into her seat and looked at Dirk's face. She saw tears form in his blue eyes. Outside the wind continued to howl and rain belted against the window. The coal fire was burning merrily now, warming and lighting the room.

'You'd better have a good explanation,' she said.

Dirk wiped his tears away. 'Gerta's husband died,' he said softly. 'An accident in the munitions factory. When you saw me that night with my arm around her, that was the night of the accident. I was bringing her home from the factory. She has no one else, no family. I'm the one she turned to for help.'

He reached for Hetty's hands again, and this time she didn't pull away. Her own grief mixed with Dirk's news was unbearable.

'I'm sorry,' she said at last. 'I don't know what to say. I made a terrible mistake.'

They sat in silence for a few moments.

'Many dreadful things are happening,' Dirk said. 'The war brings misery and grief. It makes friends doubt one another, and people are too quick to judge. Everyone is scared. My work at Elisabethville over the last weeks has been . . .' he shook his head and sighed, 'relentless. But you, Hetty . . . you are the reason I am glad I came to England. I miss my home, of course. I miss my friends. I even miss the old baker in the village who never cracked a smile. But you are my light in this darkness.'

Tears began to make their way down Hetty's face. She felt Dirk's fingertips gently brush them away.

'I love you, Hetty Lawson,' he said.

He leaned forward to kiss her, then gently stroked her hands.

'So, tell me everything that has happened in your life since the last time we met. I want to know it all, for I have missed you every single day.'

Hetty squeezed her eyes shut and gripped Dirk's hands. Then slowly, tentatively, she revealed the tragic news about her brother.

Chapter Twenty-One

Anne was working late with Mr Jack, adding the final touches to a financial report. When she'd finished typing, she placed the sheet of paper in a folder and laid it on her desk. Then she fitted the dust cover over her typewriter and headed to the coat stand to get her coat and hat. She glanced out of the window, and her heart sank when she saw tree branches bending in the wind and rain. Walking to the window, she peered out.

'Oh crikey, I haven't got my umbrella. I'm going to get soaked walking home,' she said.

'Then let me drive you home in my car,' Mr Jack said behind her. 'I've been having a spot of trouble with the engine, but I'm sure it will make it to Elm Street.'

Anne spun around to see him pick up the report and run his gaze over it.

'These figures make grim reading,' he said darkly. 'The rise in sugar tax is crippling. I just have to trust Mr Gerard's plan to advertise differently. I hope it's money well spent. I trust Gerard, of course . . .'

Anne sensed his hesitation. 'But?' she offered.

Mr Jack looked at her. 'You know me too well, Anne.

But in these uncertain times, I wonder if Gerard might be wrong. We've never gone through anything like this before. We're navigating our way as best as we can, making it up as we go along. What if we're making a terrible mistake?'

Anne thought for a moment. 'Think of the advertisements as investments, William,' she said. She used Mr Jack's first name at work now, but only when they were alone.

'But our outgoings are never-ending. Chocolate, sundry foods, printing and labels, tins and bottles, cases, stationery, carriage, rents, rates and taxes. Not to mention coal, gas and water. And then there's . . .'

'Commission, wages and salaries, travelling expenses, plant sundries, horses and carts,' Anne replied. 'Yes, William, I know how the factory operates.'

Mr Jack laid the folder on her desk and smiled. 'Apologies, dear Anne. In many ways you know the factory better than I. You've got a fresh eye, which has proved invaluable. So tell me, in your opinion does advertising during the war, when we can't make or sell as much toffee as we used to, make sense?'

He perched on the edge of her desk. Anne paced in front of the window, hands clasped and deep in thought.

'It makes perfect sense. Mr Gerard is right. If we don't advertise, and the public no longer see our brand in their newspapers and magazines, they'll think we've gone out of business. We need to remind everyone that we're open, we're here, making toffee, fulfilling our government orders. We must keep our profile high. Then, when the war is over and people start buying toffees again, we'll be the brand they turn to first. Don't you see, William? Gerard has created those astonishing pictures of servicemen eating our toffee. There are no clever slogans, mascots or fancy phrases. Just pictures of our brand with "Lady Tina" in big letters. We're making toffee for the troops and there can be nothing more important than that.'

Mr Jack jumped off the desk. 'My word, you've hit the nail on the head. Say that again, Anne.'

Anne looked at him askance. 'What? All of it?'

He rushed to her and held her gently by the shoulders. 'No, just that phrase.'

'You mean "toffee for the troops"?' she said.

'Anne! You're a marvel!' he cried. His eyes shone with excitement. 'We'll use that line in our publicity. Of course! That's just what I needed to hear. You've put it so eloquently that it's confirmed in my mind that Gerard is the genius I always thought he was. And you are a genius too. Oh Anne! Toffee for the troops! I can see it now, our brand and our logo, with your words, on the front page of the newspapers. We'll give our competitor the toffee king of Yorkshire a run for his money.'

'Mr Gerard is rarely wrong,' Anne said sagely. 'I just added the final flourish.'

'Gerard is a good man, one of the best. I'm lucky to have him on my team. However, Mr Burl seems out of sorts these days. I wonder if he's having trouble at home.'

Anne thought of the white feather she'd seen on Mr Burl's desk and guessed that that was what lay heavy on his mind. She was about to ask Mr Jack about it, as she often wondered why Mr Burl hadn't been conscripted, when he tapped the tabletop.

'Well, will you let me run you home in my car? I refuse to let you walk in this storm.'

Anne picked up her handbag and slung it over her

shoulder. She fastened her coat and placed her smart hat on her head.

'Thank you, William, I'd like that very much.'

A few minutes later, Anne slid into the passenger seat in the comfortable interior of Mr Jack's car. She felt confident that no one at the factory had seen her. And even if they had, she reasoned, what was so wrong about the factory owner giving his secretary a lift home in this storm? The wind and rain hit the windscreen and roof with such force that it shook the car. Mr Jack stepped into the driver's seat, and once again their shoulders touched in the enclosed space.

'It's steaming up in here,' he said. He produced a cloth and wiped the inside of the windscreen, then started the engine. It gave a throaty roar before tailing off into silence. He tried it three more times before the engine caught and the car moved forward.

'I really must get it looked at by a mechanic,' he muttered as they left the factory.

As he drove, the windscreen wipers swished back and forth to clear the rain, but visibility was poor. The car turned slowly onto Front Street but was met by a deep puddle in the middle of the road. A policeman directed traffic along an alternative route to avoid the flood. As Mr Jack carefully steered along the side streets, he cleared his throat.

'Anne, dear,' he began.

'Yes, William?'

'Because of the diversion, we're heading in the direction of the Deanery.'

Anne's heart skipped a beat. 'Yes, I'd noticed that,' she said softly.

There was silence for a few moments as he navigated a narrow cobbled lane. Anne looked straight ahead at the rain hitting the windscreen.

'Perhaps it might make sense for me to drive us straight there,' he offered.

'Well, I did promise to take dinner with you one night, so why not tonight?' Anne said.

'Ah, my housekeeper won't be there this evening to cook. It's her night off. She might have left me something, though,' he said.

Anne picked up on his disappointed tone, but she was far from dismayed. In fact, her heart beat a little faster learning that they'd have the Deanery to themselves.

'I could cook dinner for us, William,' she said, turning to look at him, her shoulder pressing against his. Mr Jack kept staring ahead, but Anne felt him return the pressure. She reached across and gently laid her fingers on his left hand where it held the steering wheel.

'I'd like that very much,' he replied. 'And then after dinner I could drive you home.'

He turned to look at her, and in that moment Anne felt stirrings of emotion that she hadn't felt in years. She'd kept such feelings locked up after her baby's father had left her. She'd promised herself she'd never trust another man or give herself again. And yet here she was wanting nothing more than to be with the man at her side.

'Yes, perhaps you could,' she said softly. Then she walked her fingers from his hand and gently stroked his left knee.

Mr Jack slowed the car to a stop at a junction. Across the road was the Deanery, where a welcome light from an oil lamp glowed in a window.

'My housekeeper will have left the fires burning. We'll

be warm and cosy inside,' he said. He pulled the car into the drive at the side of the Deanery, then took off his jacket and held it over Anne's head as she emerged from the passenger side. Together they ran through the rain to the house, arms around each other, holding each other tight.

As soon as they were inside, they paused, each of them waiting for the other to make the first move. At the same time as Anne reached for Mr Jack, he slid his arm around her waist, drawing her to him in a loving embrace. In the dark hallway, their lips met. This was much more than the chaste kisses they'd shared at work. Anne's heart was beating so hard she felt sure Mr Jack could hear it.

Finally they stepped apart. Anne was breathless, wanting more. Mr Jack led her by the hand into the living room, where he lit the fire that his housekeeper had set. Then, after another lingering kiss, he gently pulled away.

'Forgive me, Anne,' he breathed.

'I wanted it as much as you,' she whispered against his neck.

He looked at her and gently moved a damp strand of hair from her face. She delighted in the touch of his fingertips against her skin.

'Please, make yourself at home while I check to see if Edith has left dinner in the kitchen. I'm sure you must be hungry.'

Anne took off her coat and hat and slid her feet out of her wet shoes. She walked in her stockinged feet across the carpet. Such luxury, she thought. While William was out of the room, she took advantage of the opportunity to have a look around. The last time she'd been there, when she'd been invited to tea, she'd been so nervous she could barely take in her surroundings. This time, however, she sank into a large, comfortable armchair by a roaring fire. She noticed the heavy patterned curtains with sashes to tie each one back. The furniture looked old and solid, made of dark wood. The room was decorated in deep, masculine colours of brown and maroon. There were no cushions, flowers or ornaments.

Mr Jack walked into the room carrying two small glasses filled with dark liquid.

'My housekeeper has left one of her beef pies on the shelf. I've put it by the kitchen fire to warm, so there's no need for you to cook.'

He handed her a glass and raised his own.

'I hope you like sherry. Let's raise a toast to us, Anne.'

Anne held up her glass. The mention of sherry brought her landlady to mind, but she quickly dismissed her. Being at the Deanery with William, drinking sherry after a hard day at work, with the sweet anticipation of his kisses, and maybe more, seemed exactly the right thing to do. There was nowhere else she would rather be.

'To us,' she said.

She took a sip from her glass. Then she looked Mr Jack straight in the eye.

'If we have the Deanery to ourselves this evening, with no housekeeper to interrupt us . . .' She paused, wondering if she'd overstepped the mark, but when she looked at Mr Jack, she saw her own longing reflected in his eyes. '. . . then perhaps I could stay overnight. The rain is dreadful outside.'

She sipped her drink again and waited for his response.

'And my car may not make it all the way to Victor Street

in this storm,' he said, as a mischievous smile played on his lips.

'Then that's settled, I'll stay,' Anne said gently.

'Are you sure, Anne?'

'I'm certain.'

In the flat above the dressmaker's shop on Front Street, Jean begged Elsie not to go out in the storm.

'You'll catch your death, girl,' she warned, but Elsie wouldn't listen.

She continued putting on make-up, applying darker eyeshadow than usual and a deeper red to her lips. Jean was up and about now, no longer confined to bed, and the bruises on her face and jawline had almost disappeared. She was nearly back to full strength and itching to return to work. However, she was still under orders from Dr Gilson not to leave the flat for a few more days.

'I'll wear my raincoat,' Elsie said.

Jean threw up her hands in despair. 'I wish I'd never agreed to you walking the streets,' she cried.

Elsie stopped what she was doing and turned to face her aunt with a face full of thunder. She was still struggling with how negligent Jean had been in allowing her debts to pile up.

'If you had stopped me, what would have happened? We'd have had no money for food or coal. We'd have been thrown out by our landlord for being behind on the rent. This is all my fault. I got us into this mess and I told you I'd get us out.'

Jean sank back onto the sofa. She laid a hand on her chest and gasped. 'It still hurts, you know. Every now and then I'll get a rotten twinge of a pain that knocks me for six.'

Elsie walked to her aunt and laid her hand on her arm. 'Then relax while I'm out. I'll be back before you know it.'

She left the flat with her raincoat tied tight and the collar up. Her only protection from the downpour was her headscarf. She walked briskly to the lane behind the factory and waited in her usual spot. When a man approached, she went through her routine.

'Got a light, mister?' she asked as she stepped out from under the gas lamp so that he could see her.

The man got straight down to business, confident, almost arrogant in his approach. 'How much do you charge?'

Elsie looked at his face. She hadn't seen him before. There was something about the way he spoke that made her think he wasn't local. They exchanged the usual chat, with Elsie offering to take him to her flat, but the man refused and said he'd take her to his room instead. Elsie pocketed his money but refused to move, remembering Jean's warnings.

'I need to know where we're going,' she said.

'To Elisabethville. Do you know it? I have private accommodation there.'

His heavy accent suddenly made sense.

'Oh, you're one of the Belgian men,' she said.

He nodded along the lane. 'My car is here. I'll drive.'

And with that, he and Elsie headed off.

Chapter Twenty-Two

By the next morning, the storm had blown itself out. Hetty knocked on Dan's bedroom door.

'Mum?' she called. When there was no answer, she gently pushed the door open. Hilda was lying in Dan's bed in the dark. Hetty moved quietly around the bed and knelt in front of her. She saw Hilda's eyes were open.

'Mum? Would you like me to bring you some breakfast?'

Hilda stared ahead, gripping the eiderdown with both hands. 'Where's my boy?' she whispered. Her gaze fell on Hetty, as if just realising she was there.

Hetty covered her mum's hands and Hilda released her grip.

'Mum? I can bring you some toast, we have plenty of bread. We have eggs too. Would you like something to eat?'

'No, I don't want anything. I just want my boy,' Hilda said.

Hetty stroked her hair. 'Please, Mum. You need to eat. Have a cup of tea at least. Why not come downstairs with me? I'll help you dress and we could go out for a walk.'

'I want Dan to be here, not you,' Hilda said. She turned her head on the pillow and focused on a spot beyond Hetty.

Hetty was at a loss. She didn't have anyone to turn to or ask for advice. She'd thought about asking Elsie, but her friend seemed preoccupied these days, not the same girl she'd once been. As for Anne, she saw little of her since the factory had begun its new working schedule. Whenever she ran into her at work, Anne was always busy, running from packing store to reception, from the railway sidings to the enrobing room, delivering letters, reports and files. No, she couldn't ask Elsie or Anne. The only other person she knew was her mum's friend who lived at the end of Elm Street, but she was dealing with her own loss after her husband had been killed in the war. It would be unfair to burden her.

'Come on, Mum, please think about getting up and about. I'll help you every step of the way.'

'Aren't you working at the factory today?' Hilda asked.

'Not today. I'm due to report to Lumley Castle at lunchtime. Mrs Doughty wants to show me the ropes and introduce me to everyone.'

Hilda closed her eyes. 'If Dan was here, he'd take care of me.'

Hetty let go of her mum's hands. She stood and looked down at her lying in Dan's bed. Then she walked to the window and pulled the curtains open, letting in the spring sunshine. Light flooded into the room.

'It's finally stopped raining. There was a nasty storm last night, but this morning is bright and breezy. I'll bring up a mug of tea and a plate of toast for you,' she said, then she walked out of the room.

When she came back upstairs with breakfast, she was heartened to see Hilda sitting up staring out of the window. Hetty sat on the bed and braced herself for a conversation she knew her mum wouldn't want. However, for Dan's sake, there were important words she needed to say.

'Mum . . .' she began cautiously. Hilda took a sip from her mug and looked at her. 'We need to talk about arranging something . . . for Dan. If you're not up to leaving the house, I'll speak to the vicar to find out what we need to do. I hear the church is offering a memorial service for families of soldiers. Perhaps we could attend?'

Hilda cradled her mug to her chest. 'He's my son. If anyone should speak to the vicar, it's me,' she said firmly. Hetty was surprised by the force of her words, which came in contrast to her dishevelled, weak state.

'Are you sure?'

'I've said I'll do it and I will. My boy deserves the best and our vicar will do him proud.'

'Will you go today?' Hetty asked.

Hilda glanced out of the window again. 'The storm's gone, you say?'

Hetty looked out at a blue sky with white clouds. 'It's gone, Mum.'

Hilda took a bite of hot buttered toast. 'Then yes, I'll go today.'

'Would you like me to come with you?' Hetty offered.

Her mum looked appalled. 'You? Why would I want you when all I want is Dan back in my arms?'

Hetty felt deeply hurt by the cutting comment, but she didn't reply. She knew how much her mum was suffering, just as she was herself. She also knew that Dan had always been her mum's favourite. He'd been first above everyone for Hilda, above Hetty, all of her life. She stood, intending to go.

'Then I'll leave you to it,' she said.

That morning, when Elsie woke, she heard laughter and voices. A man was talking close by. She lay still in her bed. She heard her aunt Jean, sounding happy, flirtatious, then the man replied. She'd heard his voice before, a few times, and knew it was Alfie, Jean's special man. She realised he must have arrived last night after she'd left the flat. She could smell bacon frying, and her stomach turned with hunger. With no work at the factory that day, she didn't need to get up. But as she snuggled down and pulled the eiderdown over her head, intending to go back to sleep, there was a knock at her door.

'Elsie, come and eat breakfast. We've got bacon and eggs.'

Elsie could resist many things, but bacon and eggs was her favourite. She and Jean hadn't seen bacon in the shops for weeks. She tumbled out of bed, pulled on her dressing gown and headed into the small area of the living room they grandly called the kitchen. In reality, all that was there were cupboards, a small table and four chairs. Alfie was sitting at the table tucking into breakfast. There were blankets and a pillow on the sofa, suggesting he had spent the night there, rather than in Jean's bed. Jean's body was still too painful and fragile to be wrapped in a man's arms.

As she entered the room, Elsie looked approvingly at Alfie. He was a good-looking man with thick, sandy hair and a long, rugged face. He was broad across his shoulders and chest and was dressed in a dark shirt tucked into black trousers. Jean was sitting by the coal fire, frying eggs in a round, flat pan. Alfie looked up and smiled. Jean indicated for her to sit down and slid a plate in front of her.

'Two eggs, Elsie? Or just one?' she asked.

Elsie looked at her aunt. 'Two, if there's enough, but where's the bacon from and how can we afford it?'

Jean patted Alfie on his shoulder. 'Breakfast is a gift from Alfie.'

'My pleasure,' he beamed. 'When I got here last night and saw the state Jean was in, I thought she could do with feeding up. I went out this morning to buy bacon from the butcher. It's all I could afford.'

Jean placed two eggs and two rashers of bacon on Elsie's plate, then filled a mug with tea. As Elsie began to eat, she kept shooting glances at her aunt. Jean gave a little cough, then looked hard at Alfie.

'It's time to tell Elsie our news.'

Chapter Twenty-Three

Alfie laid down his knife and fork, then reached across the table for Jean. This shocked Elsie, as she'd never seen Jean hold hands with anyone.

'What's going on?' she asked. 'What news?'

Alfie gave a nervous cough. 'Elsie, I've been sitting here all morning working out how to tell you.' When he looked at Jean, there was a tenderness to him Elsie had never seen before. 'I'd like to make an honest woman of your aunt. I've asked her to marry me.'

'And I've said yes,' Jean added.

Elsie dropped her knife and fork in shock. She was aware that Alfie and Jean were staring at her, waiting for her response, but she found it hard to speak. She was stunned by the news and didn't feel as happy about it as they did, judging from the broad smiles on their faces. As she sat staring at the two of them, trying to gather her thoughts, Jean spoke again.

'Alfie's sister lives in London and she's offered to rent us rooms in her house. There's a garden too, Elsie, and so much space. Alfie's told me all about it. I think . . .' She gently ran her fingers along her jawline, where the last of her bruises were still visible. 'I think I need a change of scene after what Frankie did. I'm almost scared to leave the flat. I know what he put you through too, love.'

Elsie's mind whirled. She pushed her plate away, suddenly feeling sick. She couldn't believe what she was hearing.

'You're leaving me!' she cried, unable to comprehend.

'No, love,' Jean said, more gently this time. 'You're more than welcome to come with us.'

'There's plenty of space,' Alfie chipped in. 'You'd have a room of your own. And of course there's work in London. While the war's on, women are being recruited to drive trains, buses . . . There's all sorts you could do.'

He patted Jean's hand affectionately.

'And I'm going to make sure that your aunt never has to work on the streets again.'

Elsie looked at Jean and saw a contented smile on her face. She seemed relaxed and happy.

'Is moving to London really what you want?' she asked.

Jean nodded. 'I'd be a fool to turn down such a wonderful offer . . . from such a special man,' she said as she planted a kiss on Alfie's cheek. 'He proposed to me last night. It came as a shock, but I couldn't be happier. Please give it some thought, love. The three of us could make a new life in London, a new start. No more hiding from Frankie, no more walking the streets, no more working my fingers to the bone at the market for pennies. With what you've done to help, we'll be able to pay off the debt to the landlord before we move out.'

It was all too much for Elsie. 'When are you leaving?' she asked.

'As soon as we can. We'll get married in London,' Jean

replied, glancing around the flat. 'I'll have to get some packing boxes from the market and find my old suitcase. I know it's in here somewhere.'

Alfie put his arm around Jean's shoulders and gently pulled her to his side. Elsie felt as if she'd been punched in the stomach.

'What if I want to stay here?' she said.

Jean shot her a look. 'You can't stay on your own. How would you afford the rent?'

Elsie knew she'd never afford it alone. She only had her wages from the factory plus what she made walking the back lane at night. And that, she'd always promised herself, would never last a minute longer than it needed to. She realised she would have to make a decision quickly on where her future lay. She couldn't stay at the flat if she was to be free of walking the streets to pay rent. She had to strike out on her own, but how and where?

'I don't want to go to London. I like it here. I have my friends, my job,' she said. She stood from the table, pushed her chair back and barged out of the room.

She dressed quickly and brushed her hair, then ran down the stairs and out onto Front Street. She needed to be alone, to be outdoors in the fresh air; she wanted to go to the river, to sit and think and let the enormity of what had happened sink in. It was only when she was halfway down Front Street that she realised she hadn't said congratulations to Jean. She knew she was being selfish, but if she didn't think about herself and her future, no one else would.

She stormed down Front Street, anxious and worried about what lay ahead. She didn't want to leave Chester-le-Street; it was the town where she'd grown up and where her parents had lived. If she left, she'd never see Hetty and Anne again. Her breath caught in her throat when she realised she'd even miss Stan Chapman. He was the only man in her life who'd ever been kind to her. Leaving the town she loved was unthinkable, but how could she stay on her own? Where would she live without Jean? She shivered despite the warm day. Perhaps there were rooms for girls like her, girls left alone, that she could rent. But where would she go to find out? She had to think about herself and her future. Surely there must be a way.

When she reached the river, she sat down and stared across the water at Lumley Castle. She felt tears prick her eyes, but she was determined not to cry. She'd been left on her own in the world once before, when her parents died. Jean had taken her in then, but now she was being left again and this time she'd be completely alone. As she bit her lip, thinking about what to do next, she felt a movement at her side. Someone was sitting next to her, too close for her liking. The stench of beer hit her before the horror of realisation.

'Hello, Elsie,' Frankie said.

Elsie leapt up and staggered away. 'No! Leave me alone,' she yelled.

She expected him to follow her and braced herself for the dreaded touch of his hand. However, nothing happened as she began to march off. Afraid that he might follow her, she plucked up the courage to look back. She saw him still sitting on the bench with his legs crossed, as if he hadn't a care in the world. She kept a good distance away, just in case.

'What do you want?' she hissed.

Frankie inspected his fingernails nonchalantly, but Elsie knew it was just an act. She'd seen him do this before when they'd been courting.

'You're up to something. Why are you here?' she demanded.

He leered at her. 'I've been watching you, Mrs Ireland. I know what you've been up to in the back lane at the factory and overnight at Elisabethville. I know you've been selling yourself to any man who'll have you.'

Elsie felt rage building. She'd thought she'd been discreet. She tilted her chin and put her hands on her hips.

'What I do is my business,' she said, and began to march off.

'It'll be common knowledge once I tell Mr Jack what one of his toffee factory girls gets up to at night,' Frankie shouted as she walked away.

With every step that Elsie took to get away from Frankie, her rage and despair built. The only way he could have known what she'd been doing was if he'd followed her to the back lane. Was he so desperate that he was stalking her? She glanced around again and saw he was still on the bench. He even had the nerve to wave. Elsie picked up her pace and ran.

When Anne had woken, at first she didn't know where she was. The bed felt too large. The window was in the wrong place. Then the night before came rushing back, and all that had happened between her and William. She felt no regrets. It had been natural and right; their love for one another had taken its course. But now she was in bed alone. Where had William gone? She lay perfectly still, listening, hoping to hear him about the house, but she couldn't make out a thing. At Mrs Fortune's house there would be noise outside, people walking past on the street, children running and shouting on their way to school. But here there was perfect silence.

She sat up in bed, feeling the quality of the sheet against her bare skin. Then the bedroom door flew open and William appeared in his dressing gown, carrying a tray. On it was a teapot, mugs and plates piled with hot buttered toast. He got back into bed and pulled the eiderdown up, placing the tray on his knees. And that was how Anne ate breakfast on her first morning at the Deanery.

'What time does your housekeeper arrive? I'll need to leave before she gets here,' she said as she sipped from her mug.

'Why the hurry?' William teased.

'Well, it wouldn't be decent if she found me here,' Anne replied.

'It'd be decent if we were married,' he said with a cheeky smile.

Anne almost choked on her tea. 'I've told you already, William, don't rush me.'

He kissed her on the cheek. 'Then I'll wait until the end of time. Anyway, Edith's very discreet. She's been with me all the time I've lived here. We can trust her, I'm sure.'

He ran his fingers along Anne's arm.

'You know, the factory isn't open today. We could stay in bed all day if we wanted.'

Anne gave a wry smile. She put her mug of tea on the nightstand and turned to face him. 'Or we could go in to work later than normal. There's a lot of paperwork to go through to keep the factory afloat, William, even on the days when the workforce isn't there.'

William put his own mug down and reached for Anne, and she snuggled into his side.

That night, after working at the factory, Anne returned to her room on Victor Street. She had a story ready to tell her landlady about being put up at a friend's house in the storm, if she was asked why she'd stayed out. She noticed an oil lamp glowing in the front parlour as she let herself in. As she climbed the stairs, she heard laughter and voices. The women were both home, enjoying each other's company. Anne had no wish to disturb them, so she continued up to her room.

When she entered, she locked the door and looked around. The eiderdown was pulled tight across her single bed. Thin curtains hung limp at the window. The chair and dresser were old and worn; they were her landlady's furniture, not hers. She thought about the luxury of the bedroom where she'd woken. The expensive carpets and plump pillows, the warm and cosy feeling she'd had, the heavy curtains at the window . . . and the large bed. She'd felt safe there, as if she and William were the only ones who mattered.

She sighed as she took off her coat and hung it on a hook on the door. Then she walked to the dresser and pulled open a drawer. She rummaged at the back, her fingers working over silk slips and stockings until she found what she sought. She pulled out a small photograph, a tiny square picture of her baby boy. She turned it to the window to catch the remains of the light. Her child was living elsewhere now, safe and secure with a wealthy family. She had no need for worry or concern. And yet at times she felt a terrible sadness, knowing she'd never see him again. As much as she wanted to be with William, and even accept his offer of marriage when she felt ready, she knew her son would remain her secret, one she could never share. Her fear was that if William ever knew she'd borne a son out of wedlock, he – and his family – would shun her.

She slid the picture back in the drawer and pushed it out of sight. She knew she had a choice. But would she choose her future with William and the toffee factory, or crave the past, and her son?

As time went by, warmer days came often as spring began to turn into summer. The factory gardens were now planted with neat rows of vegetables. And in the middle of the garden stood Anabel's red rose bush, covered in buds ready to bloom. At home on Elm Street, Hetty did everything she could to help her mum cope with the enormity of losing Dan. Hilda was up and about now, no longer confined to Dan's room, although she still slept in his bed at night. And as she'd promised, she had spoken to the vicar about joining the memorial service for those killed in the war. However, visiting the vicar had been the only time she had left the house since Dan died.

When Hetty told Dirk the news about the church ser-vice, Dirk had offered to attend to support her. This meant a great deal to Hetty. They'd begun to see each other regularly now that the misunderstanding about Gerta had been solved. However, he'd also given her unsettling news.

'A while ago I saw your friend at Elisabethville,' he said.

'Which friend?'

'The dark-haired girl, my friends say she is very pretty. But I don't find her as pretty as you.'

'You mean Elsie?' Hetty said, surprised.

Dirk nodded. 'I saw her coming in one night.'

'Did you speak to her?'

'No. I was too surprised to see her. At first I didn't think it could be her. She was entering one of the private houses.'

Hetty was confused. 'What was she doing there? Do you know?'

'I shouldn't say,' he said cautiously.

'Please tell me,' she urged.

Dirk bit his lip. 'Your friend, Elsie . . . it's not the first time she's been in the village. There is much talk about her. She's been coming in at night, and always with different men.'

'Oh, that's just Elsie, she likes men's company,' Hetty said breezily, although deep down she was concerned. She was also hurt, because she and Elsie never kept secrets from each other, or so she'd thought.

'No, Hetty. You don't understand,' Dirk continued. 'She's been working in the village . . . spending time with men in exchange for money. I heard it from one of the men himself.'

Hetty sank back in her chair. She couldn't believe it. She wanted Dirk to be wrong, but when she looked into his blue eyes and his open, honest face, she knew he was telling the truth. Her heart sank. While she knew what Jean did for a living, she'd never imagined for one minute that Elsie would do the same. However, after Elsie had married Frankie, Hetty couldn't deny that she'd changed.

She'd become sullen and sulky. Where she'd once been vibrant and alive, she was now morose. Where she'd been chatty and willing to share gossip and news, now she kept things to herself. They saw each other less, working together only three days each week. And when they were at work, they couldn't talk to each other because of the noise in the packing room. They could hardly hear themselves think. Things had changed between them, Hetty thought. But she had been too wrapped up in her grief over Dan to notice what Elsie was going through.

Chapter Twenty-Four

The next time Hetty and Elsie met at the factory gates, heading into work, Hetty pulled Elsie to one side.

'Can we talk at lunchtime, Elsie?'

Elsie nodded blankly, and the two of them walked on into the factory.

By lunchtime, both of them were more than ready for a break after a morning spent scooping, weighing and packing. The work was more taxing than wrapping toffees as they'd done before. Plus, the atmosphere in the packing room was nowhere near as calm as when working for Mrs Perkins. They headed to the canteen for lunch. Once seated, Hetty watched Elsie closely.

'Are you all right?' she asked.

Elsie shot her a look. 'Course I am. Why wouldn't I be?'

'It's just . . .' Hetty began hesitantly, 'you seem different these days. We used to share everything and now we don't see each other as much as we did. It's like we're strangers, not friends. I've been dying to talk to you about my job at Lumley Castle. Oh, you should see the place, Elsie. It's as grand as you'd imagine.'

'Have you met the earl yet?' Elsie asked.

Hetty shook her head. 'Mum said I wouldn't, and she was right.'

'How's your mum doing?'

Hetty dipped her hand into her pocket and pulled out a squashed bread bun filled with egg mixed with salt.

'She's still sleeping in Dan's bed. We're joining the memorial service this Sunday, it's a special one for those killed overseas. Dirk's coming with us. Would you like to come?'

'I would, thanks, Hetty.'

Hetty bit into her sandwich and cast another glance at Elsie.

'You look a bit tired, if you don't mind me saying so. Not like yourself. That's why I wanted to know if you were all right.'

Elsie looked down at her plate.

'Elsie?' Hetty said, concerned. She put her arm around her friend's shoulders and Elsie's words began to tumble out.

'Jean's leaving for London. I don't want to go but I can't stay at the flat and I don't know what to do.'

Hetty gasped in shock. 'Jean's leaving . . . Why?'

'She's getting married.'

'What?'

'She's got a fella, Alfie. He's her regular man, the only one she's ever let stay overnight. He's nice and I like him. Anyway, he's asked her to marry him and go to London, where his sister lives. They want me to go with them. The house has a garden and Alfie says there's plenty of work for women, but I don't want to leave. I don't know how I'd cope outside of Chester-le-Street. I like it here.'

'Wouldn't you like to get away from Frankie?' Hetty asked.

Elsie's face dropped. 'Don't mention him to me. Anyway, why should *I* move because of *him*? Besides, I'd miss you,' she said, giving Hetty a smile.

'If you don't want to go to London, come and stay with me and Mum,' Hetty offered immediately.

Elsie pulled away and looked at her, eyes wide. 'Really? Your mum wouldn't mind if I moved in?'

'Well, I'll have to check with her first. If she agrees, we'd have to charge you rent and money for food. And you'd have to help with the chores.'

Elsie sat up straight in her seat. 'Of course I'd pay rent and do chores. I wouldn't expect a room for free. Oh Hetty, that would be perfect. Let me know what your mum says, please.'

Elsie began tucking into a meat pie. Hetty braced herself to ask about what Dirk had told her.

'There's something else I need to discuss.'

'What is it?' Elsie said.

Hetty looked behind to ensure that no one was listening then she leaned close to Elsie. 'Your aunt Jean, is she still working, you know, at nights?'

Elsie stopped eating and put down her pie. 'Why do you ask?' she said cautiously.

'Because . . .' Hetty's heart skipped a beat. She hated what she was about to say, but she had to know the truth. 'Because I wondered if she'd asked you to do the same. I know you've been selling yourself.'

Once the words were out, she closed her eyes. She'd expected Elsie to fly off the handle, to accuse her of badmouthing her, or at least challenge her and call her a liar.

But when she opened her eyes again, Elsie was staring down at the table. Hetty felt sick seeing her so cowed. She'd hoped that Dirk had been mistaken.

'I didn't want to tell you because I thought you'd judge me and I'd lose your friendship,' Elsie said quietly. 'Who told you?'

Hetty didn't want to mention Dirk, as it would seem disloyal. 'You were seen at Elisabethville, more than once,' she replied.

Elsie nodded, taking this in.

'What's happened, Elsie?' Hetty said. 'Tell me and I'll help you in any way I can. But you need to know that I can't ask Mum to take you in if you're still doing that work at night.'

'It's over,' Elsie said firmly. 'Jean couldn't work for a while and we . . . we needed the money. It was the only thing I could do.'

'Is Jean better now?' Hetty asked. 'What was wrong with her? You didn't mention she was ill.'

'She wasn't,' Elsie said, looking up at Hetty now. 'Frankie beat her up.'

Hetty's jaw dropped. 'No!' she gasped.

'She couldn't leave the flat. She was in bed for days. We had to call the doctor, so then we had to pay him, and there wasn't enough money. I was shocked when Jean told me she had debts and that she'd let them build up for months. Our rent was overdue, and we had no coal for the fire. I blamed myself for Frankie beating her up. He said it was revenge for what we did to him at Pine Street, when you, Jean and Cathy came to rescue me. I felt so guilty that I offered to take on Jean's night-time work at the back of the factory. I met a few fellas and took them back to the flat, and it wasn't too scary after the first couple of times. Then one fella drove me in his car to Elisabethville. He was an older man but polite, with nice manners. He drove me back to Front Street afterwards.'

Hetty sat in silence as Elsie continued.

'Another Belgian man came the next night, then a different one later that week, and each of them took me to Elisabethville. I didn't know I'd been seen. I suppose it was Dirk who told you.'

Hetty kept quiet.

'Anyway, it's over. I'm not doing it again. All that's left is for me to move out of the flat and find my own place. I thought about asking at the church if they knew of rooms for girls in my situation.'

Hetty laid her hand on Elsie's. 'No. I won't let you do that. You'll come to stay with us and you can live there as long as you like. It'll be good to have you there, although Jet might bark when you first move in, until he gets used to you. To be honest, having your company is exactly what I need. Life with Mum is hard. I mean, it always has been, as we've never got on. But since Dan died, she's retreated into herself. She's only left the house once, to see the vicar, and now I can't reach her. All I do is feed her and keep her warm. I never thought I'd say this, but I'd welcome some of the old Hilda back, the one who fought with me and argued. But her spirit's broken. All she talks about is Dan.'

'There's Frankie too,' Elsie said.

Hetty jerked back from her friend and stared, open-mouthed. 'He's not moving in!' she cried.

Elsie laughed out loud, and at that moment, Hetty realised how long it had been since she'd seen a smile on her friend's face.

'No, he's not moving in,' Elsie reassured her. 'I've already told you I'd never go back to him. But as we're being honest, I need to tell you something else. Frankie followed me to the river one day when I went there to think after Jean told me she was leaving. He told me he knows what I've been doing at night; he must have been hanging around the back lane, following me, watching.'

Hetty was aghast. 'Did you know he was there?'

Elsie tutted. 'Of course not. He's threatened to tell Mr Jack what I was doing.'

'He can't do that!' Hetty cried.

'Shush, keep your voice down,' Elsie warned. 'I'm frightened. If Frankie carries out his threat, I'll be sacked.'

Hetty shook her head. 'No one will believe Frankie, no matter what he says. He's a drunk, Elsie. He was sacked for stealing from the factory, remember? Who'll take him seriously now?'

'Should we tell Anne first?' Elsie suggested. 'Maybe she can have a word with Mr Jack; they always seem to be together. She's got his ear.'

'No, let's keep this our secret,' Hetty said.

Elsie pulled a handkerchief from her overall pocket and wiped her tears away. 'I've missed talking to you, Hetty. You've been grieving over Dan and I couldn't unburden myself to you. I've had so much going on and I've kept it all inside, and now it's all coming out . . .'

'Hey, come here,' Hetty said, and she gently pulled Elsie to her. 'Listen to me. We'll deal with Frankie Ireland if and when we have to. There's no point in worrying. With a bit of luck he'll get drunk one night and fall down in a ditch and we'll never see him again. Think of all there is to come instead of dwelling on him.

'I'll pick my moment with Mum to ask her about you moving in. And we'll give Dan a good send-off on Sunday at church. You can say hello to Dirk then too.'

'Will you tell him I've finished with my night-time work and I'll never return to Elisabethville? I hate the thought of him judging me for what I did there.'

'I'll tell him, don't worry. He's a good man, Elsie. He'll understand when I explain what happened between Frankie and your aunt. And speaking of Jean, when's the wedding taking place?'

'It's in London later this year, but they're leaving next week.'

'Next week! So soon?' Hetty cried. 'Then I'll speak to Mum tonight.'

Chapter Twenty-Five

As Hetty walked home from work, she ran through in her mind what she'd say to her mum about Elsie moving in. When she reached home and opened the door, Jet bounded along the hallway and jumped up. Hetty bent low and scratched him behind his ears.

'Good dog, Jet,' she said.

Jet padded along the hallway and Hetty glanced up the stairs.

'I'm home, Mum,' she called.

'About time too!' Hilda yelled in reply.

Hetty was surprised to hear her mum's voice coming not from Dan's bedroom upstairs but from the kitchen. She walked along the hallway and was stunned to see her sitting by the fire. There was a delicious smell in the air and a pan on the hearth. Hilda was fully dressed and had even combed her hair. Hetty took off her coat and hung it up, then walked to her mum.

'It's good to see you with a bit of colour in your cheeks,' she said.

Hilda stirred the coals in the fire with a poker. 'Dan wouldn't want me feeling sorry for myself,' she huffed.

'Now then, I've made broth, but it's not as nice as it could be as there's no ham in it. We can't afford to buy ham on the pittance you earn.'

'I *am* working two jobs, Mum,' Hetty replied wearily. 'I'm doing my best.'

Hilda began spooning the broth into bowls. Jet walked to them with his tail wagging.

'There's none for you, Jet,' Hetty said, and he slunk away.

As Hetty tucked into her food, she glanced at Hilda.

'Mum?' she said, bracing herself.

'What now? Can't you see I'm eating?' Hilda snapped.

Hetty kept quiet until they'd both finished. Then she took the bowls away and made a cup of tea. While Hilda relaxed in her seat, Hetty tried again.

'The broth was nice, Mum. But you're right, it'd be tastier with ham.'

'We can't afford ham, Hetty, I've already told you.'

'Well, maybe there is a way we *could* afford it,' she said.

Hilda raised an eyebrow. 'How?'

Hetty sat up straight and clasped her hands in her lap. She knew from experience that there was only one way to deal with her mum, and that was to be direct.

'It's Elsie, she needs somewhere to live. Jean's moving away to live in London, but Elsie wants to stay. So I thought maybe she could move in here with us.'

She kept her gaze on her mum as she spoke, trying to gauge her reaction, but Hilda's face gave nothing away. Hetty carried on.

'She'd pay rent, of course. And on the days when I'm working at Lumley Castle, she'd help out around the house with the chores. She'd be good company for you.

She'll even feed Jet and clean his messy footprints when he brings in mud.'

She swallowed hard. She'd said her piece and now she had to wait for Hilda's verdict. There was silence between them for a few moments.

'Mum?' Hetty asked. 'What do you think?'

'I think Elsie is a tart!' Hilda snapped.

Hetty glared at her and gritted her teeth. How close her mum had come to the truth, Hetty would never reveal.

'She's a toffee factory girl, not a tart! Elsie's not her aunt Jean. She wants to start a new life on her own. Jean will be miles away at the other end of the country.'

'I want no gossip about us, Hetty,' Hilda said darkly. 'If Elsie moves in and there's talk of her being seen with men on the street, like her aunt, she'll be out on her ear. Do you understand?'

'Yes, Mum,' Hetty said.

Hilda picked up the poker and rattled it in the coals. 'She'd pay rent, you say?'

'Enough to put ham in the broth next time we cook it,' Hetty said gently.

Hilda nodded slowly, staring into the fire. Hetty knew the next step was going to be hard.

'You could move back into your own room. Elsie could have Dan's room.'

'No!' Hilda said firmly. 'I won't let anyone have my boy's room. Elsie can have my room and I'll stay in Dan's.'

'Are you sure, Mum?'

'I'm certain. I'm not moving from my boy's room. I want it kept exactly as it always was.'

'Elsie wants to come with us to the service on Sunday,

as does Dirk. They both want to pay their respects to Dan,' Hetty said.

'Then tell her she can move in before we say goodbye to my boy.'

Hetty reached her hand out to her mum, but Hilda sharply brushed it away.

On Sunday morning there was a clear blue sky and the air was warm and still. Inside Elsie and Jean's apartment on Front Street, packing boxes littered the floor. Jean was emptying cupboards and wrapping ornaments in newspaper, while Elsie was in her room, folding her clothes into a suitcase. She packed her make-up and toiletries, her underwear and shoes, then her dressing gown. When all was done, she fastened the suitcase with its metal clasps and looked around. The wallpaper was faded, the curtains were worn and the carpet was threadbare.

'I won't miss you one bit,' she said to the room. She picked up her coat and walked out.

Jean turned when Elsie entered the living room and stopped what she was doing. She placed a glass on the table and walked towards her. They stood facing each other in silence. Elsie gripped her suitcase. She'd been dreading this moment ever since Jean had given her the news about moving to London.

'Hetty's mum is expecting me, I should go,' she said, biting back tears.

Jean walked forward and laid her hands on Elsie's shoulders. Elsie dropped the suitcase. She'd been determined not to cry, to keep her emotions in check, but the warmth of Jean's hands along with the familiar scent of her lily-of-the-valley perfume proved too much. Tears began to roll down her face.

'I'll miss you,' Jean said, as she hugged Elsie tight.

'Write to me every day,' Elsie said.

They held onto each other for what seemed like for ever.

'Elsie, love, are you sure you won't come to London with us?' Jean pleaded. 'Alfie's coming with the van this afternoon. There's still time for you to reconsider.'

Elsie stepped away and wiped her eyes with her hand-kerchief. 'You've done enough for me, Jean. You took me in when Mum and Dad died and I know it's not been easy. I know I've been ungrateful at times and I'm sorry, really I am.'

'Stop that right now,' Jean said firmly, looking into Elsie's eyes. 'You've no need to apologise. You've more than made it up to me after what you did. You got us through the worst time I've known. You looked after me and cared for me when I couldn't leave my bed. I'll never forget that. I wish you would come with us.'

'What'll happen when Alfie's conscripted and sent overseas? Who'll look after you then?' Elsie asked with tears in her eyes.

'He's too old for conscription,' Jean replied. 'Please come, Elsie.'

But Elsie shook her head again. 'It's time I stood on my own two feet. I've got to stay and forge my own future.'

'If you change your mind . . .' Jean began.

Elsie remained firm. 'I won't.'

Jean walked to the table and picked up a bottle of whisky.

'Here, take this with you. Alfie brought it as a present

for me, but I'm not keen on the taste. Give it to Hetty's mum, as a moving-in gift.'

Elsie took the bottle. 'Thanks, Jean. For everything.'

Jean tilted her chin. 'Always keep your head high, Elsie Cooper. Never let anyone bring you down.'

Elsie attempted a smile as her heart broke in two. 'I'll do my best,' she said. Then she picked up her suitcase and headed out of the door.

Elsie made an odd sight walking through the streets of Chester-le-Street that morning; a girl with a suitcase in one hand and a bottle of whisky in the other. She had to keep stopping to wipe tears from her eyes, or to move the suitcase from her left hand to her right when it became too heavy to carry. But she carried on, step by step, away from her old life and into the new.

'No more walking the streets at night,' she whispered to the morning air. 'No more going home with strange men. No more Frankie Ireland. I might have no choice but to stay married to the scoundrel, but I'll only answer to Elsie Cooper, never Mrs Ireland.'

When she reached Hetty's house, she dropped her suitcase on the ground and nestled the whisky bottle in the crook of her arm. With her free hand she rapped at the door. Hetty opened it and greeted her with a hug and a curious glance at the bottle.

'What's that?' she asked.

'It's a gift to your mum from Aunt Jean,' Elsie explained.

Hetty lifted the suitcase and carried it into the hallway, where Jet ran rings around Elsie, jumping and barking.

'Get down, Jet,' Hetty said, and the dog obediently slunk away.

'You'll get used to him,' she promised. 'And he'll get used to you. He's a friendly little soul.'

She pushed open the door that led to the kitchen. Hilda was sitting by the fire. She was wearing a black coat and hat. Her black-gloved hands gripped her handbag in her lap.

'Mum, Elsie's here,' Hetty said.

But Hilda didn't look up.

'She's in a bad way this morning,' Hetty whispered to Elsie.

Elsie walked to Hilda and crouched in front of her. 'Mrs Lawson, I know the day ahead will be difficult. I'm grateful to be allowed to come to the church service with you.' She laid her hands on Hilda's. 'And I give you my word that I'll never make you regret your decision to take me in.'

Hilda simply nodded.

'Let me take your suitcase upstairs,' Hetty offered.

Jet ran after them. Hetty opened the door to the bed-room and Elsie stepped inside.

'It's not much, I'm afraid,' Hetty said, but Elsie was overjoyed. Sunlight streamed in through the windows, lighting up the room and making it feel welcoming and warm. There was a double bed covered in a cream eider-down with a matching pillowcase. A chest of drawers stood opposite. There was a small hearth in front of the chimney breast where a fire could be set on cold days.

'I hope you like it,' Hetty said.

Elsie couldn't believe her eyes. The room was bigger than the living room in Jean's flat. She walked to the window and ran her hand down the pretty flowered curtains.

'Is this room really mine?' she asked in amazement.

Hetty nodded. 'Is it all right?'

'All right? Why, it's absolutely perfect!'

She walked to Hetty and hugged her.

'Thank you, my friend. This is just what I need to make a fresh start.'

'Come on, we'd better go downstairs. We need to leave for church soon; we're meeting Dirk there. Mum's been ready for hours, but she hasn't spoken a word or eaten anything since she got up. Be gentle with her, Elsie. Even after today, she might take a few days to get used to you being here. I doubt she's aware of much at the moment; the grief has overcome her again.'

Elsie squeezed Hetty's hands. 'Then I'll be strong for you and your mum.'

When Hetty left the room, Elsie looked around again. A wide smile made its way to her face. This was it; she was determined to put Frankie behind her. Her new life started today.

Chapter Twenty-Six

During the service, Hetty sat on one side of Hilda with Elsie on the other. Each girl held one of Hilda's hands. Dirk sat on the other side of Hetty, holding her free hand. The church was busy, and people were squashed into the pews. Hetty listened intently to the sermon, closing her eyes to pray and doing her best to join in with the hymns. However, singing wasn't easy with a lump in her throat. She had to keep dabbing her eyes with her handkerchief to keep her tears at bay. As for Hilda, she was so lost in her grief that she never opened her mouth. She had to be helped to her feet by Hetty and Elsie when everyone stood for the hymns. After more prayers, the vicar read out the names of local men lost to the war. The list was organised in alphabetical order, and Hetty braced herself as she waited. And then there it was. Her brother's name. Dan Lawson. Dirk squeezed her hand. On her other side she felt Hilda stiffen. Each time Hetty glanced at her mum, she seemed to be looking at something beyond the vicar, something far away. Hetty said a silent prayer for Bob during the service too.

When it was over, Hetty and Elsie linked arms with Hilda, almost carrying her from the church.

'I need to go back to Elisabethville,' Dirk said.

'I understand,' Hetty replied.

He placed a chaste kiss on her cheek. Then he turned to Hilda.

'Mrs Lawson, I am deeply sorry for your loss.'

Hetty watched, but her mum's face remained impassive. The girls walked home slowly, in silence, with Hilda between them. When they finally reached Elm Street, Hetty led the way into the house.

'Not now, Jet,' she said when the dog began leaping at her skirt. She turned to see Elsie taking off Hilda's coat and hat while her mum stood still, resigned.

'Come on, Hilda, let's sit you in your favourite chair,' Elsie said.

As Elsie helped her mum to her chair by the fire, Hetty filled the kettle with water and placed it on the fire. Busying herself with the teapot and mugs, then bread and tomatoes to make sandwiches for lunch, she saw Hilda's gaze fall on the whisky.

'I need a drink,' Hilda said. They were the first words she'd spoken all day.

'I'll pour it,' Elsie said, then she looked at Hetty. 'Where are the glasses?'

Hetty showed her where they kept their meagre supplies in the pantry. Elsie poured whisky into three glasses and handed one to Hilda. Hetty took her own, then raised it in a toast.

'To our Dan,' she said.

'To Dan,' Elsie repeated, and she raised her glass too.

Hilda looked at them both, and confusion flickered on her face. Finally she raised her own glass.

'To my beloved son.'

Hetty took a sip. She hadn't tasted whisky before and was shocked by how much it burned.

'You can drink it with water, it makes it easier to swallow,' Elsie explained.

'I can see I'll learn a lot with you living here,' Hetty said with a smile.

Hetty sat by the fire with Elsie and Hilda while the kettle came to the boil. She made tea in the pot, then handed round sandwiches. Immediately she and Elsie began to eat, but Hilda didn't touch her food.

'Come on, Hilda,' Elsie said gently. 'You've got to eat, to keep your strength up. Hetty's gone to a lot of trouble to make lunch.'

Hilda gripped her glass with both hands. She brought it to her lips and downed the whisky in one, then held it out to Elsie.

'Another,' she said.

Elsie cast a wary look at Hetty, who cautiously nodded her approval. Elsie poured whisky into the glass and handed it to Hilda. When Hilda downed it in one gulp again, Hetty became alarmed.

'Take it easy, Mum.'

There was a breath of silence before Hilda spoke.

'I'm not your mum.'

At first Hetty thought she hadn't heard right, but then saw the look of alarm on Elsie's face. Her stomach turned and her breathing sped up as her heart began to race. All the while, Hilda kept her gaze on the floor, on a spot beside Hetty's boot. She wouldn't look up.

'Mum?' Hetty cried, confused and stunned.

Hilda shook her head. 'I'm not your mum. I never have been.'

Hetty felt as if she'd been punched.

'Mrs Lawson ... Hilda ... it's been a difficult day,' Elsie said. 'You've not been yourself since Dan died. You don't know what you're saying.'

Hilda raised her head and looked straight at Hetty. She was still clutching the empty glass.

'I know exactly what I'm saying. It's time she found out the truth.'

Hetty felt a sudden pain in her chest. She couldn't breathe properly; there wasn't enough air in the room.

'You're upset,' she gasped. 'You're not in your right mind.'

Hilda handed her empty glass to Elsie. 'Another.'

Hetty grabbed the glass and placed it on the table. 'No more of this for you. It's making you say things that aren't true.'

Hilda levered herself out of her chair. She walked past Hetty and Elsie to the bottle and refilled her glass, then she sat at the table and faced Hetty.

Hetty couldn't think straight. 'Why are you saying these things?' she asked. She felt Elsie's arm around her shoulder.

Hilda tried to sit upright in her seat, but she kept leaning to one side. Her eyes were turning glassy. Hetty had never seen her mum drunk before and didn't know what to do. Then Hilda began to laugh, a cruel, evil sound.

'Mum? What's going on?' Hetty pleaded.

Hilda slammed the glass on the table. Jet, who'd been trying to sleep, growled and slunk away.

'It's time you knew the truth. I'm not your mother. Oh, I took you in as a baby, but you were never mine.'

'But my dad . . .'

Hilda tutted. 'Your dad was a drinker, Hetty, and a womaniser. He wasn't the man you idolise. You don't know the half of it. Those debts he left us when he died, that was just part of the problem I lived with.'

Hetty felt Elsie's arm tighten around her protectively. She realised she was rocking back and forth, trying to cope with the shock, trying to figure out the truth.

'If you're not my mum, then who is?'

Hilda threw her head back and laughed again, then she picked up her glass and poured the drink down her throat. She pointed a gnarled finger at Hetty.

'You're my sister's child. She died giving birth to you. You killed her, Hetty Lawson.'

Hetty felt as if she'd been punched. She doubled over in pain.

'When your mum died, your dad begged me to take you in and bring you up as mine. The gossips had a field day talking about me, a single woman with a baby, but I had no choice. I had to bring up my sister's child. When your dad couldn't cope on his own, he moved in with me too. And that's when I was shunned by all my neighbours and friends.' Hilda banged her fist against her chest. 'The names they called me were dreadful, but I did it because it was the right thing to do. Your dad and I fell into a routine, but we never fell in love. We lived as husband and wife in every way but name, under this very roof. We brought you up as our child. Then we had Dan. But still your dad refused to do the decent thing and marry me, so I had to live with the shame of being unwed and unwanted.

Now that he's gone and Dan's dead, there's no point in keeping secrets.'

Hetty put her hands over her ears. 'I don't believe this!' she cried, shaking her head in denial of what she'd just heard. She felt Elsie stroking her hair.

'Hilda, how can you be so cruel?' Elsie said, but Hilda wasn't finished yet.

'I've looked after you, Hetty Lawson, from the minute you were born, but I've never loved you, not like I loved Dan. He was *my* son. My child. Oh, you became useful around the house, someone at my beck and call to cook and clean.'

Hetty's shock gave way to anger as a million thoughts ran through her head. Then slowly, pieces of the puzzle began to slot into place. Everything she had suffered from Hilda during her life began to make sense. The cruel, cutting remarks. Always coming second to Dan. Never being good enough, no matter how hard she tried. Being treated as second best and criticised for everything she did. The sharp realisation cut her in two. It felt as if her heart had been ripped out, and she began to sob.

Hilda rose from her chair and walked to the door that led upstairs. But before she left the kitchen, she paused to deliver her parting shot.

'I wish with every fibre of my being that Dan was here now and you were the one that was dead.'

Hetty slumped in her chair, feeling breathless and weak, then suddenly everything went black.

Chapter Twenty-Seven

On Monday morning at the factory, Anne held her note-pad in one hand and a pencil in the other, ready to take notes from Mr Jack. This was her usual way of starting the day, going through details of his appointments and meetings. Once she had finished, she laid her notepad down on his desk.

'I have a meeting of my own this morning,' she said. 'I've finally managed to pin down Mr Burl after he ignored my previous requests. I want to discuss his behaviour towards the girls in the typing pool.'

Mr Jack looked at her. 'Are you sure you don't need me to intervene?' he offered, but Anne shook her head.

'You've more important things to do. Besides, I want to handle this myself.'

'Then you'll need this. I've signed it.' He handed her a sheet of paper with the factory logo in blue at the top.

Anne picked up her notepad and was about to head to her own office when she stopped. She thought of the white feather she'd seen on Mr Burl's desk. She cleared her throat.

'William, would you have any idea why Burl has been

excused from conscription? A fit and healthy man of his age should have been sent overseas months ago.'

Mr Jack stroked his chin. 'I understand it's a medical condition that's kept him out of action,' he said, then returned his attention to his paperwork.

Anne went into her own office and began work. Half an hour later, she heard a knock at the outer door. She glanced at the clock on the wall, then stood and smoothed down her skirt before squaring her shoulders and walking through to Mr Jack's office.

She greeted Mr Burl with a firm handshake and invited him into her office. Once he was seated at her desk, she walked to the door and closed it, then sat down directly opposite him.

He tapped his wristwatch impatiently. 'Come on, girl, get on with it. I'm a busy man. What is so important that I had to leave my office to come here to speak to *you*? You're nothing but a secretary.'

Anne sat straight in her seat and looked hard at him. She placed her hands on her desk and clasped them together defensively.

'I've received a complaint,' she began.

Mr Burl shifted in his seat, crossed his arms and glared at her as she continued.

'It's a complaint about your behaviour towards the women who work in the typing pool. I asked to meet you to demand that you moderate your language in front of them in future. I would also ask that you treat them with respect. In addition, I understand you often lose your temper and bully some of the young men in your sales team.'

She leaned forward, getting into her stride.

'This kind of behaviour will not be tolerated at Jack's toffee factory. We have always prided ourselves on—'

Mr Burl held up his hand. 'Now just a minute! How do you know what Jack's toffee factory has always prided itself on? I've worked here far longer than you. I daresay I'll be here long after you've left. Girls like you only get yourselves a job for as long as it takes to find a husband.'

Anne bit the inside of her cheek to stop herself from saying something she'd regret. To lose her temper now and fling words at the man opposite would make her behaviour as bad as his. She knew she had to keep her cool.

'Those girls in the typing pool are gossips, the lot of them,' he went on. 'Most of them can't even type properly. It takes a firm hand to manage a bunch of simpering females.'

Anne could take no more. She stood, put her hands on her hips and glared at him.

'Mr Burl, I beg you to take those words back. I also ask . . . no, demand that you treat the women in your office much better than you do at present.'

She thrust the sheet of paper towards him, the paper that Mr Jack had signed.

'What's that?' he sneered, not making a move to take it.

'It's an official warning,' she said. 'Your behaviour will not be tolerated. If it continues, we will consider further action.'

His face turned to thunder. 'I won't take this from you,' he sneered.

Anne didn't take her eyes off him for a moment. 'It's signed by Mr Jack.'

This time Mr Burl snatched the paper from her. She

watched as he read it, his face turning red. Then he leapt from his seat and stormed into Mr Jack's office.

Anne followed and stood to one side, watching the exchange unfold. She and Mr Jack had expected something like this to occur. They both knew how hot-headed Mr Burl was.

'What's the meaning of this?' Mr Burl demanded, waving the paper.

Mr Jack remained calm. 'I am sure that Miss Wright has explained everything perfectly clearly to you. Now, shouldn't you return to your office?'

Mr Burl seethed, impotent with rage because he couldn't challenge the factory boss without suffering severe consequences.

Anne moved forward. 'Mr Burl, please, let me show you out,' she said politely. She marched to the office door, pulled it open and stood to one side. At first Mr Burl didn't move, then he seemed to pull himself together and strode out without a word. Anne closed the door and sank into the nearest chair.

'It becomes easier over time to deal with such difficulties,' Mr Jack said. 'And I want to thank you for bringing the situation with Burl to my attention.'

Anne pushed a stray lock of hair behind her ear. 'Meg came to me to tell me the truth about his behaviour. I doubt she would have done so if your secretary had been a man. There are things that only women understand. She was brave to stand up for the younger women she works with.'

'Keep me updated if you hear more,' Mr Jack said. 'If Burl's behaviour doesn't improve, I'll have a word with him, man to man. I'm delighted that you take such an interest in the welfare of the girls. A happy workforce is a productive workforce.'

Anne was about to return to her own office when the door was flung open and Jacob stumbled in. His tie was awry, he was red in the face and he looked unusually flustered.

'Jacob, what on earth's the matter?' she cried.

'Anne, I'm sorry,' Jacob said, clearly upset and looking afraid. 'There's a chap, he pushed his way into reception demanding to see Mr Jack.'

A tall, thin man in a cheap suit entered the office and Anne was hit by the stench of cigarettes and beer. She recognised him immediately as Elsie's husband, Frankie Ireland. The last time Frankie had been in Mr Jack's office was when he'd been sacked from the factory for stealing tins of toffee.

'What are you doing here?' Mr Jack demanded. 'You have no business barging into my office!'

Jacob tried to take Frankie's arm, but Frankie was too strong and shrugged him off.

'Jacob, you may return to reception,' Mr Jack said calmly, then he moved to stand next to Anne, preventing Frankie from approaching any further.

'Should I call for help?' Jacob asked.

Mr Jack shook his head. 'I can handle this man.'

Jacob left and closed the door. Mr Jack addressed Frankie directly.

'Now, what is going on?' he demanded.

Frankie swayed from side to side, then gripped the back of a chair to steady himself. 'I've come to tell you that you've got yourself a common tart working at your factory,' he slurred. 'Her name's Elsie Ireland. She's giving Jack's toffee a bad name around town. I heard she's even selling her body at Elisabethville.'

'You're talking nonsense. You're drunk. Get out and never come back,' Mr Jack ordered.

Anne pulled the door open and stepped forward to persuade Frankie to leave, but he wouldn't move. He pointed a finger at Mr Jack.

'Elsie Ireland is friendly with your stuck-up Lady Muck. Or should I say Lady Tina, the one with her face on your toffee tins. She's getting your posh toffees a rotten reputation.'

Mr Jack took one of Frankie's arms and pinned it behind his back. Frankie cried out in pain, but Mr Jack marched him out of the office, along the corridor and into reception. Anne followed, watching in awe. She'd never seen him so assertive, and it gave her quite a thrill. Jacob stood and watched from behind his desk as Mr Jack frogmarched Frankie out of reception into the cobbled yard. Then he walked him all the way to the factory gates. Only when Frankie was out of the grounds did he let him go.

'If I catch you back here, it'll be a matter for the police,' he warned him.

Frankie staggered away, all the while yelling obscenities about Elsie. Mr Jack waited until he was out of sight before he returned to reception. He straightened his bow tie and ran his hand across his bald head.

'Miss Wright, any chance of a cup of coffee?'

'I'll bring it right away,' she replied.

Mr Jack headed back to his office, leaving Anne and Jacob stunned by what had happened. They looked at each other and Jacob raised an eyebrow.

'Frankie didn't hurt you, did he?' Anne asked.

He shook his head, then returned to his desk. Anne was about to turn to leave when she noticed a white feather next to his ledger.

'Jacob!' she gasped. 'Did the white feather brigade give this to you in town?'

His eyes darted to the feather. He grabbed it with both hands and stuffed it into his pocket. 'You weren't meant to see it,' he whispered.

Anne moved towards him. 'Why not? I know you're exempt from conscription because of your weak chest. Why, half of Chester-le-Street knows. So there's no shame in receiving it.'

He sank into his seat and buried his face in his hands.

'It's not my feather,' he said at last. He looked up at Anne. 'It's for Meg, you see.'

Anne was confused. What did Meg have to do with this?

'I know how much she suffers working for Mr Burl. I wanted to do something to help her; you know how stuck on her I am. She's told me what he's like, how he treats the girls in the typing pool so badly that he often has them in tears. I picked up the feather in town. I found it on the ground; someone had thrown it away.'

'Go on,' Anne said softly. Her mind began slotting together pieces of a puzzle that was now making sense.

'It's not the only feather I've found. The first one . . .'

'You left on Mr Burl's desk,' Anne said.

Jacob looked at her, astonished. 'How did you know?' he gasped.

Her mind worked quickly. 'Listen, Jacob. I spoke to Mr Burl this morning, and I swear things will change regarding the way he treats the women he works with, including Meg. Please don't leave any more white feathers for him. War is hard enough without bringing more difficulties to the factory.'

Jacob nodded, then dropped his gaze.

'Did you ever speak to Meg?' he asked. 'About me, I mean. You offered to put in a good word.'

Anne felt a twinge of guilt. She'd been so busy with her work that this had slipped her mind. Now that she understood the strength of Jacob's feelings and what he'd been willing to do for Meg, she nodded.

'I will, I promise,' she said.

Chapter Twenty-Eight

When Anne returned to the office, Mr Jack was pacing the floor. This wasn't a good sign. She entered, closed the door and waited for him to speak.

'Do you know the woman Frankie mentioned?' he asked.

'Yes, I know Elsie. She's a friend of mine,' Anne replied. 'You've met her too. If you recall, some months ago she stepped forward to take the blame when Frankie Ireland was caught stealing. He'd put her up to it.'

Mr Jack stopped dead and looked at her. 'Well, *is* she a common tart? *Is* she selling her body at Elisabethville?'

Anne thought about her friend. When she'd first met her, she'd been taken by Elsie's beauty and vivacity. She was always laughing, often flirting with the factory men and enjoying their attention. She was brassy and bold. She'd even nipped in the waist of her overall on either side with a few stitches to emphasise her shapely hips. But since she'd married Frankie Ireland, she'd changed. Anne remembered what Stan had confided to her about Elsie walking into the river when she'd not been in her right mind. Was it possible that she had reached such a depth of despair that she was now selling her body in exchange for company? Anne didn't know what to think.

'Honestly? I don't know,' she replied.

'But it's possible, right?' Mr Jack snapped.

'William, please don't speak to me in that tone,' Anne said firmly. 'Frankie Ireland is a drunk. He came in here casting aspersions on one of our girls who also happens to be my friend, and it sounds as if you choose to believe him.'

Mr Jack fiddled with his blue bow tie. His face fell. 'I'm sorry, Anne.' He sank into his seat. 'You know how protective I am of my factory and the brand. If Frankie's words contain even a grain of truth, don't you see how it could affect us? I'd be a laughing stock at Elisabethville. They'll joke about how toffee factory girls offer sweetness after hours. I won't have it. I can't risk our reputation being sullied. You know how many years my father spent building up this business. Since I took over the factory, I've dedicated my life to it.'

'Would you like me to speak to Elsie?' Anne offered.

'No,' Mr Jack said. 'I'd like you to sack her.'

She rocked back on her heels, furious. 'Now wait a minute. We've got no proof that she's done anything. All we have is the word of a drunk. I'm not going to sack anyone, and frankly, I'm appalled that you've suggested I should.'

Mr Jack leapt from his seat. 'Then I'll sack her myself,' he said.

Anne moved quickly to stand in front of the door, preventing him from leaving. She put her hands on her hips and glared at him.

'You will do no such thing! My day started badly,

having to give harsh words to Mr Burl about his treatment of women. But I never . . .' She paused and took a sharp intake of breath. 'I never for one moment expected that it would continue with harsh words to you. I will not stand by and let you sack Elsie, or any of our girls, on the basis of something we don't know is true. Besides which, even if it is true, what the girls do in their own time is their business, not ours.'

Mr Jack sat down heavily and leaned his elbows on his desk. A resigned expression clouded his face.

'You're right, Anne, of course. You always are. My emotions are running away with me. It's this damned war and the pressures it puts on the factory. I can't think straight.'

'Let me speak to Elsie in private. But I refuse to let you sack her,' Anne said.

'I need to protect the brand,' he repeated.

She stood firm. 'And I need to protect my friend.'

Anne left the office feeling sick with anxiety over her run-in with Mr Jack. It was the first time they'd argued, and she wondered if he cared more about his factory than the people working in it. She'd known other factory bosses who were ruthless and unkind, yet Mr Jack was neither of those. She mulled this over as she walked away from the office, calming herself down. She'd been surprised by his reaction. She knew times were tough, with the war affecting everyone, but he'd overstepped the mark in demanding Elsie be sacked. Well, if he could be stubborn, so could she. And looking after her friend was her priority. She'd deal with Mr Jack later, after he'd calmed down. What she needed to do now was warn

Elsie that Frankie had been bad-mouthing her at the factory.

She chided herself again for not having spent more time with her friend to find out how she was coping. She thought again of what Stan had told her about how fragile Elsie was, and knew she'd have to choose her words carefully. She thought about Meg, too. She needed to do more to help the girls in the typing pool, but she hadn't a clue where to start. She resolved to ask Mr Jack for advice. The more knowledge she gleaned about working practices and staff management, the better she could help the girls when they came to her with their problems.

When she reached the packing room, she told Mr Hanratty she needed to speak to Elsie.

'I'm not happy about this, Anne,' he sighed. 'I'm already one girl down. Hetty Lawson hasn't come to work. Elsie says she's not well.'

Anne walked to Elsie and touched her arm to get her attention. She beckoned her out and the two of them walked to the garden.

'There's a bench along here, we'll sit and talk,' Anne said. In front of the bench was Anabel's rose bush, its beautiful red flowers giving off a heady scent.

'What is it?' Elsie asked.

Anne tried to work out how to start.

'There's no easy way to tell you this, Elsie, it's a delicate matter so I'll just come straight out and say it.'

Elsie shifted in her seat.

'Your husband barged into Mr Jack's office this morning.'

Elsie gasped and her hands flew to her heart as Anne continued.

'He was drunk and . . . well, the truth is, he spoke badly of you. He said . . .' She paused and looked into Elsie's big brown eyes. 'He said you've been selling your body on the back lane of the factory. And that you've been going into Elisabethville at night, with men.'

Elsie stared at the roses.

'I had my reasons,' she said quietly.

Anne was surprised that she had confessed so easily and quickly. She was also disappointed, not in Elsie's behaviour but that Frankie had been right.

'We all have to do what we can to survive and pay our way. Times are hard, Elsie. I'm not here to judge you,' Anne said, then she thought of Mr Jack. 'But other people might. And as far as the factory goes, Mr Jack isn't happy, to say the least. In fact, he wanted me to sack you.'

Elsie turned to her, eyes wide. 'Sack me? No, please, I need this job. I don't walk the back lane any more. I had no choice, for reasons I can't explain . . . but all of them lead back to Frankie.'

They sat in silence for a few moments.

'Look, Elsie, are you all right? I mean, after what hap-pened with Frankie and your baby,' Anne said. She hated that her words were so awkward, but she had to pretend she didn't know about what had happened at the river.

'I'm fine, Anne, really,' Elsie said quietly.

'Do you swear to me that what Frankie said about you is all over?'

Elsie gently laid her hand on Anne's arm. 'I swear.'

'Then I believe you. I'll speak to Mr Jack. He's angry and upset. It's the war, it affects us all in different ways. It makes things seem a lot worse than they are. He's wor-ried that if someone saw you at Elisabethville and recognised you as a toffee factory girl, it might adversely affect future orders.'

'Please don't let him sack me,' Elsie pleaded.

'I promise to do my best,' Anne said.

As she readied herself to leave the bench, she remembered what Mr Hanratty had said about being a girl down.

'How's Hetty?' she asked.

She was confused when Elsie simply shrugged, as she was usually so chatty. Instead, she decided to try a different tack to turn the conversation.

'Have you talked to Stan Chapman lately? He's always asking after you.'

Elsie shook her head. 'I don't have much time to chat to anyone these days,' she said. 'Look, Anne, I'd better go back to work or Hanratty will complain.'

Anne stood and brought her friend to her in a hug.

'Take care of yourself, Elsie,' she said.

When work had finished for the day, Elsie headed home. After Hilda's revelation, she knew that Hetty was going through hell. She was in deep shock and had fainted twice, once in the house and again on her way to work that morning. The toffee factory held too many dangers for girls who fainted. Anabel's death loomed in Elsie's mind, and she had insisted that Hetty go home. Meanwhile, Hilda was suffering too. She'd stopped eating or even taking a mug of tea, and once more she refused to leave Dan's bed.

Elsie hurried down Front Street with much on her mind. She felt rage towards Frankie. How dare he go around talking about her? A shiver ran through her when she recalled his words about following her at night. Was he following her now? She turned around quickly, nervous in case he was there. She was relieved to see only a few of the factory men. She dug deep into her pocket, where she kept the thin band he had given her on their wedding day. It was cheap and discoloured, and she'd never been sure that it wasn't stolen. Ever since she'd removed it from her finger, it had been hidden in a hole in the lining as a reminder of how evil Frankie was. A warning never to fall for him again. However, she didn't want it anywhere near her now. She upped her pace, almost running as she made her way to the river, cursing him as she went. Reaching the bank, she brought out the ring from her pocket, raised her arm and flung it into the water.

'Elsie!' she heard.

She turned, frowning. Why was Stan Chapman there?

'Stan?' she said, trying to understand.

'Elsie love. Don't do it!' he cried. He ran to her and swept her up in his strong arms. Elsie felt herself held protectively against his broad chest.

'Put me down!' she yelled. She kicked her feet and beat her fists against Stan's back. 'Put me down this instant!'

'Everything's all right, Elsie. I've got you. I'm here,' he said as he walked her to a bench and gently sat her down. Elsie looked at him as if he'd gone mad. She pushed her hair out of her eyes.

'What's got into you?' she cried.

'Me?' Stan said. His breath left his body in bursts after the exertion of carrying her. 'Is that all the thanks I get for saving your life again?'

'Saving my life?' Elsie cried. Then, slowly, she realised

what Stan thought he had seen as she stood at the river's edge. 'Did you think I was going to walk in?'

'You were!' he cried. 'I saved you the last time, and if I hadn't been here today, I dread to think what might have happened.'

Elsie sank back against the wooden bench.

'Oh Stan, I wasn't going anywhere. I knew exactly what I was doing,' she said softly. 'Anyway, how did you know where to find me?'

Stan removed his flat cap. 'I followed you from the factory. I've got news for you, see. I'm sorry, I didn't mean to upset you. But you looked afraid and upset when you left work, and when you started running to the river, I was afraid too. I thought the worst. I remembered last time . . .' He looked down. 'I'm sorry, Elsie. I think I got the wrong end of the stick. But if you weren't going to throw yourself in, what were you doing?'

'I was saying goodbye to someone I should never have let into my life.'

Elsie looked at Stan's rugged face and his hazel eyes. She saw his strong hands grip his cloth cap.

'You're a good man, Stan Chapman. Now, you said you had news for me. What is it?'

'Ah yes,' Stan said. He sat up straight. 'I've got a message from Anne, who works in Mr Jack's office. She said to tell you that she's spoken to Mr Jack and everything will be fine. Your job is safe.'

Elsie felt relief flood through her and couldn't keep the smile off her face.

Chapter Twenty-Nine

When Hetty woke the next morning, she was still reeling from Hilda's shocking news. She'd even fainted on her way to work the previous morning, and Elsie had turned her around and marched her back home. Later, Elsie had brought her tea and tempted her with eggs on toast that she'd cooked on the fire, but Hetty couldn't stomach any food. Meanwhile, Hilda had locked herself away in Dan's room. She and Hetty hadn't spoken since Hilda's drunken outburst. Instead, Hetty had talked to Elsie, long into the night. The two girls had whispered and wondered this way and that about how Hilda had brought Hetty up, always treating her as second-best to Dan. Now Hetty felt adrift, not sure where she belonged, or to whom. She was more than grateful for Elsie's company at Elm Street and for her warm words and advice.

'We've got each other, Hetty, we'll cope,' Elsie had told her.

Hetty knew she had to get up. Ahead of her was her first full day of work at Lumley Castle. Her heart wasn't in it, but she couldn't lie in bed another day. Hilda's news had already robbed her of one day's wages at the factory.

Slowly she washed and dressed. She tied a blue ribbon in her hair and was about to head downstairs when she heard Hilda call. She stopped dead on the landing. She didn't want to see Hilda; she couldn't face her. There seemed to be too much to say, too many questions to ask.

'Hetty?' Hilda called again.

Hetty waited a moment to steady her nerves before she replied. She wanted to ignore Hilda and walk away. But something inside her wouldn't let her. She walked to Dan's bedroom and shouted through the door.

'What is it?'

'Could I have a cup of tea, please love.'

'Okay,' she said glumly. She walked downstairs, set the fire and boiled water. She toasted bread for her breakfast, then took a mug of tea upstairs and knocked at Dan's bedroom door.

'Mum?' she called. Her stomach lurched as the word automatically left her lips, as it had done all her life. 'Hilda,' she corrected herself. 'I've got tea for you.'

'Come in, love,' Hilda called.

Hetty steeled herself. Twice in one morning Hilda had called her *love* when she never would have done so under normal circumstances. It was the first time Hetty could recall her using the word except in relation to Dan.

When she entered the room it was dark. She went straight to the curtains.

'Leave them closed. I'm not up to facing the world,' Hilda said.

As Hetty set the mug of tea on the nightstand next to the bed, Hilda's hand shot out to grab her arm.

'I'm sorry,' she said.

Hetty glared at her. 'Sorry? Is that all you can say?'

'You're a good lass and you didn't deserve to find out the truth the way you did.'

Hetty softened a little, but as Hilda continued, her heart closed again.

'It was your friend Elsie's fault for bringing whisky here. It's the devil's drink. I should never have said yes to her moving in.'

Hetty peered at Hilda in the gloomy light. 'I can't believe you're blaming Elsie for your disgraceful behaviour,' she said. Then she walked out of the room and slammed the door.

'Hetty!' Hilda cried, but Hetty kept on walking.

Later that morning, Hetty made her way to Lumley Castle with Hilda's shock news turning in her mind. She felt as if she was just going through the motions. She was unaware of how warm the day was, or how chirpy the birds sounded. She walked the streets to the river not caring or noticing who was around. It was only when the castle came into view that she knew she had to pull herself together. She stopped for a moment and planted her feet firmly on the ground. She thought about Elsie back at Elm Street. It was Elsie who'd helped her cope with Hilda's news. And it was Elsie looking after Hilda now, for Hetty didn't have the heart to care for her while the shock settled in her. She was beyond grateful to her best friend. She tightened the ribbon in her hair.

'Come on, Hetty, you can do this,' she said out loud, then she marched to the service door at the back of the castle and knocked.

The door swung open and Mrs Doughty opened it, looking flustered. 'Don't just stand there, come in,' she urged.

The housekeeper was dressed as Hetty had seen her before, with a white apron over a black skirt and blouse. Strands of grey hair fell around her chubby face. Hetty watched in amazement as Mrs Doughty carried out three tasks at once. Picking up a clean apron, she flung it at Hetty. 'Here, wear this.' At the same time, she stirred a pan on the hearth while with her left foot she pointed to a sack of potatoes on the floor. 'Scrape and chop these.'

Hetty looked around. 'Where are the . . .?'

'Knives are in the top drawer, over there,' Mrs Doughty replied, returning her attention to the pan.

Hetty began work peeling a mountain of potatoes. She kept looking at Mrs Doughty, hoping for conversation, anything to take her mind off Hilda. But the housekeeper was too busy to talk about anything other than the tasks at hand. When other members of staff called into the kitchen, she barked instructions, never taking her eyes off her work.

'Jack, take the earl's breakfast!' she called to a man dressed in a smart black suit. 'Pick carrots and peas from the garden,' she said to a girl younger than Hetty.

The girl gave Hetty a shy smile. 'I'm Daisy,' she said, and Hetty said hello. She remembered the girl from the day she'd come for a tour of the castle and to learn the ropes. She supposed that in time she'd remember everyone's names, but on her first day it was important not to get on the wrong side of Mrs Doughty. She concentrated on peeling potatoes.

When Daisy returned with a basket of carrots and peas, Mrs Doughty called to her. 'Give them to Hetty, she's on vegetables today.'

'It's nice to see you again, Hetty,' Daisy said politely. She tipped the vegetables onto a large wooden table, then disappeared from the room.

Hetty's morning went by in a blur, but all the while her heart ached. The shock of Hilda's words never left her, and she struggled to process it all. Thoughts of her real mum passed through her mind. What had she looked like? Had she been caring and kind? She was saddened when she realised she didn't even know her name. She doubted her relationship with Hilda would ever improve to the point where she could find out. She tried her best to concentrate on work and not give away anything of her turmoil.

When Mrs Doughty finally slowed down, she asked Hetty if she'd like a mug of tea. Hetty was grateful for the break. She'd been peeling and chopping vegetables for hours and her fingers ached. It was harder work than wrapping or weighing toffees, and she was earning less money at the castle. It made her appreciate her factory job even more. She wiped her hands on her apron, then joined Mrs Doughty outside, where two rickety chairs sat by the door. The day was warm and she turned her face to the sun.

'Come on, out with it,' Mrs Doughty said.

Hetty was alarmed. She shot Mrs Doughty a look. 'Out with what?'

Mrs Doughty cradled her mug of tea with both hands. 'Something's eating away at you, I can tell. You're not the same bright girl who came for her interview. You seem preoccupied in a way you weren't on the day I showed you around. Now, I'm not a mind-reader, but it's clear that something's upset you since the last time you were here. What is it, a fella? It usually is. You can tell me to mind my own business. I'm not being nosy. I just like to have a happy kitchen. If anything's upset you, tell me and I'll help if I can.'

Hetty looked at Mrs Doughty, weighing up whether she could trust her. She didn't know her well but she'd been treated fairly so far. Besides, the woman didn't know Hilda, so what was there to lose? She decided to take the plunge.

'I'm not sure there's anything that anyone can do to help,' she said sadly.

'Oh now, come on,' Mrs Doughty said gently. 'Tell me what it is, then we'll decide.'

So Hetty began to reveal her difficult life with the woman she'd thought of as her mum.

'And now she tells me she's not my mum, she's my aunt,' she finished. 'I'm lost, Mrs Doughty. I don't know where I fit any more.'

There was silence between them. Mrs Doughty sipped her tea and looked ahead at the trees.

'My word, lass, you're going through the wringer,' she said at last. 'But it's not the end of the world. There are worse things that could've happened.' She cast Hetty a sideways glance. 'I thought at first you were going to tell me you were having trouble with a fella. You looked so sad and pale when you arrived this morning, I thought you might be expecting.'

Hetty was shocked. 'Mrs Doughty!'

The housekeeper patted her knee. 'Ah, calm down, lass. You're one of the good ones. I could tell that as soon as I met you and found out you were the face of Lady

Tina. By the way, the earl was impressed when I mentioned it to him. He loves those toffees.'

Hetty's heart skipped a beat. 'The earl knows about me?' she gasped.

Mrs Doughty nodded. 'He knows about all his staff who work down here. I keep him appraised of what's going on. Anyway, stop trying to change the subject.'

Hetty suppressed a smile, because Mrs Doughty was the one who'd gone off-topic. She seemed to be managing three different trains of thought, just as she managed multiple kitchen tasks.

'What'll I do about . . .' Hetty had to stop herself from saying *Mum*, 'about Hilda, Mrs Doughty?'

'I wish you'd call me Sheila,' Mrs Doughty said. 'We're all on first-name terms here.'

'It'll take some getting used to. We're on second-name terms with the bosses at the factory,' Hetty said, thinking of Mr Hanratty, Mrs Perkins and Mr Jack.

Mrs Doughty set her mug on the ground. 'You're not the first lass to be brought up by someone who isn't their mum. And you won't be the last. It goes on more often than you'd think. Me and my sisters were brought up by a woman who lived next door, after our mum died. We called her Aunt Beryl, but we didn't know we weren't related. What I'm trying to say, Hetty, is that it doesn't matter who brings us up or who they are, does it? What matters is that Hilda, this woman you thought of as your mum, she took you in and kept you safe. She put a roof over your head, fed you and clothed you. You've turned into a bonny, intelligent lass. If she's as stubborn an old fool as you say and can't see this or doesn't treat you right, then that's her downfall. If you were my daughter,

I'd be as proud as Punch. Especially with you being Lady Tina.'

Hetty felt as if she might cry, so she turned her face to the sun again. 'Thank you, Mrs . . . Sheila,' she said, touched. 'That's one of the kindest things anyone's ever said.'

Hilda had never once praised her for being chosen as the face of Lady Tina, and it still stung.

'After I learned the truth the other night, the way Hilda treated me has started to make sense. And sitting here with you, something else has begun to make sense too.'

'What's that?'

'Well, it's to do with my fella. He's called Dirk. He's one of the Belgians.'

Hetty was relieved to see not a flicker of suspicion on Sheila's face at the mention of the Belgian community. She'd been right to trust her after all.

'Does he live at Elisabethville?'

She nodded, and as she continued, it became easier to forget the word *Mum* and use Hilda's name. In doing so, she began to feel a distance from her for the first time.

'Hilda didn't like Dirk coming to the house. He's only been once, at Christmas. She was worried what the neighbours would say. That was all she was concerned about, being talked about, being judged. When I asked if my friend Elsie could move in with us, she was terrified of being gossiped about again, because of something Elsie's aunt used to do. But now I know the truth about Hilda's life with my dad, things are slotting into place. She's had a lifetime of being judged for not being married to him, for living with him after my mum died. She made me keep Dirk away because she was scared about the gossip starting again. I'm starting to understand about the shame she's carried all her life. It's turned her bitter and angry, and I realise now that she's taken it all out on me.'

Chapter Thirty

Anne remained angry with Mr Jack after he'd demanded she sack Elsie, even though she'd stuck to her guns and won in the end. She was so upset by his attitude that she kept the connecting door between their offices closed. She'd barely spoken to him since they'd argued and was too annoyed with him to pretend everything was all right. Just when she was giving serious thought to the idea of marrying him, he'd shown his true colours, and she wasn't sure what to make of him now.

When there was a knock at her door, she knew it was him, for today was a day when the factory was closed and only she and Mr Jack were there.

'Come in,' she said. She kept her tone cool, and when the door opened, she didn't look up. She waited for Mr Jack to speak, and when he didn't, she felt confused. She finally glanced up to see a bouquet of white roses tied with a blue ribbon in the open doorway. She felt her shoulders slump and lifted her fingers from her typewriter. Mr Jack walked into her office and laid the beautiful roses on her desk. At first she pretended the gesture didn't mean anything and ignored the bouquet, but then he began to speak.

'Anne, my dear. Please can we put the past days behind us? I've been so worried, I haven't been able to sleep.'

Anne looked into his tired eyes and noticed his crumpled shirt. Even his bow tie was askew. She indicated the empty chair at her desk, and he sat.

'I'm sorry, Anne. I should have listened to you right at the start instead of even thinking of believing a word that came out of Frankie Ireland's mouth. You're much better at handling the factory girls than I. You're closer to them, what with you being a . . .'

A wry smile played on Anne's lips. 'A woman?'

Mr Jack smiled now. 'And you're one heck of a woman. Will you forgive me?'

Anne ran her fingers across the delicate white petals. 'I have a vase for these somewhere, I'll put them in water.'

'Anne, please. Don't keep me waiting. This is agony.'

'Oh, William, stop making a fuss,' Anne said breezily. In truth, she was relieved that they'd made up, for she'd been toying with a major decision ever since her night at the Deanery. However, before she told him about this, there was something she needed to know.

'You won't do it again, will you?'

'What?' he said puzzled.

'Go against one of our girls when you don't know the full story.'

She stood from her desk and began pacing the room, back and forth past Mr Jack.

'If we're to be a partnership, a couple and a real team, as you want, then we must discuss matters thoroughly and work together. Do you understand?' she said.

Mr Jack fiddled with his bow tie. 'I understand.'

'Good,' Anne went on, still pacing, keeping focused. 'Because if I'm to marry you, William—'

Mr Jack leapt out of his seat. 'You're agreeing to marry me?' he cried.

Anne stopped, looked at him and held his gaze. 'Only if you promise that any decisions we make about the factory from now on will be joint ones. I want your word that you won't go sacking anyone without knowing the full details, especially when it comes to the girls. Also, I want to learn as much as I can about managing the staff. I want my office to be open to any of the factory girls who need to speak to me in confidence, on whatever matter. I intend to do all I can to help them, and I don't want you to undermine my decisions.'

'Of course. Anything for you, darling Anne. You've made me the happiest man alive!'

There was one more thing Anne needed to discuss. It would give her equality with Mr Jack at work, for she was determined not to be his secretary for the rest of her life. If he was to be her husband, she needed to hear the right reply from his lips. If she didn't ask now for what she wanted, the moment would pass and she might never again have such a golden opportunity.

'In addition, I want you to propose that I join the board of directors.'

Mr Jack didn't waver in his reply. He replied immediately and with conviction. 'I'd already envisaged that as part of our marriage.'

Anne looked deep into his eyes. 'Then that's settled,' she said.

Mr Jack reached for her. 'Settled,' he whispered, as his lips brushed hers.

'We're a true partnership now,' she murmured.

'A team,' he whispered.

Anne was racked with guilt, for she was still keeping a secret from her husband-to-be. However, she wasn't prepared to do anything that would jeopardise their future. Her son would remain a secret, one she would never share.

Their lips met in a loving kiss. Mr Jack's arm slid around her waist and he pulled her close. They were lost in the moment, lost in each other, when the office door opened and Mr Burl marched in.

'What the devil's going on!' he yelled.

Anne quickly pulled away, straightening her skirt. Her neck and cheeks were on fire with emotion from the kiss mixed with embarrassment at being caught. But Mr Jack held tight to her hand and stepped forward, composed, bringing her with him.

'I notice you didn't knock, Burl. You've interrupted an intimate moment between me,' he looked at Anne with love in his eyes, 'and my fiancée.'

Mr Burl's face turned white with shock. He looked as if he was about to pass out. He looked from Anne to Mr Jack, then swallowed hard and stepped forward with his hand out.

'Congratulations, sir.'

Anne watched the two men shake hands. Then she stepped forward too and Mr Burl reluctantly raised his hand again to shake hers.

'Congratulations,' he mumbled to the floor.

'What are you doing at the factory today?' Mr Jack asked.

'I, er . . . came to check whether an important letter had arrived,' Mr Burl replied.

'Then off you go,' Mr Jack said, dismissing him.

Mr Burl turned and almost ran from the office.

'I think we gave him quite a start,' Anne said.

Mr Jack returned to his desk, but Anne headed into the hallway and followed Burl. She suspected he hadn't come to the factory to check for post, and wanted to find out what he was up to on a day when he shouldn't have been there. She arrived at his office just as he was sweeping his desk, lifting up files and folders, moving paperwork around.

'Looking to see if another white feather has been delivered?' she asked.

Startled, he dropped a pile of paper. 'I don't know what you mean,' he grumbled.

Anne stepped inside his office and closed the door. 'You do. You see, I know you've been receiving white feathers. I've seen at least one of them on your desk.'

Mr Burl sank into his chair and ran his hands through his thick hair. 'I don't know where they're coming from, but I wish they would stop,' he admitted. 'I was nervous in case one had been delivered while I was out of the office. I wanted to remove it before my staff arrive when the factory reopens.'

Anne sat at his desk. 'Mr Burl, could I ask you a direct question?'

He looked at her and raised an eyebrow. 'Go ahead. Why not? Today has been full of surprises!'

Anne couldn't miss his sarcastic tone.

'Why haven't you been conscripted to the services?'

'It's a medical issue. None of your business,' he snapped.

She watched him squirm. She knew he wasn't telling the truth.

'You might have fobbed off Mr Jack with your tale, but not me. He's a busy man with no time to look into such things. But I'm more thorough. And you'll find that once William and I marry, we'll be working even more closely.'

'It's not a tale!' Mr Burl yelled.

'Then why isn't there a record of a medical issue on your file in my office?'

He narrowed his eyes. 'My doctor wrote the letter months ago, so there should be a copy. If it's not there, one of the typing girls hasn't filed it correctly. They're a useless bunch, those girls.'

Anne shook her head. 'Mr Burl, I've already asked you to refrain from using such words to speak about the girls in your office. I'll search again for the letter.' She stood up to leave.

'You won't find it,' he said.

She stopped dead but didn't turn around as he continued.

'I have a friendly doctor, who'll provide me with any letter I ask for in exchange for tins of Lady Tina for his wife and daughters.'

Anne turned around and looked him straight in the eye. 'Mr Burl, it seems we both have a secret, one that neither of us wishes to be made public. What you know about William and me is still to be announced. We will choose when we tell the board and our employees. Do you understand?'

'Only too well,' he sneered.

At the end of the day, Mr Jack called into Anne's office.

'How would you like to join me for a walk around the

grounds at Lumley Castle? We have much to discuss now we are to be wed. Not least about you meeting my parents again. I'm sure my mother will come around once she knows you've accepted me.'

'Will we drive to the castle?' Anne asked.

Mr Jack shook his head. 'My car is being serviced. I can't collect it from the garage until tomorrow. I've had enough of sitting in the office all day, and it's so warm outside. Let's take a walk.'

Anne tidied her desk, slipped her jacket on and picked up her handbag. She and Mr Jack walked from reception side by side. Mr Jack locked the factory gates with a heavy iron key.

'You did ensure Mr Burl has left his office?' Anne laughed. 'I wouldn't want him being locked in overnight.'

'I hope he'll keep quiet about discovering us today,' Mr Jack said.

She smiled. 'I have a feeling he will.'

They walked on together without touching, although Anne was dying to thread her arm through William's and announce to anyone who'd listen that she was his. She wanted to shout her happiness from the rooftops. Instead, it bubbled quietly inside her. They headed down Front Street, then turned right towards the river and the castle.

'I know the Earl of Scarbrough, who lives at Lumley Castle. He's a good chap,' Mr Jack said.

Anne was impressed. 'Earls and castles. My word. After we're married, my life will be quite different.'

Once in the castle grounds, out of sight of anyone, they walked arm in arm, breathing in the warm summer air. Then Mr Jack stopped and reached for Anne, circling her waist with his hands, kissing her lightly on her cheek then searching for her lips. Anne responded warmly, safe in the knowledge that they couldn't be seen.

Inside the castle, Hetty was cleaning in an upstairs room. When she glanced out of the window, she couldn't believe her eyes.

Chapter Thirty-One

The weeks went by and summer sparkled bright, with warm days lasting long into the night. At Elm Street, Hetty and Elsie formed a tight bond. Before Elsie had moved in, she and Hetty had been best friends, but now they were more like family.

Hetty was stoic around Hilda, for she had no choice but to continue to live with her. They settled into an uneasy truce. However, there was one major change between them, in that Hetty no longer sought Hilda's approval in the way she used to do. She became more independent, making her own decisions about what to cook for dinner, what to wear for work and when to leave the house or stay at home. She became determined that she'd live her life as she chose. But while Hetty became more confident and determined, Hilda remained passive, staying at home, her bad chest playing up and stopping her from leaving Dan's room. She still cried in the night for her son.

All through the summer, Hetty carried on working at Lumley Castle two days each week. She got on well with Mrs Doughty, and the work, once she became used to it, wasn't so hard. With the money she earned from her two jobs plus what Elsie brought in from the toffee factory, there was enough to buy ham at least once a week. The girls ate well and Elsie tried to tempt Hilda with their cooked meals, but Hilda ate little, only nibbling her food. Elsie was content to look after Hilda, an arrangement that suited both girls. For the first time in her life, she learned how to cook and manage the running of a house.

At work, she spurned the attentions of the men who asked her out. 'I'm done with fellas,' she told Hetty one night. Then she gave a cheeky wink. 'For now.'

On summer nights, when Hilda was in bed, the girls sat outside at the back of the house with Jet, talking and confiding. Their heads were still reeling after Hetty had shared the news that she'd seen Anne kissing the toffee factory owner. But neither Hetty nor Elsie saw much of Anne these days; she was always too busy at work.

Hetty enjoyed seeing Dirk more than ever that summer. She turned to him in her turmoil when she was dealing with Hilda's shock news, and he proved solid and robust, always there for her, putting his arm around her when she cried, handing her his linen handkerchief to dry her tears. More than that, he listened to her, asking how she was, kind and caring. She saw him at least once a week for walks along the river or tea in a café. He was a constant presence in her life and a welcome presence in her heart.

During those months, work at the toffee factory continued with reduced production. While the war dragged on and the public had less money to spend on fripperies like toffee, it was the orders from the government that kept the factory afloat. Tins of Lady Tina were shipped overseas to the forces. Mr Gerard's creative team rolled out the new *Toffees for the Troops* advertising slogans in all the newspapers to keep the brand foremost in the public's mind. Everyone worked hard, proud to be producing toffee for the forces. Even surly Jacob in reception seemed to have a spring in his step now that he was courting Meg, and Meg was happier too now that Mr Burl's temper had cooled, a little at least.

As for Anne, at home on Victor Street, she was invited once a week to have dinner with Avril and Pearl. At these informal meals, which Pearl cooked to perfection, Anne saw a different side to the officious supervisor she knew as Mrs Perkins at work. She enjoyed the women's company, although she felt guilty about not spending time with Hetty and Elsie. She missed their girlish chatter and their gossip but took heart from her new friendship with the mature ladies she lived with.

Her relationship with Mr Jack continued apace and she regularly stayed with him at the Deanery. On those nights, she simply told her landlady that she was at a friend's. Avril never once pried, and Anne was grateful for her discretion. Their engagement was still a secret at work; their intention was to announce it at the next board meeting, held in the autumn, when a vote would be taken on whether Anne would be allowed to join the board of directors. She recalled Lucinda Dalton's daring move a few months ago, when she'd simply turned up at the board meeting, sat at the head of the table and tried to force Mr Jack's hand to allow her a seat on the board. However, no vote was taken and the minutes of that meeting, which Anne had written and typed up, confirmed that Lucinda was not a member of the board.

One night at dinner at Mrs Fortune's house, Pearl placed a dish of leeks cooked in butter in front of Anne. Normally Anne adored leeks, and she'd eaten this particular dish many times before and enjoyed it immensely. However, this time her stomach turned. It wasn't the first time in the last few days she'd felt like this, but she'd ignored the signs so far, hoping against hope it wasn't what she feared. When Avril poured a small glass of sherry and handed it to her, the sweet notes of the wine made her retch. She covered her hand with her mouth.

'Are you all right, dear?' Avril asked, concerned.

Anne pushed her chair back, excused herself and ran up to her room, where she splashed cool water on her face then sank onto her bed. Her stomach was churning, and it wasn't just from the sight and smell of the leeks. She'd felt like this before, years ago, and recognised the signs. She pulled her handbag to her and took out a tiny black notepad with a calendar at the front. She counted the weeks since her last period, when she'd circled the date on the calendar, and knew in her heart there was no other explanation for how she felt now. The queasiness, loss of appetite and nausea. The way her skirt pulled tightly around her stomach and her blouse felt a little tight across her bust . . . All of this was how she'd felt when she'd been pregnant with her son.

She knew there were unscrupulous women in the dangerous back lanes of Chester-le-Street who would offer an unmarried girl a way to get rid of her child. She immediately ruled out that option, because this time she had a choice. And she had a chance. A chance to do things right and bring her baby into a world with two loving parents. This time she had a good man by her side. A man who loved her, who wouldn't disappear when she gave him the news that she was pregnant. Or at least that was what she hoped. For although she knew William adored her, as she adored him, she didn't truly know how he would take her news that they'd been caught out and were going to have a baby.

The following morning, she sipped water, the only thing she could manage for breakfast. She was sick with nerves over what lay ahead, as well as with the symptoms of her early pregnancy. She dressed carefully in her best blouse with the lace collar and took time to arrange her hair into a rolled bun. She cleaned her glasses until they sparkled. She wanted to make the best possible impression she could when she gave William her news. Standing in front of the mirror, turning her head this way and that, she noted how pale she looked. She reached into the top drawer and pulled out a brooch studded with precious blue stones, a gift from Mr Jack. She pinned it to her jacket lapel, and it shone in the sunlight from the window. Then she reached into the drawer again and took out the tiny picture of her son as a baby. He'd be a toddler now, saying his first words and counting to three. Her heart quickened.

'I will never forget you,' she said, then she kissed the picture lightly and slid it back into the drawer under a silk slip.

She walked into the factory that morning with her head held high while her stomach churned and her heart beat nineteen to the dozen.

'Morning, Anne,' Jacob called as she walked through reception.

'Oh . . . yes. Good morning, Jacob,' Anne replied, too

distracted to notice that he had something in his hands that he was offering to her.

'Anne . . . you should see this!' he called excitedly, but she kept on walking, intent on the task in hand. Her heart fluttered as she approached Mr Jack's office. He was already sitting at his desk, concentrating on paperwork. She closed the door and stood with her back to it, looking directly at him. What she had to say was something that would affect them both deeply. It was too important not to speak immediately.

'William, I have something to tell you,' she said firmly. He looked up, puzzled.

'There's no easy way to say this, so—'

The door burst open behind her, pushing her off balance, and Jacob rushed in carrying a wooden box.

'Jacob, you must always knock!' Anne reprimanded him.

His face was flushed with excitement. Ignoring Anne, he ran to Mr Jack's desk and dropped the box. Anne walked to the desk to see what was going on, disappointed that her news would have to wait. She watched as Jacob pulled a battered, scratched tin of Lady Tina from the box. There was a scorched hole in the front of the tin.

'It came with a letter,' Jacob said as he handed an envelope to Mr Jack.

Mr Jack looked in surprise from Jacob to Anne, then opened the envelope, pulled out a sheet of paper and began to read.

To whom it may concern

I received a much welcome tin of Lady Tina toffee from my home town of good old Chester-le-Street. I placed the tin in my ration bag. When advancing under open fire, I dropped flat on the ground just as a bullet entered my pack. As I felt no pain, I knew I had not been hit. The next day, to my surprise, I looked in my pack and saw a bullet had gone into the tin of toffee. I noticed the tin was penetrated on one side but not the other. The bullet had stayed in the tin, thereby saving my life. I am sending the tin to you for you to witness this miracle, for I can think of no other word. Once I return to England when war is over, I would very much like to visit your factory and collect the tin that saved my life. You may also like to know your tins are being used here as shaving tins! Last week I saw a chap having a wash using a 4lb tin of Lady Tina.

Yours,
Sergeant Gilby, Durham Light Infantry

Anne was lost for words. She ran her fingers across the bullet hole. 'We saved this man's life,' she said softly.

Mr Jack leapt into action. 'Anne, call a meeting with Mr Gerard. We need to get a picture of this tin in the newspapers. Jacob, arrange for the letter to be framed and hung in reception. Anne, get the editor of the local newspaper on the phone for me now. This is amazing news, good news that everyone will love to read.'

'It's a feel-good story all right,' Jacob chipped in. He walked out of the office, leaving Anne and Mr Jack alone.

Mr Jack continued marvelling at the tin, turning it over in his hands and reading the letter again. Anne sat in the chair at the other side of his desk, bracing herself for her announcement. But it felt wrong, too formal, sitting there. It felt as if she was about to take notes for him rather than share intimate news. She stood and walked around to his side of the desk. He was still looking at the box, shaking his head in disbelief. She put a hand on his shoulder.

'William?' she said, trying to get his attention. Finally he turned and looked at her.

'What is it, Anne? My word, you look awfully pale this morning. Are you feeling all right?'

She laid a hand on her stomach. 'I'm fine, William, really. But there's some important news I want to share. I tried to tell you a few moments ago, before Jacob burst in.'

Mr Jack pushed the box to one side and took her hands in his. 'What is it, my dear?'

Anne looked into his trusting face. She remembered the last time she'd given this same news, the same words, to a man she thought she loved. That time the man had disappeared and she'd never seen him again. She had a feeling things would be different this time . . . wouldn't they?

Chapter Thirty-Two

William's jaw dropped in shock.

'Pregnant?'

Anne kept her hand on his shoulder, retaining the physical connection between them. He looked at her, then away.

'I know it's a shock, William,' she said softly.

He stood and began to pace. Anne knew from experience that this wasn't a good sign. He only ever paced the floor when he had difficult decisions to make. She felt disheartened as she watched. She'd hoped for an immediate happy, positive reaction to the news that now felt heavy between them. She waited behind his desk. Suddenly he walked straight to her. He took her hands in his and looked into her eyes.

'I'm going to do something I should have done weeks ago . . . months ago,' he said. He kept hold of her left hand as he got down on one knee.

Anne felt relief rushing through her. For one dreadful moment she'd been worried. But when she saw him looking up at her imploringly, she knew she'd been wrong to even think he wouldn't do the right thing.

'We've already spoken of marriage, Anne, but I've never formally proposed,' he said. 'Will you, Anne Wright, do me the honour of becoming my wife?'

'I'd be delighted,' she said with a smile.

Mr Jack struggled to stand. 'I don't suppose you could help me; my knee has gone into spasm,' he said.

Anne suppressed a smile as she helped him to his feet. 'I'll help you in every way that I can, William, for the rest of my life,' she said.

Her lips found his, and soon they were lost in a kiss. At last Anne gently pulled away from him and patted her stomach.

'William, once my pregnancy shows, I'll be the talk of the factory. People will assume I'm a single girl with no husband on the horizon. There's something we need to do before our baby makes its presence known.'

'Yes, dear, of course. We've already agreed that we'll announce our engagement at the next board meeting, and I've added details to the agenda of the vote to secure your seat on the board of directors.'

But Anne shook her head. 'The meeting is weeks away. First we should speak to your parents and give them the news that we're to be wed and they're to be grandparents.'

Mr Jack rolled his eyes. 'My word. I can just imagine what my mother will say.'

'I need you to stand by me when we tell her, together,' Anne said.

Mr Jack kissed her cheek. 'I'll always stand by you. No matter what happens from now on, we're a team, all three of us.'

* * *

Later that week, Anne and Mr Jack were sitting on a floral sofa in the parlour at Albert and Clara Jack's home. Anne balanced a delicate tea cup and saucer in her hand. She was terrified she might drop it and it would crash down on the expensive carpet. The parlour was over-stuffed with heavy furniture that seemed too large for the space. The whole effect was claustrophobic. She had to concentrate on her breathing to slow her heart each time she thought of the double-shock news that William was about to deliver.

Albert was his usual cheery self, greeting Anne warmly. However, Clara was more wary, although at least this time she stayed in the same room and didn't cry off with a migraine. It was progress of a kind, Anne thought.

'You said you wanted to speak to us,' Albert said to William. 'Is everything all right at the factory?'

William set his cup and saucer on a table and took Anne's hand in his. Anne noticed Clara's eyes focus on their joined hands. From the way she frowned at this small display of affection, Anne could tell she wasn't pleased. Her heart sank. It felt as if she might never win over William's mother.

'The factory's as good as can be expected, Father. The government orders are seeing us through.'

'Good, we'll discuss it at the board meeting this autumn,' Albert said.

William fiddled with his blue bow tie. 'Ah yes, the meeting. That's what I wanted to speak to you about . . . well, partly, anyway. You see, I'd like Anne to join the board of directors.'

Clara tutted and shook her head. William ignored her and carried straight on.

'Her input into the factory is second to none; she's invaluable. I'd like the board to take a vote at the autumn meeting on whether to accept her. I've added details to the agenda.'

Albert nodded thoughtfully. 'Very good,' he said. 'I agree. Anne has proved herself an asset to the factory and will of course receive my vote.'

'Pfft!' Clara said.

Albert shot her a look, then looked at William again. 'Now, what else did you want to tell us?'

Anne glanced at William to give him her support. Then she looked at Clara, ready to gauge her reaction.

'Anne and I are to be married,' William said.

No one spoke for a very long time. Anne could hear the ticking of the clock on the mantelpiece. Her heart was beating fast. She looked at Albert.

'I love your son very much.'

It was then that Clara spoke. 'You love his money and his factory more.'

'Mother! How dare you!' William yelled.

Clara picked up her cane from beside her chair and jabbed it in Anne's direction. 'She's not worth a place on the board of directors and I won't allow it. I'll use my vote against her. She's nothing but a jumped-up secretary. She's got no family connections. I might not be able to stop you marrying this woman, William, but I won't sanction your union by attending your wedding.'

'Mother, please!'

'Clara! Please reconsider! William is our son, for heaven's sake!' Albert cried.

Clara struggled to stand, even with her cane, and Albert helped her as she walked unsteadily from the room.

'I'm sorry, Anne,' William said.

'I don't need your mother's approval to be happy with you,' she replied.

'No, but you might need her vote in order to join the board of directors.'

Albert returned alone and sat in his armchair, looking from Anne to his son.

'Your mother is still suffering the loss of connection to the Dalton family, son. I thought she'd be over it by now, but it plays on her mind. Oh, I love her and I always will, but the pain she's in with her hip and her leg manifests itself in bitterness about how she views the world. It's not easy, and the pain gets worse every day.'

'Is there nothing a doctor can do?' Anne asked.

Albert shook his head. 'I've taken her to see the best doctors in the north, but there's no hope at all.'

William squeezed Anne's hand. 'Father, we have more news.'

Anne steadied herself.

'There is to be a child. The baby is due in the spring.'

Albert's face creased into a smile, then he banged his fist on the arm of his chair. 'A grandchild! How wonderful!' he cried. He leapt from his seat and walked to a dark wooden sideboard. Anne heard the tinkle of glass and saw him bring out a bottle and three glasses. He poured brandy into the glasses and handed one each to William and Anne.

'My congratulations to you both,' he said, raising his own glass.

'You're not ashamed that the child has been conceived out of wedlock?' Anne asked, intrigued at his joyful tone.

'There's never shame where there's love,' Albert replied seriously.

'Then I propose a toast to our child,' Anne said. She raised her glass.

'To our future,' William added.

'To family,' Albert said.

Anne took a sip, but the smell of brandy didn't agree with her and made her feel nauseous. She set the glass on a table at the end of the sofa.

'Will you tell Mother about the baby? I don't think I can bear to tell her myself after her reaction to our wedding news,' William said.

'Leave your mother to me,' Albert said sagely. 'I'll choose my moment carefully. Now then, where will you be married? There's the church in Chester-le-Street, of course.'

Anne looked at William.

'We need something smaller, Father,' he said.

'Smaller? But surely it'll be a society wedding!' Albert replied.

Anne patted William's hand, a sign that she was going to explain. 'William and I have decided that because of so much hardship at the factory, our wedding will be a quiet, modest affair,' she said softly.

'Modest? Then where will it be held.'

'There's a chapel at Lumley Castle,' she suggested.

William's eyes lit up with delight. 'Lumley Castle would be perfect. When?'

Anne patted her stomach and gave a wry smile. 'I think . . . as soon as we can.'

Chapter Thirty-Three

The following day, Hetty waited outside the canteen for Elsie.

'Where have you been? I'm starving!' she said when her friend eventually arrived.

'I've been talking to Stan,' Elsie said.

Hetty saw a blush come to her cheeks and noticed that she looked unusually shy.

'You like him, don't you?'

Elsie shrugged. 'He's all right. I'm not getting involved with him, though, if that's what you think. I don't want any fellas in my life at the moment, thank you very much. I'm enjoying living with my best friend.'

Hetty threaded her arm through Elsie's as they headed into the canteen. As they queued at the counter, Anne joined them. Hetty was overjoyed to see her and hugged her tight.

'I haven't seen you in ages. You look really well, Anne,' she said.

Elsie hugged her too. 'You really do look good. You've got such a healthy glow. It must be all the sunshine right now.'

The three girls shuffled forward in the queue, each carrying a tray and eyeing the food on offer. There were plenty of salads and a vegetable stew, all made with food grown in the factory gardens. It pleased Hetty no end that she now had enough money to buy lunch in the canteen instead of bringing a soggy sandwich from home. Once they had their food, the girls found a table in the corner of the room.

'We've got so much to catch up on,' Hetty said. She wondered if Anne would reveal what was going on between her and Mr Jack after she'd spotted them kissing.

'Hetty works at Lumley Castle now, two days each week,' Elsie said when they sat down.

Anne raised her eyebrows. 'Lumley Castle? I didn't know you worked there.'

Hetty kicked Elsie's foot under the table and scowled. She'd wanted to ask Anne about what she'd seen at the castle in her own time. However, she knew Elsie was less patient, trying to force the topic with her blunt comment.

Hetty and Elsie began to tuck into their food, but Anne didn't touch hers.

'Are you all right, Anne?' Hetty said, noticing that she hadn't even picked up her knife and fork. She noticed that Anne's eyes were shining. 'What is it?' she asked.

Anne leaned forward, then looked from left to right. 'I need to trust you both with a secret.'

'It's all right, we know about you and Mr Jack,' Elsie chipped in. 'Hetty saw you kissing him at the castle.'

'Elsie!' Hetty cried. 'I'm sorry, Anne. But yes, I did see you some time ago. Are you really courting him? I thought he was marrying the tall posh woman with the blonde hair?'

'I really am courting him . . . and more,' Anne admitted.

Hetty clamped her hand over her mouth and her eyes widened, while Elsie swore under her breath.

'But that's not the only secret I want you to keep. I want to ask you both a favour.'

'Go on,' Hetty said, intrigued.

'Mr Jack and I are getting married, and I'd like you both to be my bridesmaids.'

Hetty dropped her knife in shock and Elsie squealed with delight.

'Shush!' Anne warned. 'This is top secret. You can't tell anyone. Oh dear, I should've picked a better place to ask. The canteen isn't ideal for sharing confidences.'

Hetty reached across the table for her hand. 'I'd be honoured to be your bridesmaid.'

Elsie reached for her other hand. 'Me too. Oh Anne, it's so romantic. When is the wedding?'

Anne shifted in her seat. 'Ah, well, that's the thing, you see. It's being held at short notice.'

'Because of the war, everything's changed,' Elsie said.

Anne laid a protective hand on her stomach. 'No, it's because I'm expecting,' she said.

Hetty and Elsie looked at each other, mouths open. Then they leaned their heads together over the table and Anne carried on in a whisper.

'I've missed you both so much. But I've been so busy with Mr Jack. There's a lot going on and I'm sorry I've neglected our friendship. I've been spending time with him at his home at the Deanery and I've met his parents too. And now I've got a wedding to prepare and my head's spinning.'

'Can we help?' Elsie offered.

Anne looked at Hetty. 'I suspect Hetty might become involved, behind the scenes.'

'How?' Hetty asked.

'We're getting married at Lumley Castle.'

Hetty gasped. 'No!'

Anne nodded. 'The wedding's next Saturday. See, I told you it was short notice. It'll be quiet, with just a few guests. If we held a big wedding, there'd be too many business acquaintances and society people William would need to invite because of his standing as the factory owner. So we've decided to keep it small. Plus we didn't want to be seen as being extravagant by spending money while so many of our workers are suffering under the three-day week. However, there'll be a dinner after the ceremony, which is where Hetty might come in, having to prepare food at the castle beforehand.'

'What about a wedding dress?' Elsie asked.

'I've got my cream suit; it'll have to do. I can let out a few stitches on the waistband. There's no time to make a gown.'

'Can't Mr Jack buy you one?'

'In truth, I don't want one. It's such a waste of money to wear a gown for one day then let it hang in the wardrobe for ever. I'd rather keep the money for the baby and all it will need. It'll have its own nursery at the Deanery.'

'You're moving into the Deanery?' Hetty asked, impressed. 'It's such a grand house.'

Anne nodded. 'I'm going to give Mrs Fortune my notice tonight. My room there will be free if either of you girls need somewhere to live. It's a quiet street, and while the room isn't big, it's sunny and warm. Plus there's a lock on the inside of the door.'

Hetty shook her head. 'It's a nice offer, Anne, but Elsie's moved in with me and Hilda, at Elm Street,' she explained.

'Hilda? You mean your mum?' Anne said, confused.

Hetty and Elsie shared a look, then Hetty began to fill Anne in on the news since the girls had last met. She was grateful to Anne for not interrupting or asking awkward questions about her changed relationship with Hilda. She just let her talk herself out. Hetty told her about Dirk, too, about how their relationship was progressing. She answered Anne's questions about how she was coping with her heartache over losing Dan and about coming to terms with the fact that he'd always been her half-brother. Likewise Elsie shared her news about Jean moving to live in London with Alfie. She also told Anne what Frankie had done to Jean. However, Hetty noticed that Elsie kept quiet about the night-time work she'd done to earn money to pay off Jean's debts. She knew that Elsie was trusting her alone with that secret, and it was one she would hold in her heart.

'You both sound so happy,' Anne said when Elsie finished. She turned to Hetty. 'Would you like to invite Dirk to the wedding?'

Hetty thought her heart would burst. 'I'd love to,' she said.

'I'd like to invite Stan Chapman too,' Anne said, looking directly at Elsie. 'If that's all right with you.'

'It's no skin off my nose if he's there or not,' Elsie said breezily, but Hetty knew there was more to it when she saw a contented smile on her friend's face.

'Oh, there's one more thing I should explain,' Anne continued. 'There isn't time to have bridesmaids' dresses made up. There are two cream dresses upstairs at the Co-op that I've put away in my name. Go in and try them on; the assistant will alter them for you if needed.'

'I can sew, Anne. I can alter the dresses myself,' Elsie offered.

'Would you, Elsie? That'd be grand. I'm going to ask Stan if he can create a bouquet using some of Anabel's red roses. I'll ask Mr Gerard to design the invitations.'

'I'm very happy for you, Anne,' Hetty said.

'Me too,' Elsie agreed.

That evening, when Anne reached Mrs Fortune's house, she didn't head straight up to her room as usual. She stood in the hallway and listened for the reassuring sounds of her landlady and fellow lodger, but the house was unusually quiet. Confused, she walked to Avril's parlour and knocked. Avril opened the door. She wore a dull brown dress, and her small black hat was perched on her head, as always. She also looked sad, Anne thought.

'Mrs Fortune . . . Avril, I've come to give you some news.'

Avril pulled the door all the way open and invited her inside.

'Is Pearl not with you today? It seems strange not to hear you talking and laughing together.'

'Pearl . . . Mrs Perkins . . . she's left. She no longer lives here.'

Anne was shocked. 'But why?'

Avril indicated a chair at the table and Anne sat down. Avril sat on the sofa, which sagged under her weight, then clasped her hands in her lap. For the first time since she'd known her landlady, Anne thought she looked nervous.

'There was gossip about us, you see,' Avril told her. 'I can tolerate such things, but poor Pearl couldn't.'

Anne couldn't make sense of it. Why would anyone gossip about Avril and Pearl?

'Two maiden ladies living together during the war while the men are away. You'd think no one would raise an eyebrow, wouldn't you?' Avril continued, a touch of anger coming into her voice. 'But someone saw fit to send me a nasty letter through the post accusing us of having corrupt morals. All I ever did was offer my friend a home. And . . .' She lifted her chin and looked directly at Anne, 'we held hands once walking along the riverside. Whoever sent the letter must have seen us. They weren't brave enough to sign it, of course. The coward! It was a vicious attack on our reputations. Well, Pearl decided it was best to leave. And now I've lost her as both a dear friend and a paying tenant. You've found me at my wits' end.'

Anne had seen how the women made each other happy and it hurt her deeply to see Avril upset. She was also sad that Pearl no longer lived there. It had been like having two elder sisters who looked out for her.

'I shall miss our dinners together,' she said.

'I shall miss Pearl dearly, especially our sherry nights,' Avril sighed. Then she suddenly perked up and headed to the cupboard, bringing out the sherry bottle. 'Would you join me in a sherry, Anne? We can raise a glass to Pearl and wish her well.'

Anne politely declined, knowing the smell and taste would make her nauseous.

'Oh dear, I quite fancied a little drink,' Avril said sadly.

'Avril, you've been honest with me and I need to be honest with you. I came here to tell you that I'll be moving out next week. I'll spend my last night here a week on Friday.'

'My word, that's a shock. I think I need a sherry after all.'

She downed her sherry in one, then poured herself another.

'I'm to be married.'

Avril didn't miss a beat in her reply. 'To Mr Jack of the toffee factory. Am I right?'

Anne looked into her landlady's kind face. She wasn't upset or even surprised that Avril knew the truth. Her words confirmed what Anne had guessed long ago.

'You saw me that night when Mr Jack waited outside on the street,' she said.

Avril nodded. 'It was Pearl who saw you with him, and she told me.'

'Then I thank you both for keeping my secret.'

'Is there a baby on the way?' Avril asked gently.

Anne wasn't in the least taken aback by her question. All she felt was relief that Avril knew the truth and that she could confide in her.

'Yes, there is,' she replied joyfully, thinking of the words uttered by William's father. *There's never shame where there's love.* Her hands went automatically to her stomach.

Avril smiled. 'You and Mr Jack have a special relation-ship. He respects you a great deal.'

'How do you know?'

'Pearl told me. He speaks very highly of you at work.'

'Will you see Pearl again? Do you know where she's gone?'

'She left me a forwarding address, but I'm not sure she wants to be seen with me again, after the horrid words that arrived in the post. I'm made of stern stuff, I'm as tough as old boots, whereas Pearl is more delicate. Oh, don't let her tough exterior at the factory fool you. In private, she wears her heart on her sleeve. I'll visit her when the time is right to see if we might remain friends.'

'Avril, are you free a week on Saturday?' Anne said suddenly.

The landlady thought for a moment. 'Yes, I think so. Why?'

'I wonder if you might like to come to my wedding. You see, I need someone to walk me down the aisle.'

Avril's hand flew to her heart and a tear sprang to her eye. 'Why, I'd be delighted,' she replied.

Chapter Thirty-Four

In the days leading up to Anne and Mr Jack's wedding, an official announcement was made at the factory. The news spread fast, and soon there wasn't anyone in Chester-le-Street, never mind the factory, who didn't know about it. At first Anne feared she would be gossiped about, and it was true that some of the women eyed each other and gave a knowing smile when they heard the news. Many of them wondered at the short notice given and guessed, correctly, about a baby on the way. However, what the workers said in private remained there. In public, Anne was met with congratulations. Everyone seemed happy for her and Mr Jack, all except for Mr Burl, who acted as if the wedding was an unwelcome intrusion.

When Anne told Mr Jack that she needed a few hours away from work, he agreed without hesitation. 'Anything for you, dear Anne.'

She told him she was going to Lumley Castle to speak to Mrs Doughty, the housekeeper, to ensure all would be ready for the wedding on Saturday. However, once she'd finished her business at the castle, instead of going back to the factory, she walked to Front Street to catch the Durham bus. She glanced around nervously, worried in case anyone from the factory spotted her. However, it was too early for the lunch break and for the workers to be walking about. This helped quell her nerves.

The bus arrived, and she took a seat downstairs. She paid her fare to the conductor, received her ticket and placed it in her purse. Then she thought better of it. She removed the ticket and kept it in her hand, ready to throw into the nearest bin once she alighted. If she kept it, and William found it, he'd ask questions about why she'd gone to Durham, and why she hadn't told him. Yet another twinge of guilt twisted in her gut. She hoped that one day she might feel it no more.

She looked out of the window to admire the scenery as the bus made its way into the historic city of Durham. The magnificent ancient cathedral stood tall and proud on the banks of the River Wear, and the castle high on a hill overlooked the cobbled streets. But Anne wasn't there to enjoy the scenery. When she alighted at the bus station, she made her way to the outskirts of the city, walking under a viaduct and along streets that were wide and grand, lined with large, detached stone houses. If anyone had seen her that morning, they might have mistaken her for a smartly dressed young woman heading to work, or even to study at the university. One of the Durham colleges allowed women to receive degrees. She certainly looked the part of a studious, hard-working girl as she marched determinedly on. But she had a far different task ahead.

At the end of a street, she deliberately slowed down. The house she needed was on her left-hand side. It was surrounded by mature trees, through which windows and doors could be glimpsed. She'd been here a few times, but on previous visits had always stayed on the pavement, peering into the garden, trying to see her son. This time, however, she planned to approach the house. She wasn't as nervous as she'd feared she would be; instead she felt calm and resigned as she pushed open the iron gate and walked down the path to the sturdy front door.

A young, fresh-faced maid wearing a white apron over a black skirt answered the door and greeted her politely. Anne held out a sealed envelope.

'Please, could you give this to Mrs Matthews?'

The maid took the envelope. 'Won't you come in, Miss . . .?'

'Wright. Anne Wright. No, I won't come in. I have a busy day. I'd be grateful if you could ensure Mrs Matthews receives the envelope . . . and tell her it comes with my love.'

The maid looked puzzled as Anne walked away. Each step took her further from the house, and she felt tears threaten. She'd been resolute so far, holding back her emotions, keeping them in check. But now it proved difficult. She pulled her handkerchief from her handbag and dabbed at her eyes. Pausing a moment to rest against a stone wall, she took one last look at the house, then straightened her shoulders and walked bravely on.

In the house at the end of the street, the maid knocked on the parlour door.

'Come in, dear,' Mrs Matthews called.

The maid entered the room, holding the envelope. 'A lady has just called with this for you, madam.'

Mrs Matthews was sitting on the rug while a small boy pulled a wooden toy train by a string across the floor. She took the envelope.

'A lady? Did you ask her name?'

'She was called Miss Anne Wright, madam.'

A chill went through Mrs Matthews. She would recognise the name anywhere. Anne was the girl whose child she and her husband had bought as a baby. It was a secret she would take to the grave, for her own sake and for Anne's.

'Did she ask to come in?' she enquired, trying to keep her voice light despite the turmoil that Anne's name caused. She felt nervous. What was the girl up to? How had she discovered where her son lived? It was part of their deal that she would never seek him out.

'No, madam, she declined my invitation to enter. She said I was to give you the envelope with her love.'

Mrs Matthews was curious about what it contained. She couldn't wait to open it and quickly dismissed the maid. 'Close the door when you leave, dear.'

She stood and looked out of the parlour window. She was worried in case Anne was still there, and was relieved to find the street empty. She turned the envelope in her hand. Her name was written on the front. The envelope felt too light to hold a card, letter or note.

'Mama!' the boy cried. 'Train!'

She walked to her precious son, ruffled his hair, then stroked his soft cheek. 'It's a beautiful train,' she said gently.

The boy turned away, lost in his make-believe railway. Mrs Matthews took the letter knife from her desk and slit open the envelope. Inside was a tiny square photograph of her son as a baby. She recognised him immediately and pressed the picture to her heart.

'Thank you, Anne,' she whispered.

Anne walked back to the bus station, willing herself not to cry. Leaving the only photograph that she had of her son with the woman he'd always call his mother was the right thing to do. She knew that if she repeated that enough times, she'd finally convince herself.

The bus to Chester-le-Street was waiting. She stepped inside and took a seat downstairs. As it pulled away, she made a pact with herself never to return to Durham and never to look for her son again. He was no longer hers. Finally, she'd made her decision. It was time to put her past to rest and return to Chester-le-Street, to the factory, Mr Jack, her wedding and her future.

The first thing Anne did when she arrived at the factory was head to the wrapping room. Spotting Mrs Perkins talking to the girls at one of the tables, she walked to her and gently touched her arm.

'I'm sorry to interrupt, Mrs Perkins. Could I have a word with you, please?'

Mrs Perkins excused herself from her girls and followed Anne outside. Anne led the way into the gardens and sat on the bench in front of Anabel's red rose bush.

'I hear congratulations are in order,' Pearl said.

'The news was supposed to be held back for the board meeting this autumn, but, er . . . certain events have meant that the wedding will take place quite soon. That's why our announcement was brought forward.'

'Yes, Avril has told me . . . everything.'

'You've seen her?' Anne said, surprised.

'We've spoken and we will always remain close. She and I knew about you and Mr Jack after I saw you that night outside Avril's house. We kept your secret . . .' Pearl looked at Anne, 'and I trust that you will keep ours.'

'You have my word,' Anne said. 'And I can't tell you how happy I am that you and Avril are speaking again. Did she tell you that I've asked her to give me away at my wedding?'

'She did. We keep nothing from each other.'

'Then I'd like to invite you to the wedding too. Please say you'll come. I have no one on my side, just Hetty and Elsie as bridesmaids. Jacob and Meg are coming, and Stan Chapman – and you, if you'd like to.'

Pearl's face softened. 'Thank you, Anne. I'd love to attend.'

That week, on the days when the factory was open, Anne began to notice some strange behaviour. When she walked into the wrapping room or packing room, girls stopped what they were doing and looked away. Conversations stopped dead. She began to feel paranoid and upset, before giving herself a talking-to. She had a lot on her mind with her wedding just days away, plus the stress and worry caused by war never eased. She knew her mind was running away with itself. But still she couldn't shake the feeling that something odd was going on. She'd followed Hetty and Elsie into work through the gates one morning and asked if she could meet them for lunch, and they'd looked at each other strangely.

'We can't, sorry, Anne. We're so busy in the packing room that Mr Hanratty won't allow us a lunch break.'

Anne was upset to hear this. 'He must let you have a break. I'll speak to him!'

But Hetty and Elsie had already walked off. Then she saw Stan Chapman cycling into work.

'Morning, Anne. Anabel's roses are looking perfect for your bouquet. I'll make it up first thing on Saturday morning so it's as fresh as can be.'

'Could I take it home with me late Friday afternoon instead? I can keep it in water overnight.'

'Can't do Friday. Sorry, Anne!' And with that he cycled off, leaving Anne puzzled. Why was everyone avoiding her?

She walked into reception and was further confused when even Jacob wouldn't look her in the eye. She marched to his desk and put her hands on her hips.

'Are you going to tell me what's going on, why every-one's whispering about me or excusing themselves from talking to me?'

She saw Jacob's mouth twitch into a smile before he composed himself.

'You'll find out in time,' he replied.

'You're infuriating!' Anne exclaimed. 'Come on, Jacob, tell me, please or I'll sit you next to Mrs Perkins at my wedding dinner instead of next to Meg.'

Jacob just tapped the side of his nose. 'You'll find out very soon.'

The day before her wedding, Anne made her way to the canteen at lunchtime. She was expecting to find the place as usual, with a queue of factory workers at the counter. But the sight that greeted her turned her legs to jelly and made her heart pound. Suddenly Mr Jack was at her side.

'What's going on, Anne? Jacob told me you needed me urgently in the canteen. Are you all right?'

The two of them looked ahead, unable to believe their eyes. The canteen was decorated with blue and white streamers. Banners were pinned to the walls with messages of congratulation. The whole workforce seemed to be there, and when Anne and Mr Jack entered, the place erupted into loud applause. Anne knew then that this was why the factory girls had been acting strangely. They must have been planning this in secret. Jacob appeared and beckoned Anne and Mr Jack to the front, where a makeshift stage had been erected.

'Speech! Speech!' was yelled from the floor as deafening applause continued.

Anne saw Mr Gerard and Mr Burl standing next to Jacob and Meg. She saw the girls from the typing pool, the enrobing room, the packing room and wrapping room, all of them smiling and cheering. The men from the sales office clapped long and loud, the sugar boilers and the railway workers cheered, Stan and his team of gardeners doffed their cloth caps. The ladies working in the canteen raised their mugs of tea.

Mr Gerard carefully stepped onto the stage and raised his hands for quiet.

'Thank you, everyone, for coming, and thank you also for keeping today's event a secret. I know it hasn't been easy. I did suspect at one point that Anne had guessed what was going on.'

He turned to smile at her, then faced the workforce again. As he spoke, Anne looked out and saw Hetty and Elsie at the front, next to Mrs Perkins and Mr Hanratty.

All of them were smiling. They looked as happy and excited as she felt.

'In honour of the wedding tomorrow of Mr Jack and Miss Wright,' Mr Gerard continued, 'my design team have created a special tin of Lady Tina, and everyone at the factory has signed a card, which the artwork team has created. It's a wedding gift for both of you . . . from all of us.'

Jacob walked onto the stage carrying a parcel wrapped in blue paper. Mr Jack and Anne held it between them and Anne carefully unwrapped it. She gasped when she saw the unique design on the tin. In place of Lady Tina's picture was her own image, next to a man who was clearly Mr Jack. She was overjoyed, and Mr Jack's eyes shone with delight. It was then that she noticed a tiny detail on the box that made her heart swell with love.

'Thank you! You've even painted his blue bow tie!'

Chapter Thirty-Five

On the morning of the wedding, Anne was getting dressed in her room. She wore her best cream suit with a pair of silk stockings, and she'd shined her shoes. On her jacket lapel she wore her brooch from Mr Jack with its blue and white precious stones. Her hair was swept up in a bun with blue ribbon laced through. She put on her small wire-framed glasses and looked into the mirror. She smiled at her reflection, pleased at what she saw. There was a knock at her door and she heard Avril's voice.

'Anne, there's a gentleman called Mr Chapman downstairs to see you. He's brought your bouquet.'

Anne opened the door and greeted her landlady. 'How do I look?'

Avril inspected her from her shiny shoes all the way up to her freshly washed hair. 'Perfect,' she beamed.

Anne looked at Avril's outfit. She wore a green velvet dress with a lace collar. It fitted well and made her look slender. However, she still wore her black hat. Avril caught her looking and touched the hat lightly.

'You'll never see me without it, Anne, not even on your wedding day.'

'And I'd never want you to change,' Anne replied. 'Tell Mr Chapman I'll be down in a moment.'

Avril left and Anne looked around her room. Once she left it today, to head downstairs to take her bouquet from Stan, she knew she'd never return. The small room had been her safe haven and bolthole. A place to read, think and plan. So much had happened since she'd first moved in. She'd been taken on at the toffee factory, working for Mr Jack himself. She'd made good friends in Hetty, Elsie, Jacob and Meg. She'd also made an enemy in Mr Burl, but he was far from her mind today. Although he and his fiancée had been invited to attend the wedding and dinner, he'd declined, citing a prior family engagement that he couldn't miss. Anne was relieved he wouldn't be there.

She looked at the bed where she'd spent sleepless nights worrying about the right thing to do once she realised she was falling for Mr Jack. The bed where she'd thought of her son often . . . and cried. The bed where she'd finally made her decisions. Where she'd chosen to look forward and be with Mr Jack rather than live in the past. She looked at the chest of drawers, empty now. All her clothes had been taken to the Deanery, ready for her to move in after the wedding dinner that night. She went to the chest and pulled open the top drawer, where she used to hide the photograph of her son. She felt content knowing it was with Mrs Matthews now. She closed the drawer and sighed. Then she turned to head out, noting the lock on the door that she'd installed to keep her nosy landlady out. She gave a wry smile thinking of how far she and Avril had come.

'Goodbye, room,' she whispered, then she walked onto the landing.

When she arrived downstairs, Avril called her to her parlour, where Stan stood by the window holding a beautiful red rose bouquet. She was surprised to see him looking so smart and handsome. He wore a grey suit and tie.

'My word, Stan. You look a treat.'

'Not half as much of a treat as you. You look beautiful. Mr Jack is a lucky man.'

He stepped forward, offering Anne the bouquet.

'I hope it's all right.'

Anne took the flowers and gazed admiringly at the arrangement. Anabel's red roses were mixed with frothy green leaves and tiny white flowers. The bouquet was neither showy nor mean. It was perfect. The effect was spellbinding. She brought it to her nose and breathed in the sweet scent.

'I didn't take all of Anabel's roses, just the ones that were ready. There's still plenty of buds to bloom,' Stan said quickly.

'Why, Stan, this is gorgeous. You've done an incredible job and I can't thank you enough.'

'Elsie helped me tie the blue ribbon on the stems,' he explained.

'You've seen Elsie this morning?' she asked, surprised.

Stan blushed. 'Yes, she asked me to call on her if I needed help, and of course I did. I'm all fingers and thumbs with things that don't grow out of the ground.'

'How is she? I hope Frankie's kept away.'

'We didn't talk about him, but she looked well and happy,' Stan said. 'Now then, while I'm here, is there anything I can do to help you before your wedding car arrives?'

'No thank you, Stan. Mrs Fortune and I have everything covered.'

'Then I'll be off. I'll see you when you arrive at the castle.'

Anne followed him to the door, carrying her bouquet.

'Thank you, Stan, for everything.'

'My pleasure,' he said.

Stan left, and Anne was about to head back inside when she saw Pearl walking along the street. She smiled, then waved.

'Avril, you've got a visitor,' she called.

Avril walked to the door just as Pearl arrived. She stuck her hand out in greeting to Pearl, who shook it heartily.

'It's good to see you, my dear,' Avril said.

'What a pleasant day for a wedding,' Pearl replied, looking at Anne.

Anne noticed their handshake went on longer than necessary, neither of them willing to let the other go. Suddenly she felt like she was intruding, and she headed back to the parlour, taking one last look at herself in the mirror above the fireplace.

'The car's here, Anne!' called Avril. 'Hetty and Elsie are sitting in the back. Oh, they look as pretty as a picture. The chauffeur's even wearing a hat.' She laughed out loud. 'Of course, all the neighbours have come for a look, just when I was hoping not to provide them with gossip for a while.'

Anne walked to the door and saw a sleek silver car. The driver left his place behind the wheel and walked around to the passenger door. He held it open and stood to one side.

'Avril, you can slide onto the back seat with my brides-maids,' Anne said.

Avril turned to Pearl. 'I'll see you at the castle. If you hurry, you can catch up and walk with Stan, the chap who created Anne's bouquet. He's on his way there now and only left a few moments ago.'

Anne looked from Avril to Pearl with tears in her eyes. The kindness and discretion the women had shown her meant a great deal, and their obvious happiness for her melted her heart. As Avril climbed into the back of the car to sit with Hetty and Elsie, Anne carefully slid into the front.

'You look beautiful, Anne,' Hetty said.

'And Stan's done a wonderful job with the flowers,' Elsie added.

The driver closed the door, walked around to his seat and started the engine.

'Goodbye, Victor Street,' Anne whispered as the car headed off.

When the bridal party arrived at Lumley Castle, Stan and Pearl were already there, heading into the chapel. The chauffeur opened the door and Anne stepped out.

'How are you feeling, Anne?' Avril asked.

Anne looked ahead and tilted her chin. 'Determined.'

'Most brides would say they feel happy,' Avril noted.

Anne gave her a smile. 'Oh, I'm happy all right, I've got the whole world at my feet and a man I love. But more than anything, I'm determined to have a good life with my new family.'

Avril held out her arm for Anne to take. Hetty and Elsie followed in their matching cream dresses decorated with blue ribbons. Each girl held a smaller version of Anne's rose bouquet with ribbon wrapped around the stems. As they walked to the chapel, sunlight warned the honey-coloured stones of the castle walls and glinted from its windows.

Anne stood in the doorway of the chapel with Avril at her side and Hetty and Elsie behind.

'Are you ready, Anne?' Avril asked.

Anne nodded.

'Hetty? Elsie? Are you girls ready too?' Avril said.

'We're ready,' they chorused.

Avril caught the eye of the organist, who launched into the opening bars of the Wedding March. Anne stepped inside the chapel with Avril at her side, a smile on her face and hope in her heart as she walked towards Mr Jack. She was so lost in her happiness and in her own world that at first she didn't notice William's mother in the front pew. It was only when the vicar called everyone to stand to sing the first hymn that she realised she was there. She saw Clara being helped to her feet by Albert, struggling with her walking cane, and felt a lightness in her chest, happy and relieved that she had decided to attend. Standing side by side with Mr Jack, she felt that anything was possible, even getting along with his mother.

Chapter Thirty-Six

Much later, after the wedding service ended, everyone was seated for dinner in a spacious room in the castle. Elsie sat between Hetty and Stan. She felt happy and safe there with her two favourite people. In front of her, a large table was laid with gleaming platters. She saw roast chickens, a side of roast beef and all kinds of vegetables. Carrots were piled high, steaming in melted butter. There were mounds of potatoes and peas, and she counted four gravy boats. Four! Oil lamps on the wide windowsills let a warm glow into the room, which was beginning to darken now the sun had disappeared. Domestic staff bustled around asking the guests whether they would like chicken or beef. When a small girl with long hair approached them, Hetty beamed. Elsie watched with interest.

'Do you know her?'

Hetty nodded. 'She's called Daisy. I work with her in the kitchen.'

'You're not working today,' Daisy teased. 'I'm waiting on you, but don't get used to it, Hetty Lawson.'

Elsie looked around her. On the table in front of each guest was a placeholder with their name on it. They had been designed by Mr Gerard, and the names were in blue script. Anne sat at the head of the table with her new husband. Mr Jack looked relaxed and more friendly than he ever did at work. He was laughing and joking, and every now and then he kissed Anne on the cheek or lifted her fingers to his lips. Beside him sat an older man and woman who Elsie guessed were his parents, for the gentleman looked a lot like Mr Jack.

Next to them were another elderly couple Elsie didn't know. She'd heard they were Mr Jack's aunt and uncle. Then there was a young woman with a pointed nose and a haughty look – Elsie understood she was Mr Jack's cousin – and Mrs Perkins from the factory sitting next to a woman called Avril Fortune. She knew Mrs Fortune was Anne's landlady, for Anne had talked about her at work. Elsie noticed she was getting on very well with Mrs Perkins, even making her smile, which was a rare thing indeed. However, Elsie didn't quite understand why Anne had invited Mrs Perkins to her wedding; she hadn't thought the two women close.

Beside Mrs Perkins was old Mr Gerard from the factory, and next to him his son David. He was a handsome young man who Elsie liked the look of. Under normal circumstances, before Frankie had left her disillusioned, she might have tried to catch his eye and smile, even flirt. Beside David were Meg and Jacob, making polite small talk and laughing at each other's jokes. Then came Dirk and Hetty, who were chatting to each other non-stop. On Elsie's left was Stan. He seemed awkward at the table.

'There's so much cutlery here. Why do we need six knives, for heaven's sake?' he whispered. Elsie stifled a smile.

'You look very smart in your suit,' she said.

Stan glanced down at his grey jacket as if it was the first time he'd ever seen it.

'This old thing? I just threw it on this morning,' he teased.

They fell silent again, not knowing how best to continue. All around them people were chatting to partners and friends. Anne and Mr Jack were stealing kisses when they thought no one was looking. Hetty and Dirk were holding hands and gazing into each other's eyes. Elsie began to tuck into her food, picking up the knife and fork furthest away from her plate. Stan watched and followed suit. As they ate, she could tell that he kept looking at her, as if he had something on his mind.

'How is your food?' she asked, trying to break the awkward silence.

'It's good. The carrots are particularly nice. They're from the factory garden. I grew them from seed. Had a bit of a problem with carrot fly, of course, but that's to be expected.'

Elsie smiled. 'This time last year if anyone had told me that I'd be eating dinner in a castle, that Anne would marry Mr Jack, that I'd be seated at a table where there's four gravy boats, sitting next to you and hearing you talk about carrot fly, I'd have thought they were mad! And yet . . .' She paused and looked at Stan. 'And yet here we are. I've had a rough time since I married Frankie. You saved my life, Stan, and I'll always be grateful.'

Stan laid his knife and fork down. 'I'll always be grateful I was there. I think the world of you, Elsie.'

Elsie was about to reply when a member of staff began buzzing around the table, refilling wine goblets and water glasses, attending to everyone's needs. The moment had gone and her words froze on her lips.

After the plates were cleared, a liqueur was brought out.

'You have a dog now,' Stan said. 'I saw it this morning when I called by with the bouquets.'

Elsie thought of Jet. She was starting to grow fond of him.

'Oh, it's not my dog, it's Hetty's, but he's a sweetheart. He sleeps at my feet when Hetty and I chat in the kitchen.'

'Do you walk him by the river?' Stan asked.

'Not usually, we just send him out on the back lane when he needs exercise. He sometimes runs off, but he always comes home when he's hungry.'

'I have a dog too.'

'Yes, I remember you've mentioned him to me before. He's called Patch,' Elsie said.

'Well, I walk Patch by the river, most evenings in fact.' Stan pulled nervously at his shirt collar. 'If you'd ever like Hetty's dog to meet Patch, we could meet up one evening for a walk.'

'I'm sure Jet would enjoy that,' Elsie said with a smile.

Suddenly Stan's face dropped. 'Unless the river isn't a good place for you, Elsie. I wouldn't want it to bring back any traumatic memories. We could meet for a walk elsewhere, anywhere. I mean, with the dogs, of course.'

'The river's fine, it holds no problems for me now. In fact, the last time I was there, when you found me, being so close to the water was healing, in a strange way.'

Elsie looked into Stan's eyes.

'I threw my wedding ring into the river.'

'Your wedding ring?'

She nodded. 'I can't divorce Frankie; I could never afford it. Even if I could, would any judge in the land give a girl like me a divorce? They'd want to know what grounds I have to consider it, and when I tell them it's because Frankie beat me black and blue, they'll likely as not tell me it happens all the time. But I'll never live as Frankie's wife. Never. So you see, if we . . . you and I . . . if we should ever find ourselves walking by the river, you with Patch and me with Hetty's dog . . .'

'I understand, Elsie,' Stan said gently.

'Do you? Because I'm not sure that I do really. See, I can't shake Frankie out of my life. He's my husband and we're legally tied, whether I like it or not, and believe me, I don't like it at all. I can never marry again because I can't afford a divorce. So the only thing I can do is protect myself from him.'

'Then let me help you,' Stan urged.

Elsie looked into his trusting face and felt on the verge of tears.

'If only it was that easy. We can never be together, not in the way you might like, Stan. If Frankie ever found out, I'd be terrified of what he might do to you. Besides, for now, I'm happy living with Hetty and her mum . . . her aunt.'

'There are four of you living in that small house on Elm Street?'

Elsie shook her head. 'No, just three of us. It's too complicated to explain. The point is, Stan, I'm learning to live my life for me. Not for Frankie or Aunt Jean, just me, for the very first time. If you and I start . . . walking by the river with our dogs, I don't want you to get hurt that I can't give myself fully. I'll never be free of Frankie for as long as I live.'

Stan was silent. He raised his liqueur to his lips, took a sip then placed the glass gently on the table.

'Look, Elsie, I need to be honest. Perhaps it's the wine that's gone to my head. Perhaps it's the emotion of the day, seeing Mr Jack and Anne so happy, but if I don't say this now, heaven knows I never will. From the first moment I met you, I've known in my heart how strongly I feel for you. But you never noticed me. You had your head turned by every man at the factory; they were in awe of your beauty and looks. And so I stood back and kept my feelings locked up. I saw you make mistakes with men and I saw you act the fool. My heart broke when you married Frankie Ireland.'

'Stan . . . what are you saying?' she whispered.

'I'm saying that whatever happens next, I love you, Elsie Cooper, and I always will.'

Elsie felt a lump in her throat. She reached for Stan's hand and held it under the table just as Mr Jack tapped a spoon against a glass.

The tinkling noise cut through the chatter and brought the table to order.

'Thank you all for coming and joining my wife and me today.'

A cheer went up at the table and Anne looked into her husband's eyes.

'Everything that Anne and I now do, we do together,' he continued. 'For the good of the factory and our future, we work as a team.'

There was a commotion at the table, and Anne watched in horror as her new mother-in-law struggled to stand.

'Mother, where are you going?' William cried.

Clara took her walking cane and hobbled from the room without a word. Mr Jack looked incredulously at Albert.

'Father? What's going on?'

In desperation, Anne jumped up and followed Clara along a corridor.

'Clara, wait,' she called.

Clara turned around with the help of her walking cane and glared at her.

'You haven't married my son today. You've bought your way into his factory! I'm only here because William and Albert begged me to come. Well, I came. But I am not going to sit and listen to my son waffle on about you and him being a team. What nonsense. The only partnership you're interested in is getting a seat on the board of directors. You don't care for my son. Go back to your guests, to the dinner that William is paying for. Tell Albert I'll wait in the car.'

Anne stepped forward. 'Clara, please don't go. You're wrong. I love William with all my heart.'

But Clara kept walking – too quickly, Anne thought. Her cane wasn't hitting the ground in time with her steps. Anne hurried after her, begging her to stay, just as the stick dropped from Clara's hand and she crashed to the ground.

Chapter Thirty-Seven

'Have you heard the latest news about Mr Jack's mum?' Hetty asked Elsie a few days later. They were in the kitchen at Elm Street and it was late. They were just about to turn in for the night.

'What's she done now?' Elsie said.

'Well, you know she fell down when she left the dinner and we had all that commotion of getting her into the car, then her husband drove her to hospital. It turns out that she badly twisted her ankle. Anne told me when I saw her at work. She's laid up at home and can't do a thing. Her husband is looking after her and he's at her beck and call.'

Hetty was mending a tear in her blue velvet skirt while Elsie scrubbed the hearth. Jet lay under the kitchen table, watching. Hilda was in bed upstairs. Lately she'd been complaining of chest pains, and although there was a little money in the house now, enough for a doctor's visit at a stretch, she was adamant that she was all right.

'I don't want a doctor coming in here looking at me!' she insisted.

'Please, Hilda, let us ask him to call,' Elsie had pleaded,

but Hilda remained firm and refused all attempts to change her mind.

Now, as the girls worked together, Elsie once again brought up the subject of asking Dr Gilson to visit.

'I don't understand why Hilda's so against it,' she said.

Hetty tutted loudly. 'I know her better than you. Once she's set her mind on something, she won't be moved, no matter how much pressure you put on her. She's her own worst enemy.'

'She's not well, Hetty. Don't you think you're being too harsh?' Elsie asked quietly.

Hetty shot her a look. 'All my life she's been harsh with me and I've had to put up with it. You know how often she had me in tears with her constant criticism and snide remarks.'

Elsie reached for her hand. 'I'm sorry, Hetty. Look, I don't mind looking after her. I could ask the pharmacist on Front Street if he can suggest anything that might help.'

'Thanks, Elsie. I can't tell you how grateful I am.'

Their conversation was interrupted by a knock at the door. Jet immediately leapt up, tail wagging. Hetty and Elsie looked at each other.

'Are you expecting anyone?' Hetty asked.

Elsie shook her head. 'It's a little late for callers,' she said nervously. 'You don't think it's Frankie, do you? What if he's discovered where I live?'

Hetty reached for her hand, trying to reassure her, but she was afraid too.

'It might be Dirk,' she said, trying to keep calm, 'but I can't think why he'd be calling so late.'

Together the girls left the kitchen and walked to the

hallway. Jet followed. Elsie reached for the door, but Hetty pulled her back.

'Don't open it until we know who it is.'

She leaned forward.

'Who's there?'

They were both surprised when a woman's voice replied. 'It's Mrs Douglas.'

They looked at each other and shrugged. Douglas? The surname meant nothing to Hetty.

'What do you want? It's late. We're about to turn in for the night.'

'Open up, Hetty Lawson. It's Marie. I want a word with you. It's about my brother, Bob.'

Hetty was shocked. Bob? She opened the door and was met by a formidable-looking woman standing on the pavement. She wore a wide-brimmed dark hat and a long dark coat. She looked a lot older than Bob, Hetty thought, but she could see a strong family resemblance. She stood to one side and opened the door fully. 'You'd better come in,' she said.

As Marie swept into the house, Jet growled and bared his teeth at her. Hetty noticed a folded newspaper under her arm.

'Please, take a seat,' she said politely. Her mind was trying to work out what on earth Bob's sister was doing there. 'I'm afraid I can't offer you a cup of tea because the fire's gone out.'

'I'll not sit down,' Marie said sternly. 'What I've got to say won't take long. My husband warned me not to come, he said it was none of my business, but I told him he was wrong.'

Hetty glanced nervously at Elsie as Marie whipped the

newspaper from under her arm. It had been opened in the middle. The page was folded and there was a photograph she recognised. It was a picture taken at Anne and Mr Jack's wedding under the headline *Toffee King Marries His Sweet Bride!* She and Elsie were in the photograph too, standing next to Anne, holding their bouquets. At Hetty's side was Dirk, and he'd slid his arm around her shoulders as she leaned in to his side. Everyone in the photograph looked happy. The scene was joyous, a true celebration of love. Only Mr Jack's mother had a sour look on her face. Hetty had seen the photograph already, as Anne had shown it to her at work.

'What does this have to do with Hetty?' Elsie asked.

'This!' Marie cried, raising the newspaper. 'This is abominable!' She threw it onto the table.

'I don't understand,' Hetty said, growing exasperated. 'I was bridesmaid for my friend. Why does it make you so cross?'

Marie pointed a long, bony finger at the picture, positioning her talon of a nail directly over Dirk's face. 'This man is not Bob!'

Hetty wondered if the woman was half mad. She looked at Elsie, hoping for support, and as always, Elsie stepped up.

'Marie, we're tired. I think it might be a good idea for you to leave.'

With a shudder, Hetty finally registered what should have hit her when Marie arrived.

'Marie, you're right, it's not Bob,' she said gently. 'You must understand . . . war is a terrible thing; it doesn't care who it takes. I'm so sorry for your family's loss.'

Marie started. She glared at Hetty. 'My loss?'

"Bob . . .' Hetty said.

'Bob?' Marie snapped.

'I received a letter from the army. It said he was missing in action, presumed dead.'

'I can assure you that my brother is very much alive,' Marie said coolly. 'And that's why I'm here. He's written to me every day. His last letter arrived yesterday. His unit was bombed, and there was a great loss of life, but Bob came through, he survived. He's in the hospital and he'll recover. When he does, they're sending him home.'

Hetty was relieved to hear that Bob was alive, but she was also confused.

'Why didn't the army write to me to let me know he was alive after I received the letter saying he was presumed dead?'

Marie's face fell. 'Because Bob asked them not to contact you again as you never replied to any of his cards. He wanted me to be registered as his only next of kin instead of you.'

'Well, thank you for telling me. Now I understand why you're here.'

Marie narrowed her eyes. 'You have no idea why I'm here, Hetty Lawson.' She jabbed her finger in Hetty's chest.

Elsie stepped forward. 'Now there's no need for that.'

Marie ignored her and carried on. 'My brother loved you. When he first went overseas, he wrote to you every week. He told me that at first you replied with cheery letters that kept him going when he was in the trenches. And then your letters stopped, without warning. You never wrote to him again. There was no explanation. He went out of his mind wondering what had happened. He was worried sick about you. He thought he'd done something to upset you, or that you were ill. He kept sending cards to you once a month, just to stay connected and let you know how he was, but he was saddened when you didn't reply. He wrote to me and begged me to ask you to write. But I told him to have some self-respect. I wasn't about to come here to beg, not even for my brother. And it's just as well I kept away. Because all this time you've been carrying on with another man. There's proof of it in the newspaper, it's there in black and white. He's got his arm around your shoulders, and you look as cosy as can be. I'll keep this picture for Bob to see when he returns. I always said he was too good for the likes of you. You're nothing but a toffee factory girl who knows nothing about the world.'

Elsie took Marie by the elbow. 'I think you should leave.'

Marie shook her off. 'Don't touch me, you tart. I knew your aunt Jean. Has she moved away because she needed fresh meat, because she'd already had all the fellas in Chester-le-Street?'

'Don't talk to my friend like that!' Hetty cried.

'How dare you!' Elsie yelled.

'I'll talk to both of you any way I like,' Marie said.

Hetty held up her hands in surrender. 'Look, Marie. I didn't ignore Bob. I wrote him a long letter to break off our relationship. Believe me, I did it as kindly as I could. Bob and I were never suited. When he went off to war, I realised I didn't miss him. In fact, if you must know, I felt happier without him. I couldn't carry on letting him think there was a future for us when he returned home. He mustn't have received my letter. All this time, I assumed he had. It's not my fault it didn't arrive.'

She pointed at the picture in the newspaper.

'I sent the letter to Bob long before I had feelings for Dirk.'

'Dirk?' Marie cried. 'What kind of a name is that?'

Hetty lifted her chin. 'It's a Belgian name, if you must know. He lives at Elisabethville.'

In one fell swoop, Marie picked up the newspaper and slapped Hetty hard across the face.

It stung like mad, but Hetty was determined not to give Marie the pleasure of seeing her cry. Every instinct in her urged her to put her hands to her face, to rub away the pain. She could feel her cheek burning, but she balled her fists and kept them by her sides.

'Get out!' she hissed.

'I wouldn't stay here a minute longer if you paid me,' Marie said.

Elsie escorted her along the hallway, with Jet nipping at Marie's ankles. Hetty sank into a chair at the table. She heard the front door close, then Jet padded back into the kitchen and jumped up onto her lap. Elsie sat opposite and the girls looked at each other, too shocked to speak at first.

'Did you really write to Bob to call things off?' Elsie asked at last.

Hetty nodded. 'I'm sure I must have told you at the time. Obviously I thought he'd received my letter, so I never understood why he kept sending the cards. They came as regular as clockwork, once a month. It felt strange that he wanted to keep in touch after I'd called things off with him, and I was relieved when they stopped. Now that I know the real reason, it breaks my heart that he kept hoping for a reply. He must think I'm cruel. Maybe I should write to him again to explain?'

'If I were you, I wouldn't. It sounds like his sister will update him on what's happened,' Elsie said. 'I guess your letter got lost in the post on its way overseas. This war makes all sorts of strange things happen.'

Hetty rubbed her sore cheek. 'You can say that again.'

Chapter Thirty-Eight

The weeks passed and summer gave way to autumn. Anne settled into her new home at the Deanery and revelled in its luxury and space. However, working with and managing a housekeeper took some getting used to. Anne had to learn to delegate to Edith and found it difficult at first. Just like when working in the factory office, she wanted to run everything herself; that was the way she was. However, her pregnancy tired her. With Edith's patience, she soon began running the Deanery as efficiently as she ran the factory office.

One morning at the factory, Anne and William were working together to prepare papers for the board meeting, to be held the following week. It would be the first meeting that Anne would attend as Mrs Jack. She was collating papers and inserting them into envelopes. Then she typed address labels for the envelopes before taking them to the post office on Front Street. For the board members who worked at the factory, such as Mr Gerard and Mr Burl, she delivered their papers by hand. When she walked into Mr Burl's office, Meg greeted her.

'You look happy, Meg. Is everything all right in here now?'

Meg cast a nervous glance over her shoulder. 'Things aren't perfect, but they're better than they were. If any of the girls have a problem with Mr Burl now, they come straight to me and I have a word with him. If he refuses to calm his temper, I threaten him with going higher.'

'To Mr Jack, you mean?'

Meg gave a wry smile. 'No, Anne. I threaten him with going to you.'

Anne laughed out loud, then looked over Meg's shoulder. Mr Burl was staring straight at her.

'I'll drop these off at his desk. See you later, Meg.'

Meg went back to her seat as Anne walked to Mr Burl's desk. She placed the heavy envelope in a tray. 'Papers for the board meeting next week,' she said.

Mr Burl looked up. 'I understand you're after a place on the board of directors.'

'That's right,' she said firmly. 'I trust I can count on your vote.'

She walked away before he could answer, crossing her fingers as she left, hoping the vote would go her way. As she and Mr Burl had never got along, his support was something she couldn't take for granted. Their relationship remained difficult, to say the least. If he voted against her, as there was every chance he would, her management role could be in jeopardy. Well, there wasn't anything she could do about that. She wasn't about to flatter him or bribe him in order to gain her seat on the board. And while it was in her power to blackmail him over his medical lie to avoid conscription, she quickly dismissed the thought. That wasn't her style. If she was elected to the board, the only woman at the table, she would earn her place by fair means, not foul.

On the day of the meeting, Anne prepared the board-room with papers and pencils, jugs of water and glasses. There was coffee to make for everyone too, but she was unusually jittery with nerves because of the vote that lay ahead.

'William, I'd like some help at the board meeting this morning,' she announced.

'Of course, what can I do?' he replied.

She shook her head. 'No, you don't understand. I don't need *you*, unless you'd like to make coffee and serve.'

'Can't Jacob help you? He often does at board meet-ings,' Mr Jack replied.

Anne knew that Jacob had a delegation of engineering students visiting the factory that morning. 'He's busy with the chaps from Durham University,' she said. 'I'd like your permission to ask Meg to help.'

William laid down his pen and looked at her. 'You don't need to ask my permission for anything, dear. You're prac-tically running the factory single-handed as it is. I feel I could leave everything in your capable hands.'

When Anne asked Meg, she was delighted to accept, but then her face dropped.

'I'll need to ask Mr Burl if I can leave the office, of course.'

'Leave him to me,' Anne said firmly.

When she put her case to Mr Burl, she gave him no option to refuse. Not once did she need to use Mr Jack's name to get what she wanted, as she'd done in the past.

Mr Burl gave a curt nod. 'Very well, you may take Meg,' he said.

Anne and Meg walked into the boardroom together.

'Blimey, Anne, I've never been in here before. This room is something else,' Meg cooed.

Anne looked around at the wood-panelled walls, the oak table and deep carpet, and could only agree.

'No matter how many times I come in here, I'm always in awe of this room's heritage and beauty. Can you just imagine the conversations that have been held at the table? Men of industry creating toffee brands, building the factory up, all of them sitting around this very table.'

Meg ran her hand along the oak tabletop and gave Anne a wry smile. 'I'll try my best not to spill coffee on it.'

Anne showed her where the trolley, flasks, mugs, cups and saucers were kept. She explained how to make flasks of coffee to bring into the meeting, and where to place them. She gave her a warning too.

'When you come in with the coffee, you pour it from a flask into a mug or a cup, depending on what the gentleman prefers. You'll need to stand close to each man while you pour. Some of them might use your closeness to their advantage and get a bit fresh. It's happened to me in the past and I've had to have words with such men. I'll be watching you, Meg. If anyone gives you trouble, indicate who it is and I'll have words with them after the meeting. I'm determined to stop this kind of behaviour. Women at the factory deserve respect, and if I get voted onto the board of directors today, I'll be making further changes.'

Meg held up crossed fingers. 'Good luck, Anne.'

* * *

When the meeting began, Anne sat at Mr Jack's side, poised with her notepad and pencil. It was a full turnout; all the board members had arrived, which was unusual. There were usually four or five men who regularly sent apologies for being unable to attend. As introductions were made, handshakes exchanged, Anne watched as Meg entered with the trolley. She was impressed by Meg's calm, polite manner when she served the refreshments. One chubby man with large hands grabbed a handful of toffees from his pockets, unwrapped two and popped both into his mouth. Anne was appalled by his greedy behaviour. When Meg served him coffee and stood next to him, she raised her eyebrows at Anne, who made a note to speak to him after the meeting.

Once coffee and tea had been served, Mr Jack banged his gavel on the table to bring the meeting to order. Anne looked around the table at the twelve men. They included Mr Gerard, who smiled kindly at her, and Mr Burl, who scowled. Albert Jack sat at the head of the table opposite his son. The rest of the men were a mix of legal and finance managers at the factory and leading businessmen from the region. Anne had little regard for many of them, apart from Mr Jack senior, Mr Gerard and the chaps from the factory's legal and finance teams. She'd seen the way most of the men blustered and bluffed their way through these meetings, each of them desperate to have his voice heard. There was a great deal of showmanship, which she detested.

Mr Jack was different. Not only did Anne love him as her husband, but she respected him as a business leader and factory boss. He controlled the board meetings with quiet confidence, ease and humour. However, he was often frustrated when no one wanted to shoulder the burden of responsibility for the way the factory was run. It all fell on him in the end. Another man at the table whose opinion was of value, Anne had long ago decided, was Albert's. She was proud to call him her father-in-law. If only her relationship with Clara was as good, then everything in Anne's world would be fine. Clara's bitter attitude towards her was the only thing stopping her from being as happy as she could be. Even when she'd helped Clara after she fell at their wedding, the woman still hadn't softened towards her. Anne had seen little of her since. When Anne and William had visited his parents, Clara had excused herself with a migraine again. She hadn't said a word to them about their baby, nor had she set foot in the Deanery. All of this made Anne feel terribly sad, and she wondered how she'd ever win Clara over.

After William brought the board meeting to order, the agenda was read then the first item tackled. Discussions took place over the price of raw materials, especially sugar, and the difficulty in sourcing them. A slight change to the recipe to make the delicious, creamy Lady Tina was suggested, and sadly accepted, for there was no other choice. Then sales and profits were considered, with Mr Burl reporting the figures satisfactory. Mr Jack suggested awarding grants to those at the factory who were dependents of men killed in the war, and his idea was passed unanimously. Then it was time to discuss the final item on the agenda.

'Gentlemen,' Mr Jack said, looking around the table at each man in turn, 'I propose that my wife, Mrs Anne Jack, join our board of directors. She has proved herself invaluable in the running of the factory. Her knowledge of the process and workings of not only our factory but the confectionery business as a whole in this country is second to none. She has already taken it upon herself to iron out problems with personnel . . .' his gaze lingered on Mr Burl, 'resulting in a happier and therefore more productive workforce. Gentlemen, I will ask each one of you for your vote. If you believe Mrs Jack would make a valuable addition to our board of directors, you should say *yay*. If not, the word is *nay*. As I'm sure you will have already assumed, my vote for my wife is a *yay*.'

Anne swallowed hard. She'd made two columns in her notepad, one for *yay* and one for *nay*. She placed her first tick in the *yay* column. Her second *yay* came from Mr Gerard, her third from Albert Jack. As each man voted, she put a tick in the relevant column. At the end of it, with only Mr Burl to go, she had 6 *yay*s and 5 *nay*s. The chubby man with the grabbing hands had voted no. He said he didn't approve of a woman in the boardroom unless she was there to serve coffee or take notes. Then it was Mr Burl's turn. Anne locked eyes with him across the table. If he said no, she'd have six votes for *yay* and six for *nay*. This would result in a tie, with no decision made. In this case, the matter of Anne being allowed to join the board would be carried over to be voted on again in twelve months' time. She crossed her fingers under the table while fearing the worst. She wasn't mistaken.

'*Nay*,' Mr Burl said.

Anne's heart sank. There was a knock at the door and everyone turned. An interruption was highly unusual, as board meetings were sacrosanct and never disturbed. It was hard to say who got the biggest shock when Clara Jack hobbled in with her walking cane.

Chapter Thirty-Nine

'Mother?' William cried in surprise.

Albert rushed to Clara's side. 'What are you doing here? Your ankle isn't fully healed. You shouldn't be walking.'

Clara placed both hands atop her walking cane and, with Albert's help on one side and William's on the other, gained her balance and stood straight. Anne stood and offered her her seat, but Clara shook her head. She cast a beady eye at the men around the table.

'Good morning, Mr Gerard.'

'Good morning, Mrs Jack,' he politely replied.

Several of the men at the table bristled at the interruption.

'Please, I insist you take my seat, Clara,' Anne repeated as she pulled out her chair. This time Clara accepted, and Anne stood behind her. William and Albert took their seats at opposite ends of the table.

'What's going on here?' Mr Burl demanded.

Clara raised her hand. 'Don't worry, I have no intention of staying longer than necessary. I'm here on official factory business, as a member of the board of directors.'

She raised an eyebrow at her husband. 'Although for the last few years I haven't received my own copy of the meeting papers; they go to my husband only.'

'I'll ensure that doesn't happen again,' Anne said quickly, making a note. She'd had no idea that Mrs Jack should have received her own papers. She'd simply carried on preparing the board papers as her male predecessor had done. She kicked herself for not checking this. She knew there was still much to learn, but she was determined.

Clara rested her cane against the oak desk. 'Gentlemen, I understand there is to be a vote to decide whether my daughter-in-law should be allowed to join the board.'

'You're too late. The vote has taken place. It was a tie: six *yay* votes, six *nay*,' Mr Burl said officiously. 'The matter will not be included on the agenda for another twelve months.'

A mischievous smile made its way to Clara's lips as she looked at each man in turn.

'So six of you at this table don't think a woman is up to the job. Is that right?'

Anne watched the *nay* voters shift uncomfortably in their seats.

'Well, let me tell you, a woman is as capable of helping run this factory as any of you men. In fact, she'd do a damn better job.'

'Mother, there's no need for such language,' William said softly.

'Poppycock!' Clara replied.

Anne suppressed a smile. She was suddenly in awe of the woman, who had the men at the table at her command. Some of them couldn't look Clara in the eye and shifted their gaze, or fiddled sheepishly with ties or pens.

Some gulped water from their glass. The chubby man stuffed another two toffees in his mouth and drool appeared at the corners of his mouth. But all of them kept silent as Clara held the room.

'Twelve votes means that not all of the votes were counted,' she said.

'It was a perfectly fair vote. There are twelve of us present and twelve votes were counted,' Mr Burl said.

A murmur of agreement went around the table.

'Ah, but there are thirteen members of the board of directors. In fact, there are fourteen if one should choose to count Miss Dalton, who forced her way in.'

Anne grew concerned. What did Lucinda Dalton have to do with this? What on earth was Clara saying?

'Miss Dalton is not a member of the board, as she was never voted in,' the legal director said.

Mr Burl stood from his chair and grabbed his lapels in both hands. 'The minutes of the meeting when Miss Dalton forced her way in here show that she has no voting power.'

'But I do,' Clara said.

Anne gasped. She looked at William, who appeared as gobsmacked as she felt. Then she looked at Clara again. The woman had a twinkle in her eye that Anne had never seen before. She's enjoying this, she thought. But still she was worried. Did Clara dislike her so much that she'd come to rub salt into her wounds and vote against her?

'My mother is right,' William said. 'She has a valid vote.'

'I'm the only woman ever to have been given a place on the board of directors at this factory. I don't count Miss Dalton, for she demanded her place by force, and that is not the Jack's factory way. As the lone woman on the team, I'm the only female to have made decisions affecting the factory. And let me remind you, gentlemen, we have far more women and girls working here now than we ever did before the outbreak of war. When this war ends and the men return, I will not allow our girls to be dismissed and sent home. I propose new ways of working, to keep our girls with their nimble, hard-working hands. Oh, I may be an old lady now. I know you see wrinkles and age spots before you. But I'm telling you that this factory wouldn't be what it is without me, and I want to ensure that our girls are looked after when war ends.'

'My wife is right, as always,' Albert said.

Clara looked at Mr Gerard. 'Those of you with long memories, who have been part of the factory for most of your lives, will know exactly how impassioned I am on the subject of staff welfare.'

'Hear, hear,' Mr Gerard said.

Then Clara turned to Anne and took her hand. Anne's heart began to race. Clara's hand was small and cold, with tiny bones visible through thin white skin. With Anne's help, she stood and picked up her walking cane.

'Help me to the door, Anne,' she said.

'Let me help you, Mother,' William said, but Clara shooed him away. Albert moved forward too, but she held up her hand, a warning not to come close.

'I'd prefer to be with Anne,' she said.

Anne thought her heart would burst with pride. Finally something had drawn Clara to her. But she didn't dare imagine it was love or friendship that her mother-in-law offered. She knew in her heart it was the future of the toffee factory that had brought Clara to the meeting.

'Mother, please don't leave without giving your vote,' William urged.

Clara stood in the doorway, holding onto Anne's arm, the two women surveying the room full of men. Anne could see Mr Burl turning apoplectic with rage. She half expected him to leap out of his seat and yell. But he stayed seated, silently fuming. Anne took a little enjoyment from watching him squirm.

'Mother, your vote, please. Is it *yay* or *nay*?'

'Dear son, isn't it obvious after all that I've said? Why, it's *yay*, of course.'

Clara patted Anne's hand.

'Could you walk me to the car, dear? My driver is waiting.'

The room erupted in a mixture of grumbles and cheers. Mr Gerard shook Albert's hand, then William's.

'Your mother always was a firecracker. It's good to see she's still got her sparkle.'

William banged his gavel on the table to get everyone's attention. 'Quiet, please. We will take a fifteen-minute break and then finish our meeting when Mrs Jack returns.'

'Your mother's coming back?' Mr Gerard asked, then slapped his hand against his forehead when he realised his mistake. 'Oh, you mean the other Mrs Jack, your wife.'

Anne slowly walked Clara along the hallway to reception. Clara indicated a chair at the side of the room and sank into it.

'My word, that took me back,' she said breathlessly. 'I used to rule those board meetings when I was your age.'

Anne sat next to her. 'Why, Clara? Why did you vote

296

me onto the team? I thought you and I hadn't got off to a good start. And yet you came all the way here, in pain from your ankle, to cast your vote.'

Clara placed both hands on the top of her cane and leaned forward. Across the room Anne could see Jacob concentrating on his ledger, busy at work. Or that was how it looked, at least; she knew him well enough to know he'd be listening.

'My dear, Albert kept the news from me about the baby. He thought the news would upset me even more than I already was about William marrying you.'

'But why were you so against us getting married?' Anne asked. This was the first time she'd had a chance to speak to Clara about why she'd walked out of the wedding. 'I understand that you were distraught about losing your connection to the Dalton family, but it felt as if you were taking your disappointment out on me, even blaming me for it.'

Clara glanced across the room at Jacob. 'You deserve a full explanation, my dear, but not here. I will come to the Deanery one day and we'll talk. But yes, I was against the wedding, and that's why Albert decided not to tell me straight away that there was a child on the way.'

'When did he tell you about the baby?' Anne asked.

'Only this morning, before he left for the meeting. I'd had my suspicions that you were expecting when the wedding was arranged with indecent haste. Oh, Albert tried to tell me a few times after you and William gave him the news, but I wasn't willing to listen. I had an inkling of what he was going to say and I didn't want to hear it, if I'm honest. But now I've had a few hours to let the news sink in. I ate my breakfast alone, pondering on thoughts of a grandchild. Then the nurse came to check on my ankle. She said it was improving.'

Clara stuck out her bandaged foot and turned her ankle a little.

'I dare say it'll be a while before I go dancing,' she chuckled. 'After the nurse left, I kept thinking of my grandchild. I knew the vote was today. Albert doesn't think I read his board papers, but I devour every word. You see, Anne, I had to come. I need you on the board; you're my legacy in a way Lucinda Dalton could never have been. She was never interested in family; all she cared about was money and what her father's wealth could buy.'

She looked around the reception room with its high ceiling and its panelled walls lined with certificates of merit for best toffee.

'Do you know what this factory needs, Anne?'

Anne didn't get a chance to reply.

'It needs an heir,' Clara continued. 'Whether male or female, it needs someone to carry on what Albert and I started. William's in his prime, as are you, but none of us are getting any younger. Now, help me stand and walk me to my car.'

Anne did as instructed, too dumbstruck to speak. When she reached the car, the driver helped her to get Clara into the passenger seat.

'Thank you, Clara,' Anne said. 'Perhaps we'll see you at the Deanery soon, one evening for dinner?'

'I'd like that very much,' Clara replied.

On Saturday morning William left the Deanery to visit an old family friend with his father. Anne was alone when there was a knock at the door.

'Don't worry, Edith, I'll answer it,' she called to the housekeeper.

She walked to the door, where she was astonished to see Clara leaning on her walking cane. Her driver and his car waited outside on the road.

'Come in, please. What a wonderful surprise to see you,' Anne said.

Once they were seated in the living room and Edith had brought a pot of tea, Clara began to speak.

'I promised you an explanation about why I was so against your marriage to my son.' She set her cup down. 'The Daltons have power, because of their money. They own a large amount of property and land, and people respect them. Albert and I learned from Lucinda's father, Bertram, that he was interested in joining his family to ours. He offered Lucinda's hand to William in exchange for a large share of our toffee factory. It was a proposal we had to take seriously, because once war threatened the country, our factory would be under threat too. We may have even lost it.'

'There's a possibility that we still might, if we're not careful about keeping costs down,' Anne replied.

Clara nodded. 'I know, my dear. It's a worrying time for us all. But William tells me that you're working hard at his side to help keep the factory open. I admire you for it. You remind me of myself at times.'

Anne raised an eyebrow. 'Oh?'

Clara gave a wry smile. 'I helped Albert set up the factory. I was at his side from the start. In fact, if you press him on the matter, he'll tell you I worked even harder than him, but because I'm a woman, my name won't be on any of the papers in the vaults. In fact, it was my

299

original toffee recipe that Albert used at the factory when production first began.'

Anne was stunned by what she heard.

'I only stopped working when I fell pregnant with William,' Clara continued. 'Even then, I offered Albert advice and support while I brought up our son. So you see, Anne, I would have done anything to help save the factory after everything we'd put in to build it up. Anything.'

'Even offer up your son to marry Lucinda Dalton,' Anne said.

Clara hung her head in shame. 'I'm afraid so. Albert and I put Dalton's proposal to William and he accepted immediately. Not because he loved Lucinda; I don't believe he ever did. He accepted because he wanted to save the factory. I thought all our problems had been solved – well, as far as the factory went. However, my heart bled for William, knowing he was going to marry a woman for duty, to save the factory. And then you came along.'

Clara lifted her teacup, took a gentle sip then replaced it on the table.

'Oh Anne, will you ever forgive me for how I treated you, and for walking out on your wedding day?'

'After you voted for me in the board meeting, I already have,' Anne said with a smile.

Clara searched for something in her handbag then held out a small blue box to Anne. 'I'd like you to have this.'

Puzzled, Anne took the box. 'What is it?'

'Look inside, my dear.'

She lifted the lid and was stunned by what she saw. There, nestled gracefully in folds of blue velvet, was a sparkling stone of deep blue set in a gold band. Her jaw dropped in shock.

'It's a sapphire,' Clara explained. 'And it's yours.'

'Why, it's beautiful,' Anne gasped.

'Albert gave it to me on our wedding day, but my fingers are too thin now to wear it. Oh, I know I could take it to a jeweller to alter the size, but dear Anne, I'd like you to have it.'

Anne couldn't keep her eyes off the blue stone; she was transfixed. 'Are you sure?' she said, glancing at Clara.

'I'm certain,' Clara said firmly.

'It's such a beautiful rich, deep colour,' Anne said.

'It's the very blue that inspired the colour of the toffee factory logo,' Clara said.

Anne stood, walked to Clara and kissed her on her cheek. 'Thank you so much.'

She was about to walk back to the sofa when Clara caught her arm.

'Welcome to the family, my dear.'

Chapter Forty

Anne wore Clara's sapphire ring with pride. It was on her finger the day she gave birth to her daughter, in late spring of the following year. The baby was healthy and chubby, and Anne named her Dinah, after her late mother. She lavished love and attention on the little girl, making up for the time she'd never been able to spend with her son.

Although she had her hands full with the new baby, she still prayed for her son's welfare. There were days when she looked into William's kind face and felt such love that she hated herself for keeping the truth from him. She suffered pangs of guilt and spent days wrapped in angst. But she knew in her heart that she'd take her secret to the grave. What had happened in her past, with the first man she fell in love with, who had broken her heart and deserted her, would remain firmly there. She had her own child now, and a loving husband, and would do nothing to jeopardise her family and their future. She had made that promise to her son's new parents and it was a promise she was determined to keep.

During those months, Anne stayed home at the Deanery to nurse Dinah with the help and support of capable, no-nonsense Edith. The housekeeper kept the Deanery spotlessly clean and cooked dinner each night. It wasn't easy, with rationing causing all kinds of problems, but Edith was resourceful. She managed to make a meal from whatever ingredients were available on the market, in the shops on Front Street or in the garden at the Deanery. The garden was extensive, with grounds to the front and rear, and these had been turned over to grow vegetables. Stan Chapman had advised Anne on how to maximise yield and shown her how to raise plants from seeds, and the gardens now flourished with rows of cabbages, carrots, potatoes and salad. Edith was an accomplished cook and made the most wonderful vegetable stews and pies, as meat was hard to come by. But best of all, she was a natural with Dinah and adored her. Anne was beyond grateful to the woman and never once took her for granted. She knew how lucky she was.

As the factory was near the Deanery, William often came home at midday to take lunch with Anne and Dinah, with whom he was besotted. Anne's relationship with him deepened with love and respect. After a day spent at the factory, William would return home tired and frustrated as further restrictions were placed on the business due to war. Anne would listen to his concerns, soothe him and offer advice. At these times, she often thought of Clara and Albert when they were setting up the toffee factory, Clara working at Albert's side to build their dream.

Anne had little free time. However, when Dinah was sleeping and she'd overseen Edith's chores, she began to read books on factory management, thick, dull tomes that contained jargon she barely understood, and not one mention of women in the pages. However, she struggled on, learning as much as she could, readying herself for her return. She was tired after Dinah's birth; she didn't have the energy she once had. She wasn't sleeping well, waking each time Dinah cried in the night. Being so exhausted, she knew she wouldn't be able to function well at work if she returned before she was ready. But she would return, of that she was sure.

Hetty and Elsie visited the Deanery many times to see Anne and the baby. They often came for tea and would bring gossip from the factory. They told Anne they'd been moved from the packing room to the enrobing room, where toffees were coated with thick, delicious chocolate before being sent to be packed. Hetty brought news about her relationship with Dirk, which was still going strong. She also spoke of Hilda, but her tone was dull, without love.

Elsie was always the first to rush to Dinah's cot and ask Anne if she could hold her or feed her. She took Dinah in her arms and nursed her, singing gently to the child and rocking her to sleep, but there was a sadness about her, and Anne could only guess at the memories of losing her own child that were going through her mind. Hetty hung back, unsure around the child, not knowing what to do. Anne placed Dinah in Hetty's arms one day and Hetty sat stiffly, not daring to move. And when the baby started crying, Hetty immediately handed her back, where Elsie would have shushed her and sent her back to sleep.

Hetty and Elsie weren't the only visitors to the Deanery. Albert and Clara visited too, bringing gifts for

Dinah. Albert gave Anne advice on the garden and the upkeep of the house. Clara was in awe of Dinah and couldn't take her eyes off her. Anne got along well now with her mother-in-law. However, whenever she was with her, she was always on her mettle, for Clara was sharp and didn't miss a thing. Anne never knew when she might come out with a prickly comment or loaded barb. But on the whole, if the conversation was kept light, they rubbed along well, and Anne was forever grateful for her vote. It gave her the confidence to think about moving on from her role as secretary when she returned to work at William's side.

As the months went by, Dinah grew stronger and bigger and Anne settled her into a routine. The child was sleeping through the night now. One evening, as she and William sat by the fire in their living room, with Dinah asleep upstairs, Anne cleared her throat.

'It's the board meeting next month,' she said.

William was sitting in his armchair with his feet on a footstool. He looked up from his newspaper.

'Yes, Meg is sending out the board papers tomorrow.' Meg had been promoted and now assisted William at work. 'She has a set for you and I'll bring them home if you wish. Or you could always call at the factory to collect them and bring Dinah in again. You know the ladies in the canteen and the girls in the typing pool love to see her. Mr Gerard always asks about her too.'

'How's Mr Burl these days?' Anne asked.

William laid down his newspaper and gave this some thought. 'If you're asking about his work, he's as productive as ever. He's an excellent salesman, as you know.

But if you're asking how he is in himself, then I suppose he's quiet, subdued. I understand his fiancée left him. It was something to do with the white feather brigade calling him out for evading conscription. It was all a bit ugly, from what I understand. Meg tells me he still treats the girls in the typing pool badly.'

Anne was incensed to hear this. 'Surely you've spoken to him about this?' she said sharply. 'He should have received a second warning for his bullying behaviour. When I gave him his first warning, you said that if he didn't improve, you'd mention it to the board.'

William nodded. 'I've tried, but it's not easy. He's a slippery character, Anne, as you well know.'

'William?' Anne said.

'Yes, dear?'

'It's time for me to return to work. Not just with Dinah for a visit, although she smiles so much when I take her there and she's made such a fuss of. I trust Edith enough to look after her here on the days the factory is open. On the days when the factory is closed, we can take her to work with us. If she cries, no one will hear her as we'll be the only ones there. I can't see a problem, can you?'

'No problem at all. But are you sure you're ready to return?' William said, concerned.

'I'm certain. I've given this a lot of thought since Dinah began sleeping through the night. I've got my energy back, I'm raring to go, and to be honest, I'm getting bored being stuck at home. Edith manages the house well, she oversees Stan's boys from the factory when they tend the garden, and she adores Dinah. I thought I'd return in time for the board meeting, what you think?'

William smiled widely. 'I think it's a splendid idea. I've

missed you at work, Anne. Oh, Meg's good enough at typing and filing, but I miss having you in the office next to mine.'

'Ah, about that,' Anne said. 'I was rather hoping to make changes now I'm on the board.'

William raised an eyebrow. 'Oh?'

'Last year you promised me an assistant, and now it's time to make good on your offer. I suggest we keep Meg and share her as our secretary.'

Mr Jack scratched his head. 'But your office is too small to accommodate both you and Meg.'

Anne looked hard at her husband, determined to have her own way. 'I don't plan on sharing an office.' She glanced down at her hands in her lap. She knew she had to hold her nerve.

'What is it you want, Anne?' Mr Jack said kindly. 'You know I'd do anything to help your return to the office go as smoothly as it can.'

She sat up straight in her seat and looked her husband right in the eye. She cleared her throat. 'When I return, I'll be working at a strategic level, with more responsibility. I'll no longer be your secretary, although I realise I was always much more. I'll have a higher profile, taking on the management of staff welfare. Therefore, I'd like my own office.'

William sank back in his seat, giving this thought.

'I want Mr Burl's office,' Anne said.

There was silence between them. The clock ticked on the mantel. Anne wondered if she'd gone too far. Was this more than William was prepared to give? She felt a shiver run down her back.

William laced his fingers together and placed them

under his chin, staring ahead. Anne knew he was giving her proposal serious thought. Then a mischievous smile reached his lips.

'You're a forthright woman, Mrs Jack,' he said. 'And that's why I love you. Your fighting spirit is what made me fall for you when we first met.'

He banged his fist on the arm of his chair.

'My word, you've got gumption and I like it!'

Anne breathed a sigh of relief but didn't dare believe yet that she would be given Mr Burl's office. Far better, she thought, to remain quiet while William mulled the idea over for a few moments more.

She watched as he stood and walked to the drinks cabinet. She heard the tinkle of glass. This was a good sign, she thought. A drink before bedtime was a celebration of sorts.

'Would you like a brandy?' he asked.

'That would be lovely,' she replied.

William brought two glasses with a generous splash of brandy in each. He handed her one and she wrapped her hands around it.

'I'd like to propose a toast,' he said. 'To your successful return to the factory. It'll be wonderful to have you back.'

'And to my new office?' she dared ask.

'Leave Mr Burl to me. I'll speak to him. There's a spare office at the end of the corridor, far away from the women and girls. I'll coat my words sweetly, and by the time I'm finished with him, he'll think it was his idea to move.'

Anne raised her glass in a toast. 'To my return to the toffee factory.'

Chapter Forty-One

As the year turned, the newspapers continued to report carnage and death from the front. There seemed no end to the conflict. At the toffee factory, further restrictions meant the price of raw materials increased again. The minutes of the board meetings noted that the financial situation looked bleak – but there was still hope. And while there was hope, the factory would struggle along. Government orders of toffees for the troops had kept it going so far. Tins of toffee were welcomed by service-men, who preferred toffee to chocolate. This was because it lasted longer in the tin and in the soldiers' mouths. A handful of soldiers even found the notes that the girls in packing had dropped into tins of Lady Tina and replied. Long-distance romance blossomed for some. A reply to Elsie's letter found its way to the flat above the dress-maker's shop on Front Street where she'd once lived with Jean. However, the new tenant had never heard of Elsie Cooper, and so tore the letter up and burnt it on the fire.

During those early months of 1918, war began to block exports and there was a real danger that the government orders might dry up if toffee exports came to an end. An emergency board meeting was called. William was at home, unable to attend, suffering from influenza and a hacking cough. He asked Anne to lead the meeting instead. She sat at the head of the table, in William's chair, and glanced around at the half-dozen men there. It was the lowest turnout of a management board she'd known. She suspected some of the men had stayed away because they'd learned she would be in charge. She waited until Meg had served coffee and kept her eye on her in case any of the men took advantage. She was relieved, and pleased, when Meg didn't indicate a problem. Then she banged the gavel on the table to bring the meeting to order.

'Gentlemen, as you know, we are in danger of losing the government orders for export. Therefore we need to focus strongly on the home market again,' she began.

'My thoughts exactly,' Mr Gerard said firmly. 'My team have already begun work on new advertising for your approval. And Mr Jack's, of course.'

He bent down and picked up a roll of papers from the floor. These he spread on the tabletop and all present leaned in to inspect them. Anne saw a domestic setting, a woman handing a tin of Lady Tina to a man seated in an armchair.

'As tobacco becomes more difficult to buy, many men have turned to sweets and confectionery,' Mr Gerard explained. 'This advertisement goes firmly after that market. Here we exchange the man's pipe for a tin of toffee, given to him by his loving wife.'

'Shouldn't this man be away fighting?' Anne asked. 'I don't want any of our customers thinking he's shirking his duty through cowardice. Why, the white feather brigade will have a field day!'

Mr Gerard made a note to draw the man in the advertisement older, too old to be called up for war, to alleviate the public's concern.

'These ads are fantastic, Gerard. But keep costs as low as you can,' Anne said, casting a wary eye at the finance report.

The meeting carried on, with Anne becoming more confident in her role. It helped a great deal that Mr Gerard and William's father were at the meeting too. She knew they both fully supported her. Mr Burl was quiet and said little except to ask for another cup of coffee, which meant that Meg had to stop taking notes at Anne's side to serve the man his drink.

'I trust that in the future we shall find peace and that it may not be too far away,' Anne said when she finally closed the meeting.

While Anne chaired her first board meeting, Hetty and Elsie worked in the enrobing room.

'It smells delicious in here. I want to scoop up chocolate with my fingers and stuff it all in my mouth,' Elsie drooled.

Hetty's own mouth began to water. 'I don't think I'll ever get used to such a gorgeous, tempting smell. When we worked in the wrapping room, the air was sweet with sugar. But here we pour chocolate right onto the toffee. It's too much temptation. We can't get cakes or sweets in the shops any more and we're not allowed to eat toffees at work. Even the misshapen toffees or the ones not the right colour are packed up and sold now. Before the war, they'd be thrown away because Mr Jack was so protective of his brand.'

'Now he's protective of his balance sheet, and our jobs,' Elsie noted.

The work that the girls did in the enrobing room was seated. It was the first time since they'd started work at the factory that they'd been able to sit. In the wrapping room and packing room they'd stood at long tables with hundreds of other girls, all doing the same monotonous job. But in the enrobing room, they sat on wooden stools, in long lines on both sides of a wide table. The supervisor was a short man called Mr Parrott. His name suited him well, for when he walked, his head jutted forward like a bird's. Hetty found him fair and had no complaints about the way he managed the room. He let the girls talk freely, unlike the silence that Mrs Perkins used to insist on. Plus, the enrobing room was calm, even with the girls talking, unlike the noise and din of the packing room, where they had to shout to be heard. While it was a relief to sit, working at the bench meant that they had to bend forward as they concentrated on covering toffees by hand, their nimble fingers carefully drizzling chocolate across each toffee, letting it ooze down the sides. Hetty's shoulders ached, and her stomach rumbled. It was so tempting to pop a toffee into her mouth. But if Mr Parrott caught her, she'd be sacked, such was the scarcity and value of sugar.

When spring came that year, it brought welcome warmth. The harsh winter had been bitter and long. In the enrobing room, Hetty kept her eyes on her work; it was vital not to lose concentration. Each girl had a metal tray of toffees to be covered; when they were done, the tray would be taken away and a new one placed in front of them. It was never-ending. The smell might have been wonderful, but the work was dull.

'Are you seeing Dirk tonight?' Elsie asked.

Hetty kept her gaze on the toffee tray. 'Yes, he's meeting me after work for a walk along the river. I thought I might ask him home for tea one day soon. Would you mind?'

'Why would I mind? It'd be wonderful to have tea with you and Dirk.'

Hetty was silent a moment. 'I meant just me and Dirk.'

'Oh,' Elsie said.

Hetty couldn't take her eyes off the toffees, but she guessed from Elsie's disappointed tone exactly how she must look.

'I'm sorry, Elsie. It's just that we never get any time to ourselves indoors. And now Hilda has disowned me, she can hardly complain about him being there, can she?'

'I understand,' Elsie said brightly. 'Let me know what day he's coming and I'll make myself scarce.'

'It'd just be for a few hours. He'll leave early evening. Where will you go?'

She felt Elsie shrug.

'I'll find something to do.'

On the day Dirk came to tea, Elsie excused herself when he arrived and said she'd go out for a walk. She took Jet with her and told Hetty she was planning to head to the river. She snapped the dog's lead to his collar and left, leaving Hetty alone with Dirk.

Chapter Forty-Two

'I hope you like cauliflower soup,' Hetty said as Dirk settled himself at the table. 'Stan Chapman at the factory
gave me the cauliflower and I got the recipe from Mrs
Doughty. I've made bread too, a stottie cake.'

'A cake that is bread?' Dirk said, puzzled.

Hetty looked at him and thought he looked particularly
handsome that evening. His blue eyes shone brightly and he
was dressed in a checked shirt tucked into black trousers.

'It's called cake, but it's bread. It's delicious. Elsie and I
made some last week, and I made more today, before you
came.'

'Thank you, Hetty. It's so kind of you to cook for me.'

Hetty sat at the table and they began to eat. Their conversation was stilted; it seemed odd and too formal to sit
next to one other like this. Normally, they'd be walking
along the river with Jet, chatting away without a care in
the world. Or they'd be having tea in a café, gazing out
of the window at the world passing by. But here in the
confines of the small kitchen on Elm Street, Hetty felt ill
at ease.

'Do you . . .' she began.

'I wonder . . .' Dirk said at the same time.

They both burst out laughing.

'Please, you speak first,' Dirk said.

Hetty broke off a piece of stottie bread to dip into her soup.

'Do you mind that Elsie isn't here?' she asked. 'I asked her to give us some time alone together, you see.'

'Ah, I was wondering where she had gone,' Dirk said with a smile. 'She is a good friend to you, no?'

'She's my best friend.'

'And Hilda . . . how is she now?' Dirk asked as he dipped bread into soup.

Hetty raised her eyes to the ceiling. 'She's up there in Dan's bedroom. She won't leave his room or his bed. It's becoming difficult. Elsie and I look after her, but Elsie, bless her, does all the hard work.'

Dirk reached for her hand. 'I understand how difficult it has been for you and I am always willing to help where I can,' he said quietly.

'You're a good man, Dirk. Without you and Elsie, I'm not sure how I would have coped. As for Hilda, well . . .' She shrugged, then changed the subject. 'What news is there from Elisabethville?' Her relationship with Hilda remained strained, and she didn't want to talk about her.

Dirk was silent a moment, eating his soup and bread.

'This stottie cake is good bread,' he said. 'But the news I hear is bad. Our families in Belgium send us word of brothers and fathers dying in the war. Our towns and cities are being bombed. We don't know what will be left or what to expect when we return home when war is over.'

He looked into Hetty's eyes. The sentence hung between them. It was the first time either of them had spoken about what would happen when the war ended. Hetty had always known that the Belgians were only in Elisabethville for the duration of the war. Their role was to work at the munitions factories. After the war ended and munitions were no longer needed, she assumed the factories would close down. She had no clue what would happen to the Belgians then, only that many of them would head home. It would be the natural thing to do. She paused with her spoon mid-air.

'And you, Dirk?' she dared herself to ask. 'Will you go home too when war is over?'

Dirk bit his lip. 'I must,' he said sadly. Hetty's heart felt as if it had been ripped open. 'My family are waiting for me. My sister, Gabrielle, has already returned as our mother is unwell. My parents are old now and can no longer work in their chocolate shop in Ghent. I was always the one who wanted to run the shop when my parents could not continue. If the shop is still standing . . . if Ghent is still intact, then that is what I must do. It is my future, Hetty, it is what I always dreamed of.'

He turned his gaze to her now and she saw tears in his eyes.

'That is, until I met you. Now I am torn, for I wish to stay with you for ever and yet my obligation is to return.'

Hetty laid down her spoon and reached for his hand.

'I love you, Hetty Lawson,' Dirk whispered.

A tear rolled down her cheek. 'And I love you, Dirk Horta.'

He leaned forward for a kiss, but as their lips touched, a loud noise from above stopped them dead. It was followed by a piercing cry.

'Hilda!' Hetty cried.

She ran out of the kitchen and pounded up the stairs, Dirk following. The door to Dan's bedroom was closed, as always, but this time Hetty didn't knock and wait. She pushed the door open, and what she saw horrified her. Hilda was lying on the floor, crying in pain. Hetty rushed to her and held her in her arms.

'What happened?' she said.

'I fell,' Hilda gasped between sobs. 'I tried to get out of bed and I fell. Oh Hetty, please help me.'

Hetty rocked her in her arms, telling her everything would be all right. Then she noticed Dirk waiting at the bedroom door. He was too polite to cross the threshold and enter.

'It's all right, you can come in. I'm going to need your help.'

He stepped into the room.

'Who's there?' Hilda asked.

'It's Dirk,' Hetty said. She waited for Hilda's reproach at the mention of his name, but Hilda kept quiet. 'We're going to lift you and put you back in your bed. I can't do it on my own. I need Dirk's help, do you understand?'

Hilda nodded. She was breathless, and Hetty grew concerned.

'We should call the doctor,' Dirk said.

'Let's get her back into bed first,' Hetty said.

Together they lifted Hilda onto the bed.

'Where does it hurt, Mum?' Hetty asked. She missed the look that Dirk gave her. She was so worried about Hilda that she didn't notice she'd lapsed into calling her by the name she'd used all her life.

'My chest,' Hilda rasped. 'I was trying to get a drink of water when I fell.'

Dirk ran downstairs and returned a moment later with a glass of water, which he handed to Hetty. She carefully tipped water into Hilda's mouth, but Hilda began coughing, a great hacking cough that shook her whole body.

'I'm going to fetch Dr Gilson,' Dirk said urgently.

'Dirk!' Hetty yelled, but he was already heading downstairs. She heard the front door open and close.

She held Hilda until her coughing subsided and she sank back, exhausted.

'The doctor's on his way, Mum,' Hetty said.

'I don't want the doctor!'

'He's coming whether you want him or not. I should have stood up to you about this months ago when you first took to Dan's bed.'

'My Dan,' Hilda groaned.

Hetty's heart went out to the woman, for their grief was shared.

'And my Dan, Mum. I lost my brother too.'

Hilda closed her eyes. 'You're a good lass, Hetty,' she whispered.

'Dirk's a good man too,' Hetty replied. 'I hope you don't mind him being here in your house.'

'I don't deserve your kindness. I've lied to you all your life.'

Hetty held Hilda's thin hand. 'The truth hurt. But it made me realise how much shame you've lived with because Dad wouldn't marry you. You tucked all your hurt away inside. It festered there and I got the worst of it. When Dan came along, you treated him differently, better.'

'I'm sorry I kept the truth from you,' Hilda said. Her voice was so quiet and hoarse that Hetty had to lean forward to hear.

'The doctor will soon be here,' Hetty said. 'Here, take more water.' She lifted the glass to Hilda's lips, but Hilda turned her head away.

'Everyone gossiped about me,' she said quietly. 'Everyone knew I wasn't married to your dad. They knew you weren't mine. They said I wasn't respectable. Oh, the names they called me. When Dan was born, they threw eggs at my window.'

Her words came out of her between heavy breaths, as if she was forcing them from somewhere deep and locked away.

'That's why I couldn't have Dirk in the house,' she continued, her voice still weak and small. 'I didn't want the gossip to start. I couldn't go through it again. Once in a lifetime to suffer cruelty from neighbours, from people I thought of as friends, was enough.'

Hetty heard the door downstairs bang open, then two sets of heavy footsteps on the stairs. She looked up to see Dr Gilson enter the room, followed by Dirk. She stood and went to stand beside Dirk, who laid his arm around her shoulder. The doctor pulled a chair to the side of Hilda's bed and began to ask questions. Hetty heard Hilda reply, her voice sounding far away. He asked Hetty to help her turn Hilda in the bed so he could check for broken bones, then said he wanted to examine her chest.

'Dirk, could you wait downstairs?' Hetty asked.

Dirk did as requested while Hetty stayed with Hilda. Dr Gilson was thorough with his examination and firm when he gave Hetty his news.

'Your mother will be sore after her fall, but I can't detect any broken bones. My examination shows she has bronchitis. She can't stay in here. I can smell damp and the air is fetid.' He looked around the cramped room. 'Isn't there a window you can open to let in some air?'

'She asked me never to open the window. She wanted the room left exactly as it was when my brother died.'

'You need to get her out of here. There's medicine I can prescribe for her chest. But she should be moved from this room. In fact, she should be downstairs, so she's closer to the privy.'

'There's a room downstairs at the front we never use. I could set that up as her bedroom,' Hetty said quickly.

'I'm not leaving my boy's room,' Hetty moaned.

The doctor was stern in his reply. 'Mrs Lawson, if you stay in this room, it will do your chest irreparable harm. It could even kill you.'

Hetty gasped in horror.

'Your daughter will arrange for you to move, do you understand?'

Hilda turned her head away.

'You should do it as soon as possible,' he told Hetty.

Hetty led the way downstairs to the kitchen, where Dr Gilson wrote out a prescription for medicine and also his bill for attending. He handed her both, then left.

'What am I going to do?' Hetty said. 'I can't move a bed downstairs, and Mum too.' She clasped her hand over her mouth as she realised how easily the word had slipped from her lips.

'You called her Mum upstairs too,' Dirk said.

Hetty was astonished. 'I did?'

Dirk nodded. He walked towards her and wrapped her in his arms.

'You still love her, Hetty, and she still loves you.'

She felt the warmth of his body through his shirt and the strength of his arms around her. It made her feel safe, warm and protected.

'I'll help you bring her downstairs,' he said. He glanced at the clock on the kitchen wall. 'I don't need to return to Elisabethville until lights out at eleven p.m. We have a few hours.'

'It's not going to be easy,' she said. 'There's Dan's bed, all the bedding, a chest of drawers. How on earth will we get Hilda down?'

'I'll carry her,' Dirk said without hesitation.

Hetty hugged him to within an inch of his life.

Elsie was sitting on a bench by the river. She'd let Jet off his lead, and he was sniffing a tree trunk when another, larger dog approached. She recognised it immediately.

The big dog lolloped to her and she rewarded him with a scratch behind his ears. She looked up to see Stan walking towards her. Patch and Jet were sizing each other up, tails wagging.

Stan raised his cap. 'Evening, Elsie,' he said. 'Mind if I join you?'

'Be my guest,' she replied with a smile.

As Elsie and Stan chatted happily on the bench, Jet sat between them looking out across the river. However, something caught Patch's eye and he began to growl. A man was walking along the riverside, calling Elsie's name. He was unsteady on his feet and held a beer bottle in his hand. Elsie froze when she saw him.

'It's Frankie,' she gasped.

Stan laid his hand protectively on her arm. 'Don't worry, lass, I won't let him harm you.'

Patch and Jet ran towards Frankie, barking and growling. He spun around on his heel and ran away as fast as his drunken legs could carry him, with the two dogs seeing him off.

Chapter Forty-Three

As 1918 progressed, the local newspaper began to print news signalling changes in the strategy of the war. Soviet Russia withdrew after signing a peace treaty. Just the mention of the word *peace* in the headlines brought hope to people's hearts. But these hopes were dashed when Germany launched an offensive, and it was feared Britain might be choked into defeat. Each week the newspaper brought more stories, as terrifying as they were hopeful. However, by summer of that year, reports from the front began to offer a real possibility that the war might soon draw to an end.

One evening at the Deanery, Anne and William were sitting together in the living room. Dinah was asleep in bed and Edith had returned home. William had his feet up on a footstool and was reading the *Chester-le-Street Chronicle and District Advertiser*. When he rattled the paper and noisily folded it, Anne looked up from her book. William was handing her the newspaper, tapping a half-page advertisement across the top of the page.

'What is it, dear?' she asked.

'Mr Gerard's done a fine job with our advertising. It's always a thrill to see our ads in the paper. Mind you, it helps that the editor's a good friend of mine. He always places them in a prime slot.'

Anne took the newspaper, glanced at it, and smiled. 'Gerard's team always hit the right spot with their wording. I said so at the meeting when this ad was approved. In fact, I was the one who suggested we begin it with an apology for altering the taste of Lady Tina.'

'Nothing else we can do, under the present circumstances,' William said ruefully. 'And the ad ends with a robust promise that once war is over, Lady Tina will go back to her full creamy taste.'

Anne returned the newspaper to William and he caught her hand.

'Let's hope the war will be over soon,' he said gently, then he cleared his throat. 'I, er . . . I wondered if I should give Gerard a pay rise once the factory's working as normal again. His advertisements have not only kept us in the public eye, but feedback tells us there's even more respect and admiration for the brand.'

'Well . . .' Anne began cautiously, 'let's not look too far ahead. War isn't over yet. We're still restricted to working three days a week and the girls are doing a tremendous job. I'd rather any money spare once war is over goes to keeping on as many of them as we can when the men return. We'll need the girls, William, if we're to ramp up production as quickly as we can.'

'I daresay you're right, Anne. You usually are.'

He laid the newspaper down.

'Father called at the factory to see me today after you left. He invited us to join him and my mother for lunch next week at the Lambton Café. Would you like to go?'

'I'd love to. Could we take Dinah too?' Anne asked.

William chuckled. 'Mother would be disappointed if we didn't. You know how much she adores her.'

The following week, Anne dressed in her smart cream suit for the lunch with William's parents. Dinah wore a blue velvet dress with a blue ribbon in her hair. The Lambton Café was on Front Street, a short walk from the Deanery. When Anne and William arrived, Albert and Clara were already there, seated at a round table in the window. Anne would have preferred to sit near the back of the café, away from prying eyes. Now that she was the wife of the toffee factory owner, she had become a woman of some import-ance in the small market town. When people passed her on the street, she could hear them comment on how she looked or dressed, and it made her feel uncomfortable.

She greeted Clara with a kiss on her powdered cheek and hugged Albert warmly. She seated Dinah in a high chair next to Clara, which cheered her mother-in-law no end, while Anne herself chose a seat facing into the café. That way she had her back to the window, out of view of passers-by. A miserable-looking waitress dressed in a green apron walked to the table. She carried a notepad in one hand and a pencil in the other.

'What do you want?' she barked.

Anne looked up, startled by such a rude voice. She rec-ognised the waitress from when she'd previously eaten at the Lambton Café.

'I'd like a waitress with good manners, if it's not too much to ask,' Clara said pointedly.

'There's only me. You'll like it or lump it,' the waitress replied without missing a beat. 'Now then, the special today is liver and onions. The meat pie is off. And we've got a new chef who can't cook poached eggs. If you want eggs, you'll have to have them fried, scrambled or boiled. Got it?'

Everyone ordered, then the waitress grabbed the menus and shuffled away.

'My word, that girl is so rude!' Clara complained.

'She's consistent, I'll give her that,' Anne muttered.

Suddenly William's eyes lit up. He was looking over Anne's shoulder, out of the window and onto the street.

'Good heavens, I don't believe it!' he cried.

Anne turned to see what had caught his attention, and her heart fell to the floor.

'Why, it's old Matthews!' he said excitedly. 'And he's coming in here! I thought he'd already moved to Scotland.'

Anne couldn't believe her eyes. Mr and Mrs Matthews, the couple she'd given her baby to, were coming into the café! Then she started shaking. She felt sick, dizzy with shock. For there, holding Mrs Matthews' hand, was a small boy. Anne's son.

She gasped in horror. This couldn't be happening. It couldn't. She could hardly breathe. She wanted to cry, scream, leap up from her seat and run. But she couldn't do anything, she couldn't move. She was glued to the spot. The room spun. She closed her eyes, willing the scene in front of her away, but when she opened them again, nothing had changed. She felt sweat break out on her forehead. Her mouth was dry. She glanced at William, Clara, Albert. None of them had the slightest clue who the child was and what he meant to her.

How could this be happening? Why now, with her family around? She'd thought she'd said her goodbyes and made her peace with her past, but now here was her son, coming into the café holding another woman's hand. Anne's heart raced, beating so strongly and loudly she felt sure William would hear it. Still sitting, she placed her feet firmly on the floor to steady herself and laid her hands on the table. She dropped her gaze, hoping to avoid eye contact with Mr and Mrs Matthews, but to her horror, William had other plans.

'Matthews, old chap, how the devil are you? I thought you'd already left for your new life in Scotland!' He greeted the other man with a handshake.

'We're leaving on the afternoon train,' Mr Matthews said, eyeing Anne cautiously.

'I wish you well in your new life, my friend. Meet my wife, Anne, and our little girl, Dinah.'

Anne looked up into Mr Matthews' steel-grey eyes and tried to force a smile. They locked gazes for a moment, each recognising the other, knowing they must keep their secret. Mr Matthews turned to his wife.

'Darling, this is Mr Jack from the toffee factory, with his wife.'

Anne knew he was being polite, going through the motions, trying to make everything appear normal when the situation was anything but.

Mrs Matthews looked like a rabbit caught in headlights. The two women stared at each other for longer than necessary, then Anne finally held out her hand.

'How nice to meet you,' she said.

'Likewise,' Mrs Matthews replied.

Anne couldn't help what she did next; it was a reflex,

automatic, maternal. She turned to the boy and gently ran her hand over his head.

'What a beautiful child,' she said softly.

'Mama!' the boy cried, staring straight at her.

Anne jumped in her chair, startled. And then she realised that he was looking past her, at Mrs Matthews. She felt her cheeks burn. How foolish she was, how ridiculous for thinking he might remember her.

'Mama!' he cried again.

Mrs Matthews picked him up and turned his face away from Anne.

'There, there, dear, it's all right. These people are friends of Daddy's. And speaking of Daddy, we really should be getting along.'

'Please join us for lunch,' William chipped in. 'I'm sure the waitress could bring more chairs to the table.'

'I wouldn't bet on her being so helpful,' Clara noted.

The boy began to grizzle, which set Dinah crying too. The sound helped Anne return to her senses. Her hands were shaking, but she managed to control them enough to soothe her daughter, her instincts directing her actions. She did her best to ignore Mrs Matthews and her son, who were now standing behind her, out of her line of vision.

'Come, let's leave William and his family to their lunch. I'm sure they have lots to talk about,' Mrs Matthews urged her husband.

Anne's thoughts were running wild. She was having to suppress the compulsion to gaze at her boy and study his face. Did he look like her? Or would he remind her of her first love, the man who'd left her pregnant and alone? She squeezed her tears away and forced herself to sit up straight. She could feel Clara and Albert's eyes on her.

'Are you all right, dear? You've gone terribly pale,' Clara said.

Anne couldn't reply for fear that she'd give herself away. Instead, she tended to Dinah, who was sobbing softly.

Mrs Matthew was heading to the door. Mr Matthews tipped his hat to all at the table, then followed his wife. Anne couldn't help herself; she didn't seem to be in command of what happened next. It was as if she was watching someone else stand from the table, politely excuse herself and follow the couple outside.

Chapter Forty-Four

Outside on the street, Anne suddenly didn't know what to do. She felt such a fool. She moved away from the café window so that William and his parents couldn't see her. Mr and Mrs Matthews were ahead of her, each holding one of the boy's hands, and he was toddling between them.

'Please, wait,' she called.

They turned. Mr Matthews' face was set stern.

'Now just listen to me. You have no right—'

Mrs Matthews stepped forward, holding the boy's hand.

'I'll deal with this,' she said quietly. Her husband turned away.

'Is it true?' Anne asked. 'Are you moving away to live in Scotland?'

'Yes, it's true,' Mrs Matthews replied. 'We think it's for the best. We're leaving on the afternoon train.'

She pulled the boy close, then gently touched Anne's arm.

'Would you . . .' Her voice broke. 'Would you like to say goodbye to Daniel?'

Anne's mouth opened, but no words came out.

'Daniel?' she said at last.

'We named him after my father,' Mrs Matthews said, her tone softer now. There were tears in her eyes. 'I want to say thank you, Anne, for the photograph of Daniel as a baby. I will treasure it always. My maid told me you left the picture with your love.'

Anne's mind raced. Finally she allowed her gaze to fall on the boy. She took in his small, round trusting face, his brown eyes and fair hair. Her stomach turned and her heart beat wildly. She felt her legs turn to jelly. She reached for a shop window to lean against, to stop herself from falling.

'Where in Scotland will you go?' she said once she'd managed to pull herself together.

'Perhaps it's best you don't know,' Mrs Matthews replied kindly.

'Of course,' Anne said, feeling her cheeks burn again. 'I should never have asked.'

Mrs Matthews looked behind her at her husband. When she saw that he was standing with his back to her, she leaned close to Anne.

'Perhaps every once in a while I could write to you. To update you.'

Anne looked again at her son, her eyes drawn to him, unable to pull her gaze away. She wanted to hold him, kiss him, smother him with love. And yet all she could do was stand and watch as he held Mrs Matthews' hand.

'Anne, dear!' William called from the doorway of the café.

Anne swallowed hard. 'I must go,' she said.

'Well . . . would you like me to write? If so, I'd need your address,' Mrs Matthews offered again, quieter this time, more hesitant.

Anne forced back tears and shook her head. She couldn't

bring herself to say the word *no*. She bent and kissed the boy on his head.

'Look after him,' she whispered to Mrs Matthews.

And with that, she turned and walked back into the café, where her family waited.

'I'm sorry, I needed a breath of air,' she said as she took her seat.

'It's a real shame old Matthews is moving to live in Scotland,' William said. 'He's a good man, one of the best engineers in the region. I didn't know he had a son, he never told me. What a pity his little boy and Dinah won't grow up to know one another. They might have become friends.'

He looked at Anne.

'Are you feeling quite well, dear? You look like you've seen a ghost.'

Anne lowered her gaze. With shaking hands she busied herself with a napkin, laying it carefully around Dinah's neck to protect her dress.

The waitress appeared, carrying a plate. 'Now then, which one of you lot ordered the liver?'

Later that week, in the factory's enrobing room, Mr Parrott strutted to the table and tapped Elsie on the arm.

'I've got a special task for you, lass. Come with me.'

Elsie cast a nervous look at Hetty. 'Why am I being singled out?' she whispered.

Hetty wasn't given time to reply as Mr Parrot marched off to his desk, expecting Elsie to follow. A girl was waiting there. She was younger than Elsie, and very pretty. She was petite and slim, her fair hair piled up in a bun, with wisps falling around her oval face.

'This is Kitty Aldridge,' Mr Parrott explained.

Elsie stuck out her hand and smiled. 'I'm Elsie Cooper. How do you do?'

'I'm a bit nervous, actually,' Kitty admitted.

'Kitty's just arrived at the factory to replace Doris, who's taken ill and will be away for a while. It's her first morning, and I'd like you, Elsie, to show her the ropes. Take her for a full tour of the factory and show her where everything is. Get her a pair of clogs from the storeroom, and an overall too. And make sure you're away no more than half an hour. Any longer than that and I'll come looking for you. I know what you girls are like once you start talking.'

Elsie rolled her eyes at Kitty, making her smile. The girl reminded her of herself when she'd first started at the factory, innocent and naive, before she'd met Frankie and he'd almost ruined her life. Before she'd met Stan, whose friendship meant the world to her now. She threaded her arm through Kitty's and leaned in close as they walked from the room.

'Have you got a boyfriend?' she whispered.

A mischievous smile made its way to Kitty's lips. 'No, but I really fancy the fella who works at the railway station in town.'

'I bet he's not as good-looking as some of the lads working here in the sugar boiling room,' Elsie said.

Kitty gave a cheeky wink and fanned her face with her hand. 'I hear the sugar boilers go bare-chested when the work gets too hot.'

'You've heard right,' Elsie agreed. 'I'll take you there for a look. Well, Mr Parrot told me to give you a full tour of the factory, didn't he?'

Then she pulled the girl close.

'Can I give you a word of warning, Kitty?'

Kitty turned her big blue eyes to Elsie. 'What is it?'

'With your looks, you're going to get a lot of attention from the toffee factory men. If any of them cause you problems, you come and tell me and I'll sort them out. I'll look after you. I've been through it myself. The fellas were like bees around honey when I first started here. Mind you, if you meet the head gardener, Stan Chapman, he's mine. Understand?'

'How long have you been courting him?' Kitty asked.

Elsie shrugged. 'We're not really courting . . . but I'm hoping we will be very soon.'

The girls walked off arm in arm.

'Where do you live, Kitty?' Elsie asked.

'In Birtley, so I get the bus to work each day. I live with my mum and stepdad, but he's got a rotten temper. To be honest, I wouldn't mind moving out and getting a place of my own in Chester-le-Street. Do you know anywhere there's a room for a girl like me?'

Elsie thought of Anne's old room at Mrs Fortune's house on Victor Street. She wondered if Kitty could afford it.

'I might know somewhere that'd be right up your street.'

Not long after eleven a.m., the factory hooter sounded: three short bursts followed by a continuous tone. The girls looked at each other, puzzled. It only blew continuously if there was an emergency. Hetty, nervous, glanced at Elsie.

'What's happening?' she wondered.

She turned and saw girls streaming from the room, running outside, a commotion at the factory gates.

'Is it a fight?' she asked, alarmed. She hung back, but Elsie, unafraid, surged forward.

'It's not a fight. It sounds happy, there's cheering,' she said. 'Come on, I want to find out what's going on.'

Hetty stopped dead when she saw Dirk waiting at the factory gates.

'You go on without me, Elsie,' she said, and Elsie ran away down Market Lane. Hetty walked towards Dirk and he wrapped her in his arms, then lifted her off her feet and swung her around.

'It's over, Hetty! War's over! It's just been announced.'

Hetty felt herself flying; she heard people cheering and clapping, some even crying with joy.

'Put me down,' she cried. She regained her balance and looked into Dirk's blue eyes. 'Is it really over?' she gasped.

He held out a newspaper for her to read a stark headline in large black print. *Fighting Finished. Armistice Signed.*

'It's the beginning of the end,' he said cautiously.

Hetty couldn't take it in. 'It's really over?' she said again, trying to make sense of it. 'I can't believe it.'

'No one can,' Dirk said, smiling as people cheered, held newspapers aloft and waved their hats in the air. 'It's too wonderful for words.'

A crowd surged past them on narrow Market Lane and Dirk pulled Hetty to him. His lips found hers and he held her for a long time in a loving embrace. Hetty's emotions were in turmoil. Excitement and relief over the war ending were edged with a darkness she couldn't explain. Something disturbing and upsetting had lodged in her heart, and from the sad look on his face when all around them people were cheering, she knew Dirk felt it too.

He reached for her hand and they began to walk, jostled by the crowds who were racing onto Front Street to head to the pubs, which had thrown their doors open for everyone to celebrate. Dirk turned to Hetty and held her gaze.

'Shall we go to the river to talk?'

Hetty nodded, swallowing a lump in her throat.

They walked in silence to the river, where Dirk indicated a bench. They sat so close together that Hetty could feel his heartbeat as if it was her own. He laid his arm across her shoulders and pulled her close. At first neither of them could find the right words.

'I know you have to leave,' Hetty said at last. 'That day will soon be a reality. I can't bear to think I'll never see you again. I don't know what I'll do.'

Dirk was silent for a long time, hugging her tight, and she began sobbing against his chest.

'Darling Hetty, I struggle too with what lies ahead. I thought my future was mapped out, that I would return to Ghent, to my family. But all that was before I met you.'

Hetty pulled away and looked into his eyes. 'What are you saying?'

'That I want to stay,' Dirk replied quietly.

Her heart skipped a beat. 'You do? But how?'

He looked out across the river. 'I can stay a little longer than the others because I have offered to help those who will leave Elisabethville first. I don't want to be on the first train out of here. I want to stay for as long as I can . . .

with you. But the fact is that eventually I will have to leave, and we have to be strong.'

'I'll be forever grateful for the extra time I spend with you,' Hetty said, wiping her tears away. 'What will become of Elisabethville once everyone has returned to Belgium?'

'We've heard that the Ministry of Labour might use the village as a training centre for returning British soldiers. The servicemen will live in the huts where the Belgian families live now.'

Hetty looked across the river at Lumley Castle. She thought of Mrs Doughty and the kitchen staff celebrating the news that the war was coming to an end. She smiled at the thought of the housekeeper lifting her apron and dancing around the kitchen with the earl's chauffeur.

'It feels so wrong, Dirk. I feel guilty. Worse, I feel shame for not being as happy as everyone else. War is ending. We should be overjoyed, and yet my heart breaks knowing we'll have to part.'

'My heart breaks too,' Dirk said as he lifted her fingers to his lips and kissed each one in turn.

Dirk walked Hetty home and they kissed. He had work to do at Elisabethville, where a meeting would take place to discuss plans for leaving the village. Hetty let herself into the house, pleased to find Elsie cooking dinner at the hearth. Her friend leapt up and ran to her.

'Isn't it wonderful, Hetty? War is over! It's ending!'

The two girls hugged for a very long time, and when they pulled away, both of them were crying. Elsie's tears were of joy, while Hetty's were mixed with sadness.

'Pie and mash all right for you?' Elsie asked at last.

'Sounds perfect,' Hetty replied. 'I'll go and see Hilda before we eat.'

She was relieved to see Hilda sitting up in bed, reading the newspaper with a huge smile on her face.

'Elsie brought the newspaper for me. Isn't it wonderful news?' Hilda said.

'It's the best news ever,' Hetty agreed, choking back her tears.

She gave Hilda a peck on her cheek. She noticed a glass on the bedside table and the whisky bottle next to it.

'Don't worry. I've just had a tot. I raised a glass to Dan's memory. May his death never be in vain,' Hilda said.

Hetty returned to the kitchen, where Elsie was singing and dancing around the room.

'I swear today is the best day of my life. I'm going to celebrate with Stan tonight. He's taking me to a party at the Lambton Arms. Jim and Cathy Ireland have opened the pub to celebrate. There'll be dancing all night, and free beer.'

'Won't Frankie be there? It's his brother's pub,' Hetty warned.

Elsie waved her hand as if she didn't care. 'Jim and Cathy have barred him. There's no chance I'll bump into him, and even if I do, I've got Stan to protect me. Why don't you and Dirk come with us?'

Hetty shook her head. 'Dirk's busy at Elisabethville, and I don't think I'm in the mood for a party.'

Elsie shot her a look. 'Hetty Lawson! You must be the only person in the world who's not in the party mood today. There's so much to celebrate. You must come, I insist. Oh, a letter arrived for you,' she added, pointing at the mantelpiece.

Hetty's heart dropped when she saw the familiar army-issue envelope and recognised Bob's handwriting.

'Oh no. It's from Bob. His sister must have told him about me and Dirk, and he'll be writing to give me a piece of his mind. Well, there's only one way to get this over and done with.'

She sank into a chair by the fire and ripped open the envelope. She read the letter in silence.

'Well, what does he say?' Elsie asked impatiently, shuffling her hips side to side as she hummed a tune.

Hetty looked at her, unblinking. 'It says he's coming home. He does know about Dirk.'

'Well, at least everything's out in the open now. That's good, isn't it?' Elsie turned away to tend to potatoes boiling in a pan.

'No, Elsie, it's not good at all,' Hetty replied dumbstruck. 'Because he says that the first thing he's going to do when he returns is arrange for us to marry. He's already written to the vicar! He's promised he'll change. He says that war has taught him the value of life, love and happiness, and that he'll do anything to win my heart.'

She gulped, thinking of Dirk, who she was about to lose overseas.

'He says he'll let nothing and no one stop him from making me his bride, and will fight anyone who stands in his way.'

Her head spun. It felt as if her life was turning upside down. The love of her life was leaving to return to his family in Belgium just as Bob, the man she no longer loved, was heading home, determined to marry her.

'Oh Elsie . . . what am I going to do?'

Elsie hugged her tight. 'One thing's for sure, you've got me to help you fight your battles from now on, Hetty Lawson. Who knows what the future holds? But whatever happens, I'm right here by your side.'